The Set-Up Girl

'With an authentic voice and a cast of engaging characters, *The Set-Up Girl* is funny, romantic and relatable – a queer delight.'
Erin Gough, award-winning author of
Amelia Westlake and *Into the Mouth of the Wolf*

'*The Set-Up Girl* is an utterly charming young adult debut. It will be all-too-relatable to anyone who's ever had a crush on the wrong person – and even more relatable to anyone who's ever had a best friend.'
Jodi McAlister, bestselling author of
Valentine and *Here For The Right Reasons*

The Set-Up Girl

SASHA VEY

ALLEN&UNWIN
SYDNEY·MELBOURNE·AUCKLAND·LONDON

First published by Allen & Unwin in 2025

Copyright © Text, Sasha Vey 2025
Copyright © Illustrations, Daniel Gray-Barnett 2025

All rights reserved. No part of this book may be reproduced or transmitted in any form or by any means, electronic or mechanical, including photocopying, recording or by any information storage and retrieval system, without prior permission in writing from the publisher. The Australian *Copyright Act 1968* (the Act) allows a maximum of one chapter or 10 per cent of this book, whichever is the greater, to be photocopied by any educational institution for its educational purposes provided that the educational institution (or body that administers it) has given a remuneration notice to the Copyright Agency (Australia) under the Act.

Allen & Unwin
Cammeraygal Country
83 Alexander Street
Crows Nest NSW 2065
Australia
Phone: (61 2) 8425 0100
Email: info@allenandunwin.com
Web: www.allenandunwin.com

Allen & Unwin acknowledges the Traditional Owners of the Country on which we live and work. We pay our respects to all Aboriginal and Torres Strait Islander Elders, past and present.

EU Authorised Representative: Easy Access System Europe, Mustamäe tee 50, 10621 Tallinn, Estonia, gpsr.requests@easproject.com

A catalogue record for this book is available from the National Library of Australia

ISBN 978 1 76118 154 2

For teaching resources, explore allenandunwin.com/learn

Cover design, text design and hand-lettering by Amy Daoud
Cover illustration by Daniel Gray-Barnett
Set in 11.75/17 pt Baskerville by Midland Typesetters, Australia
Printed and bound in Australia by the Opus Group

10 9 8 7 6 5 4 3 2 1

The paper in this book is FSC® certified. FSC® promotes environmentally responsible, socially beneficial and economically viable management of the world's forests.

For the introverted bisexuals.

1

'Kind of messed up to have a vendetta against a whale.'

Mae, who had been looking down at the maths textbook between us with a despairing expression, blinked over at me. 'Wasn't *Moby-Dick* last month? Are you still planning on finishing it?'

'No one finished it,' I grumbled. 'Tetka Sabinka chose it, and she didn't even turn up for the session.'

'Scandalous,' Mae said, attention drifting back to the textbook.

'Gotta say, I feel like you're not appreciating what I'm going through right now.'

Mae leaned her chin against her palm. 'So sorry, Amalia. You're going through … making yourself read a book?'

I shrugged, pulling a face, like *Obviously*.

'Aren't you still super close to the start?' she asked.

Leaning back in my chair, I began flicking my pen

between my fingers. 'Objection: reading is about the journey. The journey has begun. I feel like that's what we should be focusing on.'

Mae rolled her eyes at me, brushing red curls away from her face with a flick of her hand. I sniffed, tipping back further—

'Hey, Mae.'

I dropped my pen. Mae's response was lost in the scramble to get my chair back on the ground.

By the time I straightened, our unexpected guest was saying, 'Yeah, that'd be great. Thanks, Mae.'

'No worries, Kasun,' Mae said, dimple coming out in full force as she smiled up at him.

Kasun, beautiful Kasun, grinned at her, then turned and walked back down the aisle to his desk. I didn't watch him go. I did look over at Mae.

'What?' Mae mouthed, when she noticed.

'Since when are you two,' I made a gesture, which she pulled a face at, 'like *that*?'

Mae waved me off, though I could see the beginning of a flush light the hollow between her collarbones. I kept staring at her.

'We're in the same group for that bio presentation we have to do before the zoo trip,' she finally said. She added, 'It's no big deal.'

'No big deal?' I repeated. 'No big deal that your crush is coming over to our desk to say hello?'

The flush had started to crawl up her neck. 'He just

wanted me to email him my part of the PowerPoint so he can put it together before we present.'

'I bet next he'll be asking you to email him a PowerPoint about how hot you are.' I frowned at myself, tilting my head. 'No, wait – he'll be asking you to email him … he'll make a PowerPoint about—'

'I get it,' Mae half-groaned, half-laughed.

'Sex PowerPoint,' I said, with conviction.

'Stop!' Mae said, the word carried on a laugh loud enough that the teacher glanced up from her desk and shook her head in our direction, shooting us a warning squint.

We settled down, bending our heads towards the textbook in unison. Mae started copying figures into her notebook and I tried to follow suit, but I was finding it hard to concentrate. My brain was stuck on Kasun.

His smile. The way the light caught in his chestnut hair. The lean strength in his arms. Those dark eyes.

I sighed through my teeth, squeezing my eyes shut. It didn't matter. I couldn't be distracted by him. Mae had more of a chance with him than I ever would.

I was never going to be the leading lady. But I could be a supportive friend.

'Isn't summer meant to be almost over?' I complained, tugging at my collar and trying to will myself to stop sweating.

Mae and I were on the bus home, two of many students clogging the centre aisle. Though the walk from school to the bus stop wasn't far, it was a stinker of a day. By the time we had piled on board, I was already yearning for a fresh shirt and a cold shower.

Mae didn't answer, too busy trying to angle her armpits towards an imaginary flow of fresh air that happened to be about level with my own armpits.

'Give up,' I told her. 'This is our life now.'

Mae pulled a face, letting her arms drop. My pocket vibrated. Shimmying on the spot so I could reach, I pulled out my phone, checking my notifications.

> Elizabeta
> **Heads up**
>
> Elizabeta
> Mum's already asking about your university preferences, so have an answer you can give her at book club

I groaned, shimmying my phone back into my pocket.

'What's up?' Mae asked.

'It's my cousin Elizabeta,' I said. 'Tetka Mojca wants to know my university preferences. So I have to think of something believable before book club next week, which also won't lead to an entire afternoon of questions.'

'You're not thinking bio anymore?'

'I don't know,' I groaned. 'I don't know what I'm thinking. This whole ... being done with high school *thing* doesn't feel real yet. But if I seem *at all* uncertain it's going to lead to—'

'An entire afternoon of questions,' Mae finished, nodding. 'Okay, fair. What's this month's book, anyway?'

'Oh, *Emma*,' I said.

'Jane Austen? Cute.' Mae lifted her other arm in another attempt to air her armpits.

'I haven't actually read it since we did it in English,' I admitted, reaching over and pressing her arm back down. 'But it'll be fine. Something something matchmaking, right?'

'Something something,' Mae agreed.

We lapsed into silence. My mind bounced from *Emma* to *Moby-Dick* and then, unbidden, back to maths class.

I screwed up my courage – *supportive friend, supportive friend, supportive friend* – before asking, 'So, want to talk about Kasun?'

Mae squinted at me, though I could see her blush. 'We're ... just in the same bio group.'

'You sure?' I prompted. 'It seemed like he was hanging around more than someone who only wanted to swap PowerPoint slides. Maybe he wants to swap something else. Numbers, saliva—'

Mae swatted at me, mouth opening in a silent yell. I laughed, leaning away as far as I could in the crowded bus.

'Actually,' Mae said, once we had settled back down, 'he did give me his number.'

She spoke so softly that at first I thought I'd misheard. Once I processed Mae's words, though, my heart plummeted.

Still, I widened my eyes in what I hoped was a look of excited shock. 'No way! Mae, that's great!'

She shrugged, as though getting the number of her crush was no biggie. 'He probably only gave it to me for school stuff.'

'Did he *say* that?' I asked.

Mae shrugged again, clearly holding back a smile now. My heart sank to my sweaty, sweaty shoes.

'That's so good,' I said. 'That's great, Mae.'

The bus jolted to a stop, sending everyone in the aisle knocking into each other like an unruly line of dominoes. Despite finding myself even more tightly sandwiched than before, I was glad of the disruption. It saved me from having to keep lying through my teeth.

✱ ✱ ✱

For as long as I could remember, Mae and I had lived a ten-minute walk away from each other. Her house was on the corner of a main road, which wasn't great for noise, but did mean she was closer to the bus stop than me. I walked her to her door like I did at the end of every school day, and we air hugged (too hot for physical contact) before I set off on my trudge home.

Ten minutes later, I made it through my front door, sweating like I'd run a race. Sliding my shoes off by the door without bothering to unlace them, I called a cursory 'Hello!' to the empty house before heading for my room, dropping my schoolbag at the base of my bed and beelining for the shower.

By the time I had cooled down and spent almost an hour lying facedown on my bed while a podcast played and *Moby-Dick* sat waiting on the pillow beside me, staring at me with about as much accusation as my unopened bag of homework, members of my household had begun filtering in.

My sister Kamilia was the first. She announced herself by opening my bedroom door, putting her hands on her hips and staring at me. I craned my head around, not moving from my position on my stomach, and stared back. Finally, she sighed and left.

'Close the door!' I yelled after her.

She did not.

Dad was next. Despite my door still being open he was polite enough to knock, and when I grunted my approval he came into my room, resting one hand on the back of my head in hello.

Mum and Dad were around the same height, both with broad shoulders and thick dark hair that Kamilia and I had inherited. Dad was significantly rounder than Mum, though with more densely muscled arms and a moustache that seemed to grow thicker and richer the patchier the hair on top of his head became. Even though he had stopped working professionally as a builder a few years ago after a back injury, his hand was still rough with callouses where it rested against my head.

'Kako si?' he asked.

I gave him a thumbs up.

'You have homework?'

I wiggled my thumb.

Giving my head a pat, he left, closing my door behind him.

Mum was last home. I listened to her clanking around downstairs for a good half hour before the clanking paused. I heard her stop at Kamilia's room first, and then my door opened.

'Malka,' she said, from the doorway.

'Hey, Mum.' I decided it was probably time to sit up. 'What's up?'

'I was talking to my sister, earlier,' she said, crossing her arms and leaning her hip against my doorframe. 'Organising for next Saturday.'

'Tetka Sabinka?' I guessed.

Mum waved her hand like the answer was obvious, which I supposed it was.

'She wanted to do *that* book again.' Mum pointed at the copy of *Moby-Dick* that was still sitting, untouched, on the bed beside to me.

'Oh,' I said. 'But I thought we were going to talk about *Emma*?'

Mum rested her hands on her hips.

'You know what she said?' Mum asked.

I did not know what Tetka Sabinka had said. I had a feeling I was going to find out.

'She said to me,' Mum continued, my role in this conversation purely ornamental, '"Oh, Barica, why don't we do *Moby-Dick*? We didn't get a chance to discuss it." I said, "Sabinka, we did not get a chance to discuss it because *you* decided you wanted to do afternoon tennis." And she said, "But we need to talk about it. It's *great American literature*." I said, "What do I care about American literature? What do *you*? You already chose tennis over this big book and its problematic whale." And Sabinka said—' Mum pulled in a breath, eyes blazing, '—she said, "Barica, I don't understand why you would choose this silly romance book anyway."'

'Ah.'

My mother put her hands in the air, palms up. 'I said, "Fine. If this is how you feel, you don't have to come."'

'Ah,' I said, again.

This was not an uncommon type of familial argument. Ever since the book club's inception, there had been a fair degree of sniping regarding the choice of book for each session. None of us had the same reading tastes, which I thought provided a nice bit of variety, but it had a tendency to bring out the worst in my mother and ... well, Tetka Sabinka. Of the three sisters, Tetka Mojca was most happy to go with the flow.

'How was your day?' Mum asked.

'Yeah, good,' I said, adding, 'Sorry Tetka Sabinka was rude about *Emma*.'

'It doesn't matter,' Mum said.

Now that she had recounted the conversation, she seemed a lot more cheerful. 'She is only angry because she is not in charge,' Mum said, conversational, already turning back into the hallway. 'She has always been like this. She was a noisy baby, you know. Always screaming, always making sure she had the attention.' My mother looked at me properly. 'Do you have homework, Malka?'

'Yep. I'm about to get started on it.'

'Good girl,' Mum said.

She left the door open behind her and, with some reluctance, I opened my schoolbag. I figured I could, at minimum, make myself stressed about upcoming assignments – it would beat being mopey about Mae and Kasun's new connection.

2

To be clear, I hadn't set out to share a crush with my best friend.

It was the first time it had happened, as far as I knew. Mae had always liked her boys … well, unattainable. When we were kids being hustled to Slovenian Church on Sunday mornings, Mae would always moon over the one altar boy who seemed destined for priesthood. (Mae had never been made to go every week, as her link was through her maternal grandmother. I, being a full-blooded second generation kid, was made to attend every Sunday until I put my foot down at thirteen.)

All through school, too, Mae had set her crush sights high: the cutest boys; the sportiest boys; the smiling, beautiful boys who didn't seem to have a care in the world. When we started high school, it didn't take long for Mae to set her sights on Kasun. It was a crush that had fluctuated over the years, ebbing and flowing as the currents of Mae's emotions dictated. But near the end of last year …

I don't know. Maybe the stress of starting our final year of high school had made me snap. Maybe I was more easily swayed than I thought. All I knew was that when Mae had ebbed once again into the crush and begun to wax lyrical about Kasun last year, I had realised with mild horror that I was starting to think she had some good points.

It made the week following the revelation that Kasun and Mae had exchanged numbers a painful one. Every time Mae smiled down at her phone, my stomach twisted, and then I felt annoyed at myself for both assuming every text Mae received was from Kasun and also for caring.

By Friday night, I was exhausted with myself. I was, I decided, going to have a quiet night in.

After poking half-heartedly at an essay and flicking through a few pages of *Moby-Dick*, I rolled onto my stomach and picked up my phone, typing 'degrees' into my browser.

I spent the next few minutes staring with little interest at the Wikipedia page for 'Degree (angle)' before trying again and searching 'good degrees'.

When a call from Mae appeared at the top of my screen, I swiped to answer, saying, 'What are your thoughts on climate science?'

There was a pause from Mae's end, then: 'Still trying to think of a degree to tell your aunt about?'

'Yu-huh.'

'Why don't you just say bio, if it's what you're actually thinking?'

'I don't want Kamilia hearing. She'll decide I'm just copying what she's doing. She'll be so smug; I'll never hear the end of it.'

There was silence from Mae's end, and then she said, carefully, 'Is that ... not what made you consider it?'

I groaned. 'I mean obviously hearing Kamilia talk non-stop about what studying science at uni is like has had *some* influence on me. But that's not the point.'

Mae hummed in an *only child* kind of way.

'And how's the whale?' she asked.

I could hear the faint sound of crickets in the background, as well as the *shush*-ing of fabric.

I glanced guiltily at my closed copy of *Moby-Dick*. 'Are you going somewhere?'

The cricket sounds paused, as did the sound of fabric, so I assumed Mae had stopped moving.

'Okay, so,' Mae said, 'speaking of bio – you know how I had the bio presentation today?'

How could I have forgotten? Mae had been giddy all day because at the end of the presentation Kasun had apparently hugged her. In her own words, it hadn't been: 'One of those awkward one-armed things – he actually like *fully hugged me. In front of everyone.*'

'Yes?' I said.

'So after the presentation,' Mae continued, 'Kasun and I were talking a bit and he was like, "Hey, Jake is going to set off a bunch of fireworks at Mill Hill Park tonight." *And* he was also like, "It would be cool if you came, as a celebration for doing our presentation."'

Mae paused, which I took as my cue to speak.

I floundered for a moment, before landing on what I hoped was a sincere sounding, 'Wow!'

'So I sneaked out,' Mae said.

I sat up in bed.

'You what?' I asked, sure I had misheard.

'I sneaked out,' Mae repeated. 'My parents have a date night today, anyway, so as long as I'm back before, like, eleven, I should be fine.'

I blinked at the phone. This was … new.

'You sneaked out,' I repeated, trying the idea out for size. 'Okay. You sneaked out. Okay.'

'You're freaking out,' Mae said.

'I'm a little bit freaking out,' I confirmed, leaning forwards and tucking my arms into my stomach. 'What if they catch you? Mae, you're not even allowed to date, let alone—'

'We're eighteen!' Mae interrupted, voice rising.

It sounded like she had started walking again.

'We're eighteen,' Mae repeated, dropping her voice. 'We're technically *both* eighteen, and it's our last year of high school, and we've never done anything like this before and my *crush* is actually *talking* to me—'

'You said we.' I tucked my arms more firmly into my stomach. 'Why did you say we?'

There was a beat of silence.

Then Mae said, 'I'm outside your house.'

'No.'

'C'mon,' Mae wheedled. 'It's an adventure.'

'I don't even know how to sneak out!' I whisper-yelled. 'My parents are downstairs watching some American tennis competition!'

'So they're distracted,' Mae said. 'Ames, c'mon. If you don't come I'm going to turn right around and go home, and I don't want to do that. I need you. I can't do this alone. I don't *want* to do this alone.'

Groaning, I scrubbed my palms over my face, thinking of all the ways this could go wrong.

Then I blurted: 'Okay.'

'Okay?' Mae sounded both excited and nervous.

'Okay,' I confirmed. 'Wait there. I'll be out in – I'll be out soon.'

After pacing around my room, I did the only thing I could think of: I picked up my copy of *Moby-Dick* and went to my sister's room.

'Kamilia,' I whispered.

When there was no answer, I pushed her door open.

My sister glanced up from where she was sitting cross-legged on her bed, her laptop open in front of her. She shot me an unimpressed look.

'I need your help,' I said.

She raised her eyebrows slowly, tilting her head, which I took to mean 'make your case'.

'I want to sneak out,' I whispered.

Kamilia's eyebrows dropped back down. Then she grinned.

'Oh, this is so cute.' She closed her laptop and propped her chin on her fist. 'What's the game plan?'

'I ...' I opened and closed my mouth a few times. 'Not sure. But Mae's waiting for me outside, like ... right now. So.'

Kamilia's grin broadened.

'Exciting,' she said, in a tone that felt more mocking than I'd like. Then she stood up, looking me up and down. 'Is that what you're going to wear?'

I glanced down at my black T-shirt and baggy jeans that I had rolled up at the ankles in concession to the heat. 'Yes?'

Kamilia sighed like that was the wrong answer, but all she said was: 'Fine. Follow me.'

I drifted after her as she headed down the stairs, tensing as we got to the kitchen. Was Kamilia about to walk us to the living room and announce my plans to our parents? Instead, though, Kamilia took a left turn at the kitchen, hustling me into the laundry and pointing towards the door that led into the garden.

'I'll make sure this stays unlocked for you,' she said. 'It's quieter than the front door. You'll have to climb over the back fence and loop back around to the front of the house – just use the tree at the back, it's super easy.'

When I nodded and made to move towards the door, Kamilia put one arm out, barring my way.

'You have your phone, wallet and keys, right?' she asked.

I patted my pocket, then gave her what I hoped was a very cool, calm and collected thumbs up.

Kamilia's gaze dipped down to my other hand – I was still gripping *Moby-Dick*.

'And you're bringing that?' she asked.

I looked down at it, then back at her. 'Yeah. In case I …'

In case Mae and Kasun start making out and I need a distraction.

In case someone tries to talk to me and I need an out.

In case I want to talk to someone, but need a conversation starter.

In case a rogue firework shoots towards me and I need to hold something in front of me as a shield.

'Weird safety blanket, but whatever,' Kamilia said, opening the door and then shooing me towards it.

'You owe me,' she whispered, as *Moby-Dick* and I hustled out into the dark.

✱ ✱ ✱

Mae was sitting on the low brick wall outside my house, knee jiggling. When I rounded the corner she shot up, wiping her hands on her knees and grinning at me. She looked like a cute cat burglar in a black singlet and skirt, her red hair up in a messy braided crown.

'This is exciting, right?' she whispered.

'Sure,' I said, letting her loop her arm through mine as we started down the road.

Of all the places to sneak out to, Mill Hill Park was a fairly tame first outing, which was one of the reasons I had agreed so quickly. It was a fifteen-minute walk from my house through dark suburban streets, the streets sloping up and up until we made it to the peak of the hill, where the park spread out in front of us.

The closer we got, the more nervous I became.

What were we doing? What was *I* doing? Kasun hadn't invited me, he'd invited Mae. What if this was a small, intimate gathering? What if, by coming along, I was about to wreck the group dynamics? And hadn't Mae said something about fireworks? Fireworks were not legal for private use in this state, which I knew from a single ill-fated family New Year's celebration five years ago. Was I about to get myself involved in potentially *criminal* activity? I was eighteen, which meant if this went to court I would be tried as an adult—

I felt Mae squeeze my arm, and realised my breathing had picked up.

'It'll be fine,' she mouthed, and then we were stepping onto the path leading into the park.

I thought it might be difficult to find the right group of people, as it was a big park with plenty of dark corners, but Mae seemed on top of it, pulling her phone out as we walked and directing us via texted instructions.

It didn't take long for a clump of familiar people to come into view.

'I will bet money that what's-his-face did *not* get a license for his fireworks,' I whispered to Mae, as we drew closer to the group.

It wasn't a huge gathering, but I could see enough people to put to rest the fear that I would be crashing something intimate. Still, anxiety hummed through me, rising in pitch the closer we got.

'It's going to be fine, Ames,' Mae said, gaze fixed ahead.

Then she stepped up onto her toes so she could wave at someone ahead. When she started tugging me more firmly, I dug my heels in.

'Um, no,' I managed. 'Not right now.'

Mae looked over at me, forehead crinkling. 'Not right now?'

'Too many people, Mae,' I said, gripping my copy of *Moby-Dick* hard enough that I could feel the cover crease. 'Too many ... what ifs. I'm going to ... to stand right here for a bit, and ...'

This was the second time tonight I'd lost my words. Mae watched me, patient, as I sorted through my thoughts.

'*You* should go say hello and try to find Kasun,' I said finally, disentangling from her and giving her a pat on the arm with *Moby-Dick*. 'I'm going to stand here and look very cool and calm while I take some deep breaths, and then I'll come right over.'

Mae's forehead was still crinkled. 'I can stand with you, if you like? We can be cool and calm together?'

I shook my head. 'It's fine! I'm going to check my phone. I'll be right here where you can see me. Just – give me a sec.'

It took some more coaxing, but, eventually, Mae turned and headed towards the group. I took a deep breath and then glanced down at my phone. It was with some relief that I saw I actually had notifications, so I wouldn't have to pretend to be busy while I worked to calm my racing brain.

Kamilia had sent a message to the cousin group chat a little less than half an hour ago:

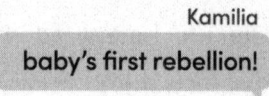

Under the message was a blurry picture of me disappearing out the back door. Kamilia's hand was in the foreground of the picture, giving my retreating figure a thumbs up.

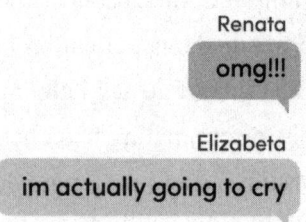

> **Elizabeta**
> never thought id see the day

> **Renata**
> where you going, girly?

> **Elizabeta**
> look at her go

> **Elizabeta**
> she's hustling

Smiling to myself, I texted back a winking face, then put my phone away. The exchange had done more than any deep breaths could have: it left me feeling almost pleased at my own daring, even if the catalyst for my actions was something totally outside myself.

Suddenly, and with a crackling bang, the world lit up. Turning my gaze skywards, I watched a haze of pink sparkle to life. Another crack, and the pink was swallowed by smoke-wreathed flares of gold. The sight coaxed a smile out of me.

When I sensed somebody coming to a stop beside me, I glanced over, expecting to see Mae.

My smile was still in place, which was good, because otherwise my expression would have crashed into blank shock. Kasun, looking stunning, was standing beside me, also with his head tilted back. When I glanced over, he caught my eye, and we smiled at each other for a moment – his smile was a quirk at the corner of his beautiful mouth, mine frozen. He looked back towards the fireworks. I didn't. After a few seconds of staring at his profile and feeling my pulse vibrate in every point of my body, I turned my gaze upwards as well.

After a moment, Kasun said, 'Mae said she'd bring you along. Glad you could make it.'

I made a small noise in the back of my throat – maybe a scream, I wasn't sure. The fireworks drowned me out, thank goodness. Tilting my head towards him, I nodded. Kasun nodded back.

'I like fireworks,' he said, after another moment had passed.

Was he still talking to me? I looked over – his head was still tilted towards the sky, but his gaze was slanted in my direction.

Was this real?

I cleared my throat. 'Yeah?'

'I like loud celebrations,' Kasun elaborated.

We were looking at each other now, the fireworks a dim light in my periphery.

'They remind me of family celebrations,' he continued.

'Loud family,' I said.

Great. I had managed to string together two words from his sentences to form one of my own. I was doing *so* well.

'Yeah,' Kasun agreed, smiling a little wider. 'Big one, too. It's pretty hectic.'

As I smiled back, nodding like a bobblehead, my mind was reeling. Was Kasun … confiding in me? Had the three whole words I'd managed to get out fooled him into thinking I was successfully engaging in conversation? Well, it wouldn't fool him forever. I'd have to step up my game.

'What are we celebrating?' I asked.

'Oh, so,' Kasun glanced up and, in the same motion, took a small sidestep towards me, his arm brushing up against mine for one heart-stopping moment, 'Jake's sister got a promotion. She's doing her own thing tonight, so he's celebrating for her.'

Oh, yeah. Jake. Mr Fireworks himself.

'Fireworks are illegal,' I commented.

Kasun winked, and both Jake and the legality of his fireworks suddenly seemed less important. 'Not everywhere.'

I laughed a little at that. This was okay. I was doing okay. As long as I didn't look directly at him.

I opened my mouth to speak, and then closed it. It felt traitorous, somehow, to talk to Kasun without Mae around. Traitorous, and also pointless. Why fan the flames of my own crush, when Mae actually seemed to be in with a chance?

With some reluctance, I said, 'Have you talked to Mae yet?'

'Not yet,' Kasun said, 'but I saw her.'

'Sounds like you two did pretty well in your bio presentation,' I said, wincing even as I spoke – *ah, yes, school; the thing everyone wants to talk about on a Friday night.*

'Yeah,' Kasun said with a laugh, seemingly unfazed. 'We make a good team.'

My smile felt tight on my face.

'Speaking of Mae, I should probably find her.' I reached for my phone as I spoke.

'Oh, damn,' Kasun said.

He was staring forwards, one hand raised towards my arm. I looked around and noticed that people were starting to move. Some were running. That couldn't be good.

'What's happening?' I asked.

My phone lit up with Mae's name. I put it to my ear and repeated my question.

'The cops are here,' Mae said. 'Where are you?'

I breathed through a flush of panic.

'Um, okay. Okay.' I drummed *Moby-Dick* against the side of my thigh, squinting at my surroundings. 'I'm … basically where you left me. Where are you?'

'Uh,' Mae said. 'Sorry, so, I sort of got pulled along with some people. We're going to Jake's … sister's house, apparently? Do you want me to—' There was a rush of sound from Mae's end, which cut her off as effectively as pressing mute.

I swatted at Kasun's shoulder with *Moby-Dick* before I could overthink the action, saying, 'Mae's going to Jake's sister's house.'

Kasun nodded, then turned around, striding away. Lacking other options, I hurried after him, phone still pressed to my ear. Mae's voice was cutting in and out.

'What?' I said, a little breathless. 'Mae, I'm – I think I'm on my way.'

Then, lacking a better option, I hung up, slipping my phone back into my pocket and upping my pace until I was level with Kasun. We power walked to the edge of the park, where there were a string of cars.

'Over here.' Kasun pointed towards a grey seven-seater. Seeing my expression, he added, 'I told you I had a big family.'

I managed a smile, even though my hands were shaking.

Was this happening? It felt like a fever dream. I had snuck out. There were police. And I was about to share a car with Kasun. For however long, it would just be me, him—

—and four other people who had noticed Kasun and were jogging towards us. Kasun, who was in the process of unlocking the car, grinned at them, waving them over.

The reality I had constructed faded back into daydream.

As I stood there marinating in the horror of my situation – car full of strangers, park full of cops, destination adjacent to a firework-lighting delinquent – one of the girls turned towards Kasun, asking in a low voice, 'Who's she?'

'This is Amalia,' Kasun said. 'We have geography together.'

It was maths, actually, but I wasn't about to point that out. I smiled a lipless smile, avoiding the glances shot my way and focusing on my reflection in the car window instead. It didn't make me feel much better. I looked washed out and almost green under the streetlight, my expression half-distorted in the tinted glass.

'Amalia, you're the guest, so you can take shotgun,' the other girl in the group said to me, flashing me a smile as she spoke.

I smiled back at her, knowing my relief was clear on my face, and she winked. Then one of the guys raised a hand, pointing at the other boy beside him.

'Hold on,' he said. 'Dave-O gets carsick, so he should be up front.'

'Should be right,' Dave-O muttered.

'Mate, no offence, but I'd rather not risk it – don't want you puking when we're stacked like sardines.'

Everyone looked over at Dave-O, who nodded in stoic acquiescence. 'Yeah, all right.'

'That's fine,' I said. 'You take shotgun and – the rest of you can sit together, so – I'll – I can sit right at the back.'

There were nods all around, and I nodded back, trying not to listen to my brain as it screamed: *Never let them take you to a secondary location!*

I am not *being kidnapped*, I reminded myself. *I am going to a stranger's house because my best friend is going to a stranger's house.*

I slipped into the car before I could keep second-guessing myself, wriggling into one of the two small pop-up seats at the back of the car. Once I was situated, the others piled in. I was in the process of pulling on my seatbelt when Dave-O started hollering and pointing.

Someone had appeared at the tree line and was running towards us. He had the broad, stockily muscled look of a rugby player. His curly hair was buzzed back close to his skull, his dark eyes bright. A large bag swung from his fist.

Jake.

I watched, stomach sinking, as he pulled to a stop in front of the group, exchanging a complicated handshake with Kasun.

'Thought you wouldn't make it, mate,' Kasun said.

Jake grinned. 'Better late. Also, I might have company coming, so we should go.'

I watched Jake's gaze rove across the interior of the car. He paused when he saw me, but didn't comment, looking back at Kasun.

'You driving?' he asked.

'I'm driving,' Kasun confirmed, swinging a set of keys around his finger.

Jake's gaze returned to me – no, not to me. To the empty seat beside me. Then it flicked to my face.

'Mind if I join you?' he asked.

Me. He was asking *me*.

I stared at him, at the small seat beside me, and then at my phone as it buzzed in my lap.

Mae

on ur way??

I took a deep breath, then tapped back:

Amalia

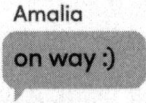

I couldn't chicken out. Not when Kasun and Mae hadn't even got a chance to talk yet.

'Sure,' I managed.

3

Jake swung into the car, pulling the sliding door closed behind him and collapsing into the seat beside me, his thigh knocking against mine.

The moment the door closed, Kasun reversed and swerved out of the parking spot, speeding towards the main road. The force of the turn jerked us and Jake grabbed the back of the seat in front of us to stop from sliding into me. His thigh pressed more firmly against mine as he adjusted the bag in his lap and clicked his seatbelt into place.

'Okay?' Jake asked.

I didn't answer, too discombobulated by the press of his leg against mine. I wasn't used to touching people other than Mae or my family, so this was throwing me for a loop. Thankfully he wasn't damp with sweat from his sprint across the park, and he didn't smell like rotten eggs from the fireworks. He smelled ... fine, actually. Nice, even. Woody, almost earthy, with a hint of musk which was probably just teenage boy sweat. Did all boys smell woody? The only man in my life who I had ever really smelled was my dad (not that I spent a lot of time smelling my dad), so I wasn't exactly up to date on what boys smelled like.

'Okay,' Jake said, more to himself this time.

I realised he was doing his best to tuck himself into the small seat – a losing battle, as he was significantly larger than both me and it, and the back of the car wasn't exactly roomy. I appreciated the thought, though. Shooting him a smile that probably looked more like a grimace, I crossed my legs, trying to make myself smaller.

Now that we were on the road and it was clear nobody was following us, everyone was much more relaxed. Kasun had passed his phone behind him, provoking a lighthearted squabble over the music selection from the seats in front of us. Dave-O had the window down, and seemed to be focusing on not throwing up.

I could relate. I felt – and probably looked – like a caged animal. I stared ahead, tapping the tips of my fingers against *Moby-Dick*. This was fine. This was fine and not at all spiralling out of control.

Oh god, why did I get in this car? Where were we even going? How was I going to get home?

I was calm. I was *calm*.

I thought of the texts from my cousins and sister: *baby's first rebellion*. I could do this.

Jake tapped a finger against the cover of my book, interrupting my thoughts. 'What are you reading?'

'*Moby-Dick*,' I muttered, lifting my hands so he could see the cover.

'Just some light reading, then?' Jake asked, the hint of a smile in his voice.

'Yep.' I darted a glance at Jake, then said, 'It's for a book club, actually.'

'Oh, a book club girl, are we?'

I wasn't sure whether the edge to his voice was mocking or joking, but it made my hackles rise either way.

'Sure,' I said, going for breezy, 'you know how it is. *Moby-Dick*, red wine, recurring discussions about Brenda's divorce that normally segue into discussing the merits of castration. Usual book club stuff.'

Jake let out a choked sound that I realised was a laugh. I glanced around me with sudden anxiety, hoping no one else had heard me. Thankfully, the squabble over the music was still going; Dave-O's head was hanging fully out the window now, and Kasun looked focused on driving.

'How do I get in on this book club action?' Jake said. 'Brenda sounds like a riot.'

'It's a pretty exclusive group,' I said with a sniff.

It was actually just a family book club: me, my mum, my sister Kamilia, my aunts Tetka Mojca and Tetka Sabinka, and my cousins Renata and Elizabeta. Any discussions of castration needed to be strictly plot-relevant, and I didn't think I'd met a single Brenda in my life. Not that I was about to tell Jake any of that.

'Pity,' Jake mused. 'So, what brought you and *Moby-Dick* out tonight?'

'Favour for a friend,' I muttered.

'Mae, right?' Jake guessed, and I nodded.

I hoped Mae was okay. She'd have texted me if she wasn't, though. Unless she couldn't. Unless—

'And how are you liking it?' Jake asked.

It took me a moment to process Jake's question, and another moment after that to answer.

'I could have done without the bit with the cops,' I said finally, and Jake coughed another laugh.

'I meant, how are you liking the book? But that's … good to know,' Jake said, a smile playing at the edges of his mouth. 'I'll make a note of that. For next time.'

'Thanks,' I said, tart, hoping my tone covered for my blush. I added, after a beat, 'The book's fine.'

I had read about three pages in the last week, but that was, once again, none of Jake's business.

We drove for another ten minutes or so before Kasun pulled up in front of a tall, white-painted brick complex. I figured it was the right place as a small group of familiar teenagers were loitering outside the front gate.

'Better let everyone in then,' Jake said. I wasn't sure if he was talking to me or not, so I nodded to be safe.

Once Jake had swung out of the car, I scooted after him, scanning the group outside the building for a familiar head of red hair. When I spotted Mae, I felt my expression crack with relief.

Mae was leaning against the wall, the embodiment of a technicolour film noir character with a cigarette dangling between her fingers, her hair shining like a beacon in the lamplight. She laughed as I crashed into her, wrapping me up in a hug.

'Are you okay?' she asked, after we had clung to each other in silence for a good thirty seconds.

'You would not believe the night I've had,' I muttered into her hair.

Mae pulled back, looking both amused and concerned. 'What did I miss?'

I widened my eyes. 'You. Would not. Believe.'

When we disentangled, I held her at arm's length and then leaned back in to give her a sniff. 'Were you smoking?'

'Oh, ew, no,' Mae replied, wrinkling her noise. 'No, I was just waiting out here for you and one of them was like "do you want a cigarette", and I didn't want to be rude.' She shrugged, wriggling her eyebrows. 'Wow, though. Like … wow. Tonight's been …'

'Stressful as hell?' I finished.

'Kind of amazing,' Mae corrected.

I thought of talking to Kasun at the park, and felt myself smile. 'I guess it could have been worse.' Forcing my smile down, I pointed a single finger at Mae. '*But* it could have been better.'

'But it could have been worse,' Mae singsonged, batting my hand down and lacing her arm through mine.

Together we followed the group through the entrance and down a tiled path that led into the building itself.

'How did you get here?' I asked Mae, as we filtered single file down a hallway and towards a lift.

'I was chatting to some people and then the cops came, and I guess I sort of ended up in someone's car,' Mae said. 'You?'

'Same.'

We quietened as we piled into the lift, though we kept our arms threaded, Mae bumping her hip against mine. In the silence, I berated myself for not telling Mae whose car I had been in. I knew she wouldn't think anything of it, but there was something about the fact that I'd both talked to Kasun before her and been in his car that felt like a betrayal, especially because there was a nasty part of me that felt … glad. Glad that I had talked to Kasun first tonight. Glad that I'd got a glimpse into his life, even if it was just finding out that he had a big family and a car to match.

Glad that I had snatched a piece of him for me and me alone.

These were nasty thoughts, and pointless too.

Once we were out of the lift and had sighted the right door, I pulled Mae aside. Mae looked faintly puzzled, but let me direct her.

'Game plan,' I said, pulling us to a stop. 'We're going to get you in there and talking to Kasun.'

Mae bit her lip, shoulders curling in. 'Oh, I don't know ...'

I flicked her upper arm, and she wrinkled her nose at me.

'No!' I said. 'Don't do that. Kasun invited you. He's the reason you're here. You said it yourself – your crush is actually *talking* to you. You're in with a chance. *This* is your chance.'

The words were as much a reminder for me as they were a pep talk for Mae, and they seemed to do the trick, for Mae at least. Pushing her shoulders back, Mae nodded.

'Okay, we can do this,' she said.

'*You* can do this,' I corrected.

Mae nodded again.

'I can do this,' she murmured.

With that, we headed for the apartment.

'Was this an official afterparty?' I whispered to Mae, once we were inside.

The apartment was dimly lit, the music a thumping undercurrent of sound – I assumed they were keeping it down for the sake of the neighbours. Clumps of people were gathered around the doorways, a group of girls from our year sitting on a red leather sofa pushed back against the far wall of the living room. Next to the living room was a doorway cloaked by a bead curtain, the shape of a kitchen visible beyond it.

'I think it's more of a ... lowkey hang,' Mae said.

'A lowkey hang,' I repeated. 'How is that different from an afterparty?'

'You're talking to me like I'm queen of the parties,' Mae said, from the corner of her mouth.

We had made our way to the sofa now.

Mae, ready with a smile, exclaimed, 'Hey, ladies!'

The girls returned the greeting, a few sparing me a smile, too. I smiled back, but hung behind Mae, letting her lead the conversation. She had always been the more socially outgoing one, whether it was approaching strangers in the street to compliment their outfits or instigating conversations in class with people we barely knew.

As I looked around the room, I heard a familiar laugh from the kitchen. A moment later, the bead curtain was pushed open, someone I didn't know moving back into the living room. I peered through the temporary gap in the swinging curtain, confirming my suspicions.

Showtime.

'Sorry,' I said, interrupting one of the girls on the sofa with an apologetic wince before turning to Mae. 'I think I found him.'

Mae, eyes widening, stared at me and then towards the kitchen when I flicked the bead curtain a meaningful glance. 'Oh. Oh, that's okay, I might just stay here for—'

'Excuse us,' I said to the girls.

Taking Mae by the shoulders, I propelled her through the bead curtain. Her protests were lost in the clatter of plastic.

'You can do this,' I muttered.

Once I managed to disentangle myself from the final few strings of beads, I surprised both myself and Mae by saying, 'Hey, Kasun!'

Kasun, who had his head stuck in the fridge, pulled back and turned towards us, a plate of flatbread balanced on one hand.

I wasn't sure where my confidence had come from. Or my lack of nerves. Maybe it was because I was approaching him on behalf of Mae. Maybe it was because I knew I didn't have a chance. Either way, the personal stakes were non-existent, which meant there wasn't anything for me to be anxious about.

This self-congratulatory musing ground to a halt when Kasun's expression brightened in recognition, and he said in that velvety, velvety voice, 'Hey, Amalia!'

'Bread,' I replied.

'Oh, yeah.' Kasun laughed like I'd said a full sentence about his snack and not a single word. 'It's bazlama. Jake's mum makes it, it's so good. Want some?'

I managed to shake my head.

Kasun, whose expression bloomed into a full smile the moment he caught sight of Mae, said, 'Mae! What's up? Did you want some?'

I glanced at Mae, who blinked at Kasun.

Oh, no. No, no. She wasn't allowed to be as bad as me.

Right. Desperate times, etcetera. It was time for me to leave the love birds alone so Mae had a chance to sink or swim on her own.

I disentangled myself from Mae. Turning towards the exit, I raised my hand, exclaiming, 'Oh, hey!'—

—just as Jake stepped through the bead curtain.

4

'Oh, hey,' Jake echoed, raising his eyebrows at me.

I did my best not to melt into the floor. That had not been the plan. The plan had been to pretend I had caught the attention of a 'friend' outside the kitchen I could go and join, giving me an excuse to leave Mae and Kasun to it. Instead, I had accidentally summoned our host.

'Oh, hey,' I repeated weakly, adding, 'Jake.'

'Amalia,' Jake said, eyebrows drifting higher, if that was possible. 'Do you ... want me to say "hey" again?'

I managed to smile, then shot a glance at Mae. To my dismay, she was watching us and not even trying to talk to Kasun.

'Hey,' I said, then winced at myself. 'Um, hello. Do you want to go to ...' I floundered, my face heating as my brain caught up with my mouth.

Go to? Go to *where*?

'… go to the living room?' I finished.

Jake stared at me, and then his gaze flicked to Mae and Kasun. Something that I hoped was understanding crossed his face.

'Sure, Amalia,' Jake said, a smile playing at the edges of his mouth. 'Let's go to the living room.'

I shot Mae what I hoped was a covert thumbs up, then made a beeline for the bead curtain. Jake held it open for me, gesturing for me to go first with an expression I could only interpret as lightly mocking.

'That was smooth,' Jake commented, once we were through the curtain.

I shot him a glare. He smiled back.

'So, playing matchmaker, are we?' he asked, leaning against the wall beside the curtain and crossing his arms.

'Shh,' I muttered, glancing at the curtain and then gesturing with my head that we should move further into the room.

Jake shrugged at me, smile broadening – but, to my surprise, he followed me across the room.

'Not that it's your business, but yes,' I said, once we had made it to the opposite wall.

'Hey,' Jake said, putting extra emphasis on the word – as though I could have forgotten my own embarrassing repetition of it a few moments earlier. 'No judgement from me. I love love.'

I made a face at Jake, and he grinned back. A moment passed, and I realised I wasn't sure what else to say. Jake looked at me for a beat longer, grin relaxing into something smaller. Then he said, 'I should go check on some people. Make sure they're not making a mess.'

'Oh, sure,' I said, suddenly feeling even more awkward.

'You and *Moby-Dick* enjoy yourselves.' Jake nodded at the book still clutched in my hand.

'Thanks,' I managed.

When Jake was gone, I leaned back against the wall, my gaze drawn to the bead curtain. I imagined Mae and Kasun standing together in silence, Kasun's smile slowly dropping as Mae failed to speak. Then, instead, I imagined Mae launching into conversation, beautiful in her animation. My mind spiralled out, imagining the texts they must have exchanged before today to lead to Kasun's invitation tonight. Mae probably hadn't needed me to push them together. Kasun was probably half in love with her already.

'Hey, are you okay?'

Someone pressed their hand against my shoulder, and I looked over to see one of the girls who had been in the car with us – the nice one, who had offered to let me take shotgun. She was smaller than me, with long black hair and one deep dimple in her left cheek. She was also, I realised, extraordinarily beautiful.

'I'm Laeli,' she supplied with a smile, though her eyebrows remained drawn together. 'Amalia, right?'

'Yeah.' I smiled back, hoping I wasn't goggling at her – she was maybe the most beautiful person I'd ever laid eyes on, and I wasn't sure how I'd managed to miss it at the park. 'I'm fine. Just ... tired.'

She tilted her head, smile softening. 'So, you and Kasun have some classes together?'

'Oh, yeah,' I said.

'And you know Jake too?'

'Not really,' I confessed. 'I don't really ... know anyone here very well, except for Mae. Mae's my best friend. She was the one who was invited. By Kasun. So ... sorry for crashing. Um.'

I bit down on my lower lip to stop myself from speaking. For some reason Laeli wasn't looking at me weirdly, though, just smiling a little. Her eyes were dark, rimmed by thick lashes.

'You have kind eyes,' I blurted, then felt myself flush.

Laeli glanced down and then back at me, lips pursing around a smile, her dimple deepening. 'You're sweet. And don't apologise. I mostly know Kasun and Jake here, so I'm feeling a bit out of place, too.'

'How do you know Jake and Kasun?' I asked.

Laeli moved to stand next to me, putting her hands behind her back and leaning against the wall. 'We've been friends since we were kids.'

'Same with me and Mae.'

'It's nice, isn't it?' Laeli said, eyes crinkling. 'Having old friends.'

'I don't know what I'd do without her,' I said, honestly.

Laeli opened her mouth to speak, but then she looked past me, her expression slipping into something expectant.

I followed her line of sight – Jake was heading back towards us.

'So one of the guys is messed up,' Jake said, coming to a stop next to Laeli. 'We're taking him home. I know it's early, but want a lift?'

'That's okay,' Laeli said, smiling up at Jake. 'Mum knows where I am. I've already given her a call.'

'Easy,' Jake said. Then his gaze moved to me. 'You?'

'Me?' I echoed.

'Do you need a lift?' Jake asked.

'I …' I shot a glance at the bead curtain, then turned my attention back to Jake. 'Yes. Okay. Um, now?'

'Now,' Jake confirmed.

'Okay, one sec.'

I headed back to the kitchen.

Mae and Kasun were still there, deep in conversation. Mae was leaning back against the kitchen counter, saying something that involved a lot of hand movements, and Kasun was watching her with the kind of smile that made my heart ache.

I hovered in the doorway for a moment, then blurted, 'Mae.'

Mae spun to face me. 'Amalia?'

I stepped further into the kitchen, and Mae moved to meet me.

'What's up?' she asked.

'I'm going to head off,' I said. 'Someone's giving me a ride home. Do you want to go, or …?'

Mae slipped her phone out of her pocket, and we both looked at the time: 10.06 pm.

'I might stay a bit longer,' Mae said.

She seemed surprised at her own words, her gaze darting towards Kasun and then away.

I felt a frisson of anxiety. 'How are you going to get home?'

'I'll make sure she gets back okay,' Kasun said, choosing that moment to jump into the conversation. 'I can take her home when she's ready to go.'

I glanced at him, then back at Mae.

'Are you sure?' I asked.

Mae took a deep breath, then smiled. 'I'm sure. I've got time.'

'Okay,' I said, even as I felt another sharp jab of anxiety in my stomach. 'Be safe. Give me a call if you need.'

Mae nodded, and we exchanged a tight hug. Then I turned for the exit, smacking at the bead curtain to get through and making my way back into the living room. Laeli and Jake were where I had left them, Laeli smiling when she caught sight of me.

'I'm ready,' I said.

Jake nodded, pushing off the wall and heading for the front door. Offering Laeli a parting wave, I followed.

Outside the building, I suffered a serious bout of deja vu: three guys were leaning up against the side of Kasun's car, one of them appearing on the verge of collapse.

'Who's driving?' I asked.

Jake, who had just pulled a set of keys from his pocket, raised his eyebrows at me.

'No,' I said.

'No?' Jake repeated, already moving for the driver's door. 'Don't let the fireworks fool you, Eyebrows. My parents raised a responsible young man.'

Jake grinned at my dubious expression, then turned towards the guys, raising his voice: 'Amalia gets shotgun.'

Three pairs of eyes slid over to me, a grunt or two of affirmation following the appraisal. I watched the other two guys manoeuvre their drunk friend into the centre seat, one of them holding a bucket under his arm.

Once we were all in the car, I huddled back against the seat, turning my face towards the window. The guy behind me gave my seat a kick, which I ignored, assuming (generously) that it had been accidental.

'I'm going to drop these guys off at the nearest train station,' Jake said to me, turning the keys in the ignition. 'Where should I drop you?'

I drummed *Moby-Dick* against my thigh, pondering my options. 'Back near the park is fine.'

Jake nodded. He looked like was going to say something else.

Our companions were getting rowdy now – a wayward elbow prodded me in the back of the neck, and I jerked forwards with a wince. Jake's eyes narrowed, and he twisted so he could glare behind him.

'Oi! Settle down,' he barked, slapping his palm against the back of his seat.

All noise and action behind me quietened. Their sound levels stayed at a low murmur for the rest of the drive.

Jake had flicked on the radio instead of plugging in his phone, so I spent the drive to the train station tuning out the conversation from the backseat and trying to ignore energetic ads for cars and baby formula. I glanced at Jake only once: his gaze was fixed on the road ahead, a faint crease between his eyebrows.

When we reached the station, the boys slid out, one of them yelling to Jake something I chose to hear as 'Thanks, ya mad aunt'. Another chortled a 'Bye, Emily', which I appreciated – if not for its accuracy, at least for the sentiment. Jake turned towards me.

'So, still want me to drop you off at the park?'

'Yes?' The reply stretched into a question.

'Okay.'

As we pulled out onto the road, the ad break finally came to an end. The music that replaced it was slow and whining.

I grimaced at the radio, gaze flicking between the dashboard dials. 'How do I change the channel?'

'Dunno,' Jake said, with a shrug. 'Not my car, remember?'

I stared hard at the dials, giving one a toggle – okay, that was air conditioning. I tried another – volume! I was getting there.

'Why are you driving Kasun's car?' I asked, once I had located the radio scanner.

'To use up his petrol.'

I managed to tune us onto some frantic country music. 'Why?'

'So many questions. Change the channel, would you?'

I did so, running us through a few bursts of static before I found something classical and string-heavy.

'He's eating my sister's bazlama,' Jake said.

'He's eating your sister's bazlama?'

'Yeah. He always eats my family's bazlama.' Jake merged onto the main road near the station.

Our pace slowed to a crawl – clearly, we weren't the only ones doing late-night drop-offs.

'And that ... really gets to you?' I shot Jake a look out of the corner of my eye as I started scanning radio channels again.

'He's a goddamn bazlama thief. He's cost my family thousands in yeast. In return, I'll cost him thousands in petrol.' Jake flashed me the edge of a smile, and I felt myself snort out a laugh.

Jake tapped the edge of the steering wheel. 'So, Eyebrows, why are you playing matchmaker?'

I glared at Jake – which he missed, because he was checking his blind spots before making a turn. The responsible dickhead.

'Why are you calling me that?' I asked.

Jake ignored me, saying, 'You were staring at the bead curtain pretty intensely after we left the kitchen.'

I shrugged, twiddling the scanner in an attempt to recapture a missed radio station. I hadn't realised I had been that obvious.

Ignoring his statement (it felt only fair), I said, 'Did you really light those fireworks to celebrate your sister's promotion?'

'What do you want me to say?'

'What?' I could feel heat rise up my throat, though I wasn't sure why.

Jake shot me another half-grin. 'Do you want me to lie to you?'

'No?'

Where was he going with this?

'Okay. I'll be honest.' Jake drummed his fingers against the wheel. 'Hell yeah, I did. She's too responsible for that kind of thing now, but someone has to celebrate properly. Dream jobs deserve fireworks.'

I settled on a classic rock station and turned it up for good measure. 'Right. Sure.'

'Now *you* have to answer something honestly.'

I resisted the urge to start station-scanning again, putting my hands in my lap and side eyeing Jake. 'Okay?'

Jake pulled the car to the kerb, and I realised we had arrived at Mill Hill Park. 'Why are you helping your friend hook up with a guy you're into?'

5

I cupped my hand against the back of my skull, bunching the hair there against my palm as I let out a nervous laugh. Jake raised his eyebrows.

My entire body felt hot. 'I'm not responding to that. I don't – why would you even think that?'

I paused for a moment, waiting for him to speak, then realised I didn't actually want to hear what he had to say. With a huff, I slid out of the car, stepping out into the night.

'Kasun and I have been friends a long time,' Jake said, getting out of the car a beat later. 'He's a good-looking guy. Likeable. He gets attention. Let's just say I know the signs.'

I didn't say anything, beginning to walk in the direction of my house. Frustratingly, Jake followed.

'I'm not trying to be mean, Eyebrows—' Jake continued.

'Are you calling me that because you've forgotten my name? Is that it?'

'—I'm just curious.'

'My name's Amalia,' I said.

Jake shot me an indulgent smile, and I smiled back. Both our smiles said we weren't about to engage on terms other than our own.

The night had become surprisingly chilly, and I was glad I'd decided to wear jeans. Jake didn't have anything on beyond a slightly baggy T-shirt with a faded logo and a pair of shorts, and I could see the way his flesh pimpled in the cold, even if his expression and posture didn't reveal any discomfort. Despite my frustration, I felt a pang of sympathy. We walked for a few more minutes before I spoke.

'This is far enough,' I decided, coming to a stop. 'You can go back to Kasun's warm car now.'

Jake shoved his hands into his pockets, squaring his shoulders. 'Sure?'

'Yeah. It's my street.'

What was the protocol here? I wasn't about to hug him. I barely knew him – we had interacted more in one night than in almost six years of schooling. We stared at each other, and then Jake nodded, taking an awkward step back.

'Thanks for the ride,' I said, doing the same.

'Thanks for being entertaining, Eyebrows.' Jake did that crooked grin again. 'I still want in on that book club.'

'Sure,' I muttered, as Jake turned and headed back up the street, raising a hand in farewell.

'See you around, Eyebrows!' he called.

I watched him retreat, then turned back to my house with narrowed eyes. Taking out my phone, I called my sister.

The call almost rang out before she picked up. 'What's up, baby rebel?'

'I'm outside,' I said. 'Is it safe for me to come in?'

'One sec.' I heard the sound of shuffling from Kamilia's end, then: 'Yep, I'm in the kitchen. Come now.'

It was harder getting back over the fence, as I didn't have as much help from the tree this time. Finally though, I made it back into the yard, slipping through the laundry door and into the kitchen. Kamilia was waiting for me, a mug of tea cupped between her hands.

She surveyed me, then said, 'You're so red.'

'That fence is a workout,' I said.

'Why are you two still up?'

I whipped around – my mum was standing in the doorway between the living room and the kitchen, hands on her hips. As I stared at her, probably looking like a deer in headlights, she narrowed her eyes.

'Why is this?' she asked, gesturing at my face. 'Have you been running a race?'

'Yep,' Kamilia said, before I could stammer my way through an incriminating answer. 'I dared Malka to race me to the kitchen. She's so slow I had time to make a cup of tea before she even got down the stairs.'

'Shut up,' I snapped instinctively, and Kamilia grinned at me over the rim of her mug.

'You girls,' Mum sighed.

Kamilia winked, and I pulled a face at her.

What a night.

What a day.

Or: what, day? That felt more accurate.

I attempted to blink the sunlight out of my eyes, making a noise of disgust. Rolling onto my stomach, I peered at my blaring phone with some difficulty. When I worked up the strength to swipe one finger across the screen, Mae screamed, *'Ames!'* so loudly that I hung up.

A moment later, the phone rang again.

'Ames,' Mae said, 'last night was so …' She let out a screech.

I winced. 'Good night?'

'Yeah,' Mae said, breathlessly.

'I'm glad,' I said, feeling a twinge, and then another twinge – that had been a lie, and I didn't like that it had been a lie. 'You made it home before your parents?'

I had received a text at 11.01 pm the previous night from Mae that only said: *Home*, so I had been on edge ever since, glad she had made it but nervous that her parents had caught her coming back in.

'Yep, beat them by like five minutes,' she said. Then, in a husky, insinuating tone, 'And how was your ride home?'

In a similar though less effective husky voice, I said, 'We rode *all* night.'

'Oh, baby!' Mae cried. Then, in a normal voice: 'So you had sex with Jake?'

'Yeah, Mae,' I replied, flopping onto my back, 'and then we went back to the park and lay on our backs on the grass, and he set off a bunch of fireworks just for me.'

Mae snorted. 'You need to work on your "joking" tone.'

'Who said I was joking?' I said, keeping my voice neutral.

'Ha-ha.'

'I don't know why you're laughing. Jake and I are in love.'

'Okay, but seriously,' Mae said, and I could imagine her doing spins in her desk chair, catching herself against her desk before launching herself into another circle. 'Thank you for pushing me into a conversation with Kasun. We talked for a *super* long time. He was laughing at basically everything I said, and he was standing *super* close …'

I zoned out as Mae gave me a rundown of her night, focusing instead on stopping my thoughts from drifting and spiralling.

'So, are you … going to go on a date now?' I asked, once Mae had run out of steam.

There was a pause, and then Mae said, the edge of hurt audible in her tone, 'Were you listening to me just now?'

I was quiet for too long, and she laughed before I blurted, 'Yes! Yes. I just don't get … like. What's the protocol?'

'The protocol?'

There was rustling from her end, and I could imagine Mae getting up from her chair only to flop back down on her bed, shoving one of her many small, fluffy pillows under her head to get comfortable. While she rustled about, I grabbed the water bottle on my bedside table, chugging the stale water like it was the nectar of the gods.

'Yeah,' I said finally, running my finger around the rim of the bottle. 'You flirted, you … hit it off.' I tried not to let the curdling feeling in my gut reach my voice. 'What comes next?'

Mae went silent, like she was thinking hard.

'Well, he actually invited me to another party next weekend at some beach, so I'll go to that, and then … we'll see how it goes.' I could almost hear her shrug. 'And … I guess that's it.'

I lay back, blinking at my ceiling. 'Honestly, I'm underwhelmed.' I felt my eyes narrow. 'When you say another party—'

'I'll make it work,' Mae said firmly.

'And when you say beach—'

'I'll come up with a plan,' Mae said, with enough confidence that my eyes narrowed further.

I didn't like the sound of that.

※ ※ ※

By Tuesday, Mae was yet to tell me her grand plan for sneaking out for the second week in a row, which had left me with an ever-growing pit in my stomach. Mill Hill Park on a Friday night had been one thing, but 'some beach' (I didn't even know which beach) on a 'weekend' (when on the weekend, Mae? *When?*) was another thing entirely. The unknowns were setting off all my internal alarms.

I didn't know how Mae was being so calm about this. One successful sneak-out did not make her an expert. I was bracing myself for this to blow up in our faces – and yes, it would be *our* faces, because wherever Mae went, I went. That was a given.

My cousins, on the other hand, were ecstatic. It seemed like me sneaking out for the first time was the most exciting thing to happen to them all year (though, to be fair, we hadn't had much year yet, so maybe it was).

Kamilia had barely reported back to the group chat that I'd got home safe before they were asking if I would do it again.

Renata

also how would u rate the experience?

Elizabeta

ten out of ten would sneak again??

When I grudgingly confirmed that there were, possibly, plans to sneak out again, Elizabeta sent a series of skull emojis followed by a single dancing woman emoji. I think she meant for the skulls to convey that she'd died from excitement (I wasn't sure what to do with the dancing emoji), but every time I opened the chat the sight of them only contributed to my sense of foreboding.

'Ames.'

I snapped back to reality, staring at the pencil being waved in front of my face.

'Was that just in your mouth? Gross.' I batted at her wrist.

'Kasun's going to be in our next class,' Mae said, voice dropping to a whisper as the teacher's stare swept the room. It was our first class of the day, and the mood was low. 'What do you think I should do?'

'What do you *want* to do?' I replied, trying to ignore the nasty voice in my head hissing: *nothing, leave him alone*.

'You *know* what I want to do,' Mae said, pitching her voice lower so her whisper became suggestive.

'You'd definitely get suspended if you did *that*. Probably expelled. Maybe wait until after maths.'

'Super unhelpful, Ames. Thanks.'

'You're so welcome.'

I glanced down at my workbook, then back at Mae. She was still staring at me, chewing on the end of her pencil.

'Gross,' I repeated.

I considered asking about the party again, but decided against it. I wasn't sure I even wanted to know – there was no guarantee that the plan Mae was cooking up would make me any less stressed on her behalf.

'You didn't actually tell me how your ride back was,'

Mae said, 'other than texting me that Jake had dropped you off.'

'Yeah, me and a few other people,' I replied, focusing back on my work.

'Kasun said he gave you a lift there. To Jake's,' Mae continued.

I peeked at Mae from the corner of my eye, bracing myself for an expression somewhere between angry and upset. Instead, she was grinning.

'Kasun also said the car was pretty full,' she said, oh-so-casual. 'That you and Jake probably had to get pretty … up close and personal in the back.'

So this was what was happening.

I decided my best defence was silence.

Mae disagreed.

'When the sides of your thighs touched in the back of that dark, dark car, did you see fireworks?' she whispered.

'I'm going to kill you in real life,' I whispered back.

✳ ✳ ✳

When we walked into class the next period, my stomach lurched the moment I caught sight of Kasun. Mae tightened her grip on my arm, so I knew she had noticed him too. We lingered in the doorway for a few moments, Mae holding me in place, but Kasun didn't seem likely to glance our way anytime soon. I tugged at Mae, trying to get her moving.

To her credit, once she started walking again, she moved fast. Unfortunately, she seemed to have been overcome by the ghost of someone who sat in the back row, because before I knew it, we were bypassing our usual seats and heading towards Kasun.

'Our seats are back there,' I prompted, using my head to gesture at the window seats we had just passed.

Mae didn't respond, plonking us down in the row behind Kasun.

'Mae,' I hissed.

She ignored me, sitting down and taking out her books. After glaring at her for a moment longer, I sat down beside her. When the seats' usual occupants appeared in the doorway, stalling and shooting us incredulous looks, I offered a weak smile in return and sank lower in my seat.

'Mae,' I said, reproachful, as I tracked the pair's huffing path across the room to another pair of seats.

She was still ignoring me, her gaze focused on the whiteboard at the front of the room, her pen jiggling between two fingers. I sighed and started taking out my books.

I could pinpoint the moment Kasun noticed us: Mae's back straightened, and she leaned forwards, her pen stilling. Without checking, I knew that she had directed her gaze to her book, which she was staring at with studied nonchalance. I couldn't blame her for that. I was doing the same thing.

'Oh hey, Mae,' I heard Kasun say, and I looked up to see him turn so he was facing our desk, his beautiful brow crinkled in a frown. 'Did sir make a seating plan?'

I rested my elbow on the desk, chin on my palm, so I could stare pointedly at Mae.

'No,' Mae said, though I could see the beginning of a blush spotting her collarbone. 'We just felt like a change.'

'Oh, okay,' Kasun said.

I flicked Mae's arm at the same time Jake appeared in the doorway. I tried to bat down the prickle of awareness I felt as he walked down the aisle between desks. He seemed less concerned by the seat change than Kasun, throwing his bag beside his friend and then turning towards me, startling me by bracketing the sides of my desk with his hands.

'Hey, Eyebrows,' he said. 'Get home safe the other night?'

I wasn't sure if that was meant to be a joke or not, so I stayed silent. Mae pinched my thigh, and I let out a squeak.

I sent up a silent thank you when the teacher arrived.

By the end of class, I wasn't sure what Mae had managed to achieve, beyond dragging me into a feud with our seats' regular owners. Kasun headed for the door the moment the bell rang without a backwards glance.

As students streamed out, the teacher said, voice raised, 'I've been told to remind those of you in biology not to forget your permission slips for the zoo visit in Week Six. Please return your slips so I can stop talking about a subject I do not teach.'

'Didn't we go to the zoo in, like, Year Seven?' Mae said, hiking her bag onto her back and joining the stream of students. Then, in a different voice: 'Oh! Hey.'

I noted with dissatisfaction that Jake had appeared beside us, and seemed intent on keeping pace with me.

'Eyebrows and I have geography together,' Jake explained, flashing Mae a grin.

'Oh!' Mae said again, smiling at Jake and then looking at me, tilting her head.

'I have a name,' I said, trying to remember if we actually did have our next class together or not – and then recalling, with some bitterness, an entertaining presentation Jake had done earlier in the year. 'Yeah. Okay. We do.'

Mae widened her eyes at me. 'I'll see you later, then.'

Before I could stop her, Mae had turned around and was pulling her phone out of her pocket. She shot me one last wide-eyed stare over her shoulder, before hurrying in the opposite direction. A few seconds later, my phone buzzed in my pocket. I ignored it.

'So, new seats, huh?' Jake said.

'I don't want to talk about it.'

We walked on in silence.

Finally, not looking at Jake, I said, 'It wasn't my idea.'

'After the wingwoman skills you flexed on the weekend?' Jake said. 'Not sure I believe that.'

Something in my gut curled and soured, and I threw Jake a look.

Jake took a few long strides, and I thought – hoped – that he was about to stride away. Instead, he turned so he was half-walking backwards, eyebrows pulled down in thought.

'I just don't get why you're trying to push them together,' he said.

I glared at him and hoped he would trip. Was he actually curious? Or was he just trying to get on my nerves?

'I don't get why you're talking to me about this,' I said.

Jake raised his hands, falling back into step beside me. I wasn't done.

'And *also*,' I continued, wrapping my hands around the straps of my backpack, 'I never even said I had a crush on – you know. So. So! Frankly.'

I ran out of steam.

'You want to run that by me again?' Jake asked, sounding amused now.

'No,' I snapped.

A lifetime later, we reached the door of our classroom.

Jake gestured for me to go first. I narrowed my eyes at him, but stepped through, glancing over my shoulder to make sure there were no shenanigans happening behind me. Jake raised his eyebrows at my expression, hooking his fingers into the lintel above the door and taking a swinging step through the doorway. I watched his shoulders bunch under his school shirt, and then sniffed and looked away.

'Are you coming on Saturday?' Jake asked.

'What?' Then, connecting the dots: 'The party? Mae is. Or wants to.'

Jake nodded. I still wasn't sure what to make of him or his questions. Why did he want to know?

'How's *Moby-Dick*?' he asked – another question I didn't know what to do with. As though I might have forgotten, he added, 'For your book club.'

'Oh, um, okay?' I glanced into the classroom – the teacher still hadn't arrived, thankfully – then back at Jake. I found myself saying, 'Actually, it's not even this month's pick. We're doing *Emma*. I just didn't finish *Moby-Dick*, so I'm reading both at the moment.'

'Ooh, rule breaker,' Jake said, with a smile that was either teasing or mocking – I still couldn't tell with him.

The teacher appeared behind us, and, finally, Jake broke away from me, heading for the back of the room. With some relief, I slumped into my regular seat near the front, slipping my phone out of my pocket.

I sniffed again and put my phone back in my pocket.

'Hey, where's *Moby-Dick*?' Mae asked at lunch.

Munching on her sandwich, she gestured at the copy of *Emma* in my lap. I blinked down at it before turning my attention back to her.

'I'm taking a break from *Moby-Dick*,' I said.

'Is that because of your mum and your tetka's latest … disagreement?' Mae asked.

She insisted I keep her updated on book club drama, and she had been particularly thrilled by the latest saga.

'No,' I said, 'I just thought I should refresh *Emma* before its session.'

Not that I'd been making much progress. Jake's 'wingwoman' comment had struck a nerve, and reading about matchmaking wasn't exactly helping to distract me from my current stresses.

'Can't believe you'd abandon the whale like that,' Mae said, snorting out a laugh when I jabbed her in the side with my elbow.

I pursed my lips, then blurted, 'What's your plan for Saturday?'

Mae went quiet. Her wide, puppy dog eyes made me instantly wary.

'What's your plan for Saturday, Mae?' I repeated.

'You know how in movies when people sneak out they have, like, another friend who sneaks out with them, and they're each other's alibi?' Mae said coaxingly, her eyes becoming, if possible, wider and more puppy-like.

'I know that people are always caught when they do that,' I shot back, adding, '*and* I wasn't invited.'

I was arguing a losing case, I knew. (Although … did Jake asking me if I was going count as an invitation? I pushed the thought aside. That wasn't the point.) The moment Mae had accepted Kasun's invitation, my fate was sealed.

'My parents trust you, so if I said I was staying at your place they wouldn't care, and they wouldn't ask any questions,' Mae said, pleading now. 'You know it's the same for your parents with me.'

I narrowed my eyes at Mae. She wasn't wrong. Outside of my family, Mae was the only person in the world I could mention I was seeing without my parents asking a thousand and one questions about my plans and the person I was with. It came with the territory of growing up together and being from the same tiny ethnic community. Also, my parents thought Mae was an angel who had never done anything wrong in her life – a reputation she was at risk of testing now.

'Didn't you have fun on Friday?' Mae asked.

I opened my mouth, then closed it. It had been stressful, yes, but …

'You did,' Mae said, and I found I couldn't disagree.

'It was … new,' I conceded.

'Think about it,' Mae said, scooting forwards, apparently emboldened by my lack of denial. 'We tell our parents we're heading to each other's houses, then we meet up and go to the party. At the end of the night we can just choose the safest house to sneak back into. Or ... whatever. We'll work it out.'

Whatever, we'll work it out, wasn't a phrase that filled me with confidence. Still, despite it all, I found myself groaning but nodding.

Mae pumped her fists, and I felt my lips twitch up in a smile. Maybe this wouldn't be too bad.

Maybe.

6

By Friday, I was jittery enough that my sister spent most of dinner sending me narrow-eyed looks across the dining table. I nodded absentmindedly through the meal to whatever was being said, only managing to catch hold of the thread of conversation when Mum suggested I join Kamilia and my cousins on one of their regular weekend camping trips soon. I managed to wriggle my way out of that by implying (not totally untruthfully) that I was too busy with school work.

When we were clearing up the plates, Kamilia muttered, 'What is up with you?'

I didn't say anything, instead gesturing upstairs with a tilt of my head before carrying a pile of plates to the sink. Once we had finished tidying, I headed for the stairs. I knew that Kamilia would only be a few steps behind.

When we got to my room, Kamilia closed the door

behind herself for once, heading for my desk chair and sprawling out on it.

'Where's the body?' she asked.

'You know how I mentioned in the group chat I might possibly be planning on sneaking out again?'

Kamilia's eyebrows shot up. 'You want to do that tonight?'

'Tomorrow.' I nibbled at the edge of my nail and then dropped down on my bed, tucking my hands under my thighs. 'I told Mum and Dad I'm going to Mae's for a sleepover, but we're going to—' I glanced at the closed door, whispering, '—a beach party.'

'Which beach?' Kamilia asked.

'MacKenzies,' I said.

Kamilia sucked air in between her teeth. 'That's not easy to get to. A bold choice, baby rebel.'

'Thanks?' The word twisted into a question. 'I mean, it's not like I chose the location.'

Kamilia nodded once, then stood up, putting her hands on her hips. 'Still, I'm impressed, Malka. Keep this up, and we might have something to talk about.'

I stared at Kamilia as she headed for the door. 'But … we *are* talking.'

'You'll see,' Kamilia said. 'Or maybe you won't. We'll see.'

'I don't know what that means,' I said.

Kamilia shrugged enigmatically from the doorway, then disappeared down the hall without another word.

In contrast to my bundle of nerves, Mae spent the entirety of Saturday buzzing with excitement. I wouldn't see her until the evening, but she kept me updated via text throughout the day, starting strong with:

A few minutes later, she sent back a throwing up emoji with the text:

> **Mae**
> raspberry vodka does NOT taste like raspberry

Around noon, she sent me a screenshot of a map showing our bus route for the night, which I stared at with some anxiety: the route was winding, and involved a bus change on a random side street. I spent close to an hour after that mapping our route using street view, counting the streetlights and trying to work out how dark and skeevy the route was going to be, while Mae sent me screenshots of hair and make-up styles followed by either question marks or exclamation marks.

Before I knew it, I was heading 'for Mae's' dressed in jeans and a T-shirt, which I felt was an outfit that could pass as both 'I am going to a sleepover' and 'I am going to a party'. From Mae's pursed lips (and texts leading up to our evening) I knew she had been hoping I'd go for something a bit more daring. We had met up at a kebab place on the main road near our first bus stop, and munched our way through a halal snack pack while Mae used her phone as a mirror to do her make-up.

Summer was officially coming to an end, so while the days were still hot, the nights were starting to get cool and windy. I had bundled my hair up in what I hoped was a stylishly messy bun in anticipation of the sea winds, and Mae had braided her hair around her head, but it seemed like only I had thought to bring a jacket.

By the time we got off our first bus, the evening had settled into darkness, and we were close enough to the ocean that I shrugged on my jacket as we exited the bus.

Twenty minutes into waiting for bus number two, Mae started stomping her feet. I wondered for a moment if I was about to witness a tantrum. When I looked at her properly, though, I realised that she was just stepping from side to side, hands bundled under her armpits.

'Can I have your jacket for a bit?' she asked, when she noticed I was watching her.

'I told you before we left that it'd get cold,' I said.

'Okay, *Mum*,' she said. 'I don't have any jackets that go with this top.'

I gave Mae's top a pointed look. It had thin golden chains for straps that crisscrossed over her otherwise bare back, the glittery golden material itself done in the style of a scarf shirt that barely covered her midriff.

'What's that saying?' I said, shoving my hands into my pockets. 'Beauty is pain? Listen to your best friend when she says it'll probably be windy?'

Another ten minutes passed without the bus. Mae kept bouncing from side to side, lightly jangling with the movement.

I shrugged off my jacket and handed it over.

Another five minutes crawled by. A bus that was not the right bus pulled up.

'I wish one of us had a car.' I stared mournfully into the bus window. 'Imagine how warm and comfortable we could be right now.'

'Maybe you should have brought a jacket.'

That was not Mae's voice.

'Hello,' I said to Jake, who was making his way across the bus shelter towards us.

He was wearing a big black hoodie and a pair of shorts, which in my books negated any warmth gained from the hoodie.

'Hey, Eyebrows,' he said. 'Waiting for the bus?'

Mae, leaning past me with a much friendlier smile than mine, said, 'Yeah! Are you?'

'Nah, just got off,' he said, totally straight-faced like *I* was the one with a dirty mind. 'I'm heading to Kasun's.'

'Kasun's?' Mae repeated.

Jake settled back on his heels, rolling his shoulders – which absolutely did not draw my attention to how broad they were.

'He's giving me a lift,' Jake said, glancing at me and then Mae. 'Lives right around the corner from here. I bet there'll be room – a few people are going from his. We should have at least two cars.'

'Are you sure?' Mae asked, though her tone was telling me she had already decided she was getting into one of those cars, even if it meant she had to kill someone for a spot.

Jake looked over at me and smiled a slow smile. I narrowed my eyes at him, and his smile widened into a grin.

'The more the merrier,' he said.

Kasun lived in a red brick complex set back from the road. The door leading inside from the car park was already propped open, and Jake, after gesturing for us to go first, directed us up to the third floor. Even without his help, I think we could have guessed the right direction –

the sounds of music and laughter intensified the closer we got.

'Must have nice neighbours,' I muttered, as Jake rapped on the door.

'No one lives next door. It's a holiday rental,' Jake replied, like I was trying to have a conversation with him or something.

A moment later, the door was thrown open by Kasun, who grinned at Jake and then, taking us in, threw out his arms.

'Maths girls!' he said.

I felt my face heat again. What was I supposed to do? Did he want a hug? Was this a group hug situation?

Before I could short circuit, Mae acted. I got a waft of her strawberry-scented shampoo as she ducked by me, going in for a squeeze.

'Hi,' I said, when she stepped back and Kasun's gaze turned to me. 'Sorry. We're here.'

Well. It was a better opener than 'bread'.

'We bumped into Jake at the bus stop,' Mae filled in. 'He said there'd be space with you guys? Totally cool if not.'

'The more the merrier,' Kasun said, ushering us in.

Mae followed without hesitation.

I paused. The thought of entering an unfamiliar space filled with an unknown number of people was doing a number on my heart. I flexed my fingers and took a few deep breaths.

'There's going to be space,' Jake said from beside me, misreading my pause.

When I didn't respond, I felt his hand brush my shoulder. Without meaning to, I flinched. Jake pulled away immediately.

'Okay, Eyebrows,' he said, circling around me so we were facing each other.

His tone – like he was talking to a baby animal who had wandered into the middle of the road – rubbed me the wrong way. I let out a sharp breath, glaring at him.

'You know I have an actual name,' I said.

Jake looked at me in a way I hadn't seen before. His dark eyes had gone ... soft.

'Amalia,' he said. 'I know.'

We stared at each other. I didn't know what to do with this Jake, who was watching me with the kind of patience that made me feel like it would be all right for us to just ... keep hanging out here, for as long as I needed.

'Good,' I said, finally.

Looking away from Jake and focusing on the wall behind him, I took in another deep breath.

'It's not ... too much, us being here?' I asked the wall.

'You were invited,' Jake said.

'Mae was invited,' I corrected.

'You were invited,' Jake repeated, gentle but firm.

I blew out a sigh. 'How did Kasun get his family to agree to having a bunch of people over anyway? My parents would never.'

'They're down the coast with Kasun's younger siblings,' Jake said. 'Kasun normally stays here when they go away for short holidays, so he has the place to himself. There aren't many people in there, though.'

I took another breath. 'How many?'

'Five,' Jake said. 'Seven including you and me. It's just pres.'

I didn't bother saying I had no idea what that meant.

Jake leaned against the wall by the door, shuffling his feet forwards so the toes of his shoes stopped in front of my own. The position made the height difference between us less stark.

'Everyone inside is super chill,' he said, 'and you're not stressing anyone out by being here. Okay?'

I stared at Jake, surprised by how easily he had cut to the centre of my anxieties. Something about it made me feel raw, like he had cracked me open in a way I wasn't sure I liked.

I nodded – to Jake or to myself? I wasn't sure – and walked past him into the apartment. He didn't say anything, following a few steps behind me. I tried not to feel embarrassed by that distance, or his silence. Should I have said something else? Should I have denied it?

(What did it matter? We weren't friends. Who cared what he thought of me?)

Mae wasn't hard to find: she was chatting to Kasun in the living room, fiddling with the zip of my jacket with one hand and using a cup to gesture with the other. Not an inspiring sight for me and my crush. I was happy for her, though. (Really.)

Not wanting to intrude, I all but tiptoed around them, heading for what looked like the kitchen.

I wasn't as sneaky as I had hoped, though, because Mae came in behind me as I was staring at the array of drinks on display.

'Why are you making that face?' she asked.

'You should be talking to Kasun,' I shot back, though I knew it was half-hearted.

Mae surveyed the selection of drinks, then looked at me with a growing smile. 'Are you thinking about … drinking?'

'I don't know.' My gaze jumped from the bottle of Baileys to the box of Vodka Cruisers sitting on the countertop. 'I … maybe?'

'I'm having vodka and lemonade,' Mae offered. 'Kasun mixed it for me. Much nicer than straight raspberry vodka.'

I could feel myself shaking my head as Mae spoke. 'My parents would kill me if they knew I was drinking tonight …'

'If they knew you were at a party, they'd assume you were drinking anyway,' Mae said, which was … a good point.

'Have whatever you want,' someone said from behind me, and I turned to see Kasun in the doorway, smiling – at me.

'Oh,' I managed, feeling my heart begin to thump against my ribcage hard enough to hurt.

Both Mae and Kasun were watching me expectantly.

I looked back at them, then at the drinks. 'I …'

C'mon, baby rebel.

'I'm curious about the, um, the Baileys?'

If nothing else, I would have something to say in the family group chat.

7

Somehow, that single question led to Kasun, Mae and me spending the next forty minutes in the kitchen sampling and mix-and-matching the drinks present. At one point, I laughed so hard at Mae imitating her parents at a wine-tasting that I felt the burn of my drink in the back of my nose.

When it was time to leave, Jake stuck his head into the room, took in the sight of us giggling over a monstrous concoction, and sighed before saying, 'Guess I'm driving.'

After taking the smallest sip imaginable of the monster blend, which was a mess of all the alcohols and mixers we could find in the kitchen – it was so, so bad – I snapped a picture of it to send to the group chat. Kasun ducked into frame just as I was taking the picture, and I felt my face go hot, even though there wasn't anything particularly intimate about the moment, and his smile was for the camera, not for me.

As I opened the photo, I felt Kasun step up next to me. His shoulder brushed mine as he looked down at my phone.

'Can you send that to me?' he asked. 'Hang on—'

Before I could process what was happening, Kasun was slipping my phone out of my hand, opening my messaging app and typing something into it. Then he pulled out his own phone.

I felt mine vibrate in my hand: Kasun had sent me a waving emoji. With fingers I hoped weren't visibly shaking, I sent Kasun the picture, before sending it to the group chat. He sent back an emoji of two glasses clinking, then grinned at me in a way that made his eyes crinkle adorably.

I glanced at Mae, wondering if I'd find her looking at us, but she was making a face at the monster blend, smacking her lips in a way that suggested she had made the unfortunate decision to take a sip. Feeling my eyes on her, she wrinkled her nose at me playfully.

'Bad,' she announced.

'Yuh-huh,' I agreed.

I glanced back at my phone as I felt it vibrate again. Renata had already responded to the picture:

> Renata
> ALCOHOL???

> Renata
> alsooo

Her next message was just a line of eyes emojis, which I assumed was in reaction to Kasun's photobomb. I sent back a single eye emoji, which she reacted to with an even longer line of eye emojis.

'Hey, you're going to get cold,' Kasun said suddenly, which was a weird thing to say to Mae, who was wearing my jacket.

It took me a moment, and then I realised: Kasun was talking to me. His expression was expectant, and when we locked eyes he gestured for me to follow him before heading out of the kitchen. I looked at Mae. She shrugged, unconcerned.

If I was a better friend, I would have said something like: *Oh, Mae's wearing my jacket, actually. I can wear that, and Mae can go with you.*

Instead, I swallowed and followed Kasun.

I caught up with him as he paused at the doorway of one of the rooms off the living area.

'You can borrow one of mine,' Kasun said, stepping inside.

I couldn't tell if my head was buzzing from the alcohol or this interaction. Feeling like I was having an out-of-body experience, I floated through the door after him. I anchored myself against the doorframe and let my gaze roam greedily across the room as he headed for a built-in wardrobe on the far side of the space.

'My sister said girls get colder than guys,' Kasun said conversationally, as I took in everything.

Kasun's room was a little smaller than mine, with a queen-sized bed in the centre, done up in navy blue. He had a desk in the corner of his room with two large monitors, a PC tower glowing green and purple under his desk. The room wasn't particularly clean, but it wasn't particularly dirty, either. There were a few clothes near the base of his bed and a pile of textbooks and workbooks on the floor next to his bedside table. I crept closer to the table, trying to see what books were there: he had a small pile of what appeared to be either well-loved or second-hand volumes. I felt my eyes widen as I took in the authors: Aristotle, Immanuel Kant, Peter Singer. These were ... adult books. Serious books.

'Is this okay?'

Kasun was holding up an orange puffer jacket that would look cute on him, but I was sure would make me look like a traffic cone.

'Great,' I managed.

Kasun handed it over, then followed my gaze to his bedside table. He rubbed at the back of his head, almost sheepishly.

'It started as kind of a joke,' he said. 'I didn't ... I don't read much. I prefer movies. Then one day, Jake, Laeli and I were at this second-hand bookstore place. Laeli was like, *I got something for you*, and it was this book about philosophy with this really long title, with all these words in it I had no idea about. One of them was ... um ...' Kasun squinted at the ceiling, then looked back at me with a grin. 'Ratiocinative. Sounds like a fake word, y'know?'

He laughed in a way that seemed almost self-conscious, rubbing at the back of his head again. 'It was a joke gift, cause I'd got her an astrology book because she wants to study astronomy and it's a running ... thing. So she got me this weird book and then ... I actually liked it. Took me like six months to read and I think I read every paragraph five times and I still don't really get it, but it ... it made me think about things I didn't know were ... even ... things, y'know? I was kind of hooked after that.'

I hoped my heart wasn't too visible in my eyes.

Sure, yes, my crush on Kasun had always been about more than looks – I had started to notice that Kasun was a casually kind person after Mae had pointed it out last year, and kindness was my kryptonite. My crush on him had really solidified late last year after seeing him comfort a girl he wasn't friends with after a particularly brutal maths test.

But to find that, on top of that, he liked to read complex things that challenged him and made him think? In that moment, I struggled to think of anything hotter.

'That's so cool,' I said, instead of, *Are you a real human man or a fictional dreamboat created to be specifically hot to me?*

Kasun shrugged, like he was embarrassed by the compliment – which only made him cuter, god help me.

'So that's okay?' He pointed at the jacket he had given me in a clear attempt to change the subject.

'It's great,' I lied, shrugging it on.

Kasun nodded. When he turned away I tilted my face towards my shoulder, giving the jacket a sniff.

Disappointingly, it smelled like the detergent my aunts used. I felt like I had my nose pressed against one of my cousins.

Still, my heart was full as I headed back into the living room. I had the feeling that my night had peaked. How could it get better than this?

✱ ✱ ✱

The 'party' was in a public park beside MacKenzies beach. By the time we arrived, the alcohol I had sampled had hit me, and not in a nice way: the noise and lights across the road were making my head pound, and I was feeling fuzzy and dizzy in a way I couldn't shake by focusing really hard. I couldn't tell if the noise of the waves behind us was too quiet, or if my brain was selectively reducing my ability to take in stimulation so I could conserve a few last dregs of sobriety.

I was sitting on one of the two swings in the park's play area – the one that was made to fit a toddler, not half the butt of a teenager – beside a group of people that included Mae. Mae was in conversation with one of the girls we'd carpooled with, and had been talking to her and her friends for most of the time we'd been at the beach. I had seen Kasun glancing over at her a few times, but Mae hadn't seemed to notice.

Was she playing hard to get? I would have to ask if she was working on some sort of ... *seduction strategy* later. Not right now, though, when I had been so recently reminded of my own feelings. My conversation with Kasun in his room had added salt to the wound of my crush: the closer Mae and Kasun became, the more of Kasun I was getting to see. Unfortunately for me, the more of Kasun I saw, the more I found to like.

'Did you want to come?'

Was that addressed to me? Blinking, I looked over at the girl smiling at me – oh, the friendly girl I had talked to at Jake's sister's house. Something. Name. Laeli. Laeli? Yes, Kasun had been talking about her. Laeli.

'You look bored,' Laeli said, as my brain tried to launch, failed, restarted and finally flickered back to life. 'We're going for a walk along the shore, if you want to come?'

'Oh,' I said. Then, realising I had been staring at her in silence for too long, I added, 'A walk would be nice, sure.'

Two other girls joined us and soon outpaced us, disappearing towards the beach, but Laeli stayed next to me as we walked out of the park and down towards the water. Further down the beach, some of the boys from the party were doing various nonsensical things at the water's edge. I squinted at them, decided my brain was too blurry, and focused on the sand at my feet instead.

'So, what brings a girl like you to a beach like this?' Laeli asked, slipping her hands into her pockets and glancing over at me with a small smile.

'You did,' I said, confused. Then, after my brain had filtered through the words again and managed to lock onto their non-literal meaning: 'Oh, um. I'm here with my friend? Mae.'

Laeli made a noise of recognition. 'Oh, yeah. Your friend Mae. I remember you mentioning her.'

I glanced at Laeli curiously. The way she had said 'friend' … was she trying to work out what I thought she was?

'Mae,' I said. Then, throwing caution to the wind: 'My best friend. Basically my sister. Definitely just … my friend.'

Laeli nodded, smiling a little. 'Cool.'

Did she …?

'And you're here with your … *friends* Jake and Kasun,' I said, leaning on 'friends' with the same inflection I had before, even though doing so made my face warm.

Was I …?

Laeli nodded again, teeth scraping over her bottom lip as she glanced at me and then away.

Oh?

I felt at once sober and too drunk for this conversation.

Over the last year, I had come to terms with two things about myself: I didn't much enjoy reading domestic thrillers (thank you, Tetka Mojca, for that curveball book club choice last August), and, arguably more importantly: I didn't just like boys. This last one was my own private revelation. I hadn't said it aloud yet, content to keep it to myself until it felt like the right time.

(And maybe I could admit that there was an element of fear there too – what if people didn't believe me? I couldn't prove it. How would I even prove it? And what if they *did* believe me but rejected me for it? I had heard the throwaway comments from some people in my community. I knew the things that were said when people thought they were safe to say them. Was I ready for that?

And what about Mae? Yes, she was my best friend, but—

What if?)

'Amalia?'

I blinked over at Laeli, realising belatedly that my expression had slipped into something blank. I wasn't sure how long I had been quiet for. It had clearly been long enough for the mood to shift. Laeli was still smiling, except her face had shuttered a little, like she'd taken a step back from the conversation.

'You okay?' she asked.

'Sorry, I think I'm a bit drunk,' I blurted.

Laeli's eyes warmed by a fraction, her lips pursing to cover a smile. 'I did guess.'

'I don't normally drink,' I said, realising one of my hands had decided to start waving around and not sure what to do about it. 'I don't ever drink, actually. Kasun, Mae and I got sort of carried away—'

As I talked, I watched Laeli's expression relax back into something open. Her shoulders, which had tightened, dropped by increments.

'That sounds gross. Is it bad that I'm curious about the taste?' she said, when I took a breath.

'It isn't,' I said. 'I don't think I can recommend it, though.'

We smiled at each other, any lingering discomfort from my accidental silence gone.

'Hey,' Laeli said, 'I wasn't sure how to bring this up, but—'

Suddenly, the group of boys who had been doing shenanigans by the water were upon us. I had been so engrossed in our conversation that I hadn't even noticed they were nearby. Laeli's words faltered as Jake jogged over, slinging an arm around her shoulder.

'You kids having fun?' he asked, giving her a gentle shake.

Laeli let him jiggle her back and forth with a long-suffering expression. 'Yes, Dad.'

Jake looked at me then, narrowing his eyes slightly, though not in an unfriendly way. 'You two have met before, right?'

I nodded. Jake nodded back, glancing at Laeli and then back at me. I stared at him, wondering why he was looking at me like that. There was something about his expression that I could only describe as scheming.

'Yeah, cool,' Jake said finally. 'Enjoy. I'm gonna go.'

'Bye, Jake,' Laeli said, directing a look at me that said, *what a goof.*

Catching up with the boys on the beach had also meant catching up with the other two girls who had set out from the park with us, and when one of them pulled Laeli into their discussion, I let myself drift to the outskirts of the group, embracing dizziness.

Once we returned to the park, I toppled down beside Mae, who gave me a nudge and raised her eyebrows. I nudged her back, then dropped my head onto her shoulder. Mae gave the side of my head a kiss and returned to her conversation.

I wasn't sure how long I sat there, lost in the static, but at some point I realised Jake had squatted down beside me.

'Did you and Laeli have fun?' he asked.

I fixed him with a look I hoped was convincingly sober.

'Yes?' I said, the word twisting into a question right at the end.

Jake nodded, seeming both distracted and thoughtful. Then he asked, 'Talk about anything ... interesting?'

I squinted at him. 'I really, honestly don't know what you want me to say, Jake.'

'Yeah, that's fair. I'm being weird.' He sat back on his heels and stared at the air beside my head, then nodded like he'd made a decision. 'I'm going to go now.'

'Okay,' I said slowly, watching him push himself up and head over to a group of people that included Kasun.

Mae swatted at my arm. Once she had my attention, she waggled her eyebrows.

'No,' I said.

She waggled them harder.

I gave up and dropped back onto her shoulder.

8

For the second week in a row, Kamilia snuck me in through the laundry door, ferrying me back to my room and shushing me every second step for some noise or another I was apparently making. Once I was alone, I managed to wriggle into my pyjamas, my limbs leaden with tiredness, and fell asleep to a world that spun to black behind my eyelids.

I had set an alarm for eight in the morning so I could dramatically make my re-entrance to the house after my 'sleepover with Mae', but managed to turn it off without quite meaning to, spiralling back into sleep and waking instead at eleven to find my dad standing in my doorway.

'Muh?' I managed.

'I knocked,' Dad said. 'Tvoja Mama te kliče.'

I frowned, smacking my lips. My mouth was dry and my head pounded.

'Mum's on the phone?' I rasped.

'No, Malka,' Dad said, 'she has been calling for you. She wants you to come downstairs.'

I smacked my lips again, gaze roaming around my room before coming back to my dad, who I realised was frowning.

'When did you come home, Malka?' he asked.

My head hurt too badly for me to feel anything more than a brief twist of worry at his expression.

'Early,' I said, groping around in the dark crevices of my mind for a convincing lie. 'Mae made me … go for a run in the morning. She's … doing that kind of thing now. I was tired so I went back to bed.'

Dad looked at me for a moment longer, then nodded, his moustache twitching as he glanced behind himself and then back at me.

'A hot shower will relax your muscles,' he said. 'But be fast.'

'So fast,' I confirmed, propping myself up on my elbows and arranging my face in an expression I hoped conveyed: *I'm about to leap out of bed right this minute.*

Dad only snorted, pulling my bedroom door closed behind him.

✱ ✱ ✱

The reason Mum was so keen on having me up and ready was because it was book club today, which meant my aunts and cousins were about to descend on the house. (While hosting was technically meant to be passed around, our house had become the unofficial home of the meetings.) It was important, Mum thought, to show a united front – as though she, me and my sister were in an alliance against an invading force rather than members of an interfamilial discussion group – hence why I needed to be up, ready and present to welcome our guests alongside her and Kamilia.

As I creaked down the stairs and into the living room, my mouth still dry despite the water I had slurped directly from the tap and my head still pounding, I was finding it hard to remind myself why I cared.

Book club signalled the only time we were allowed to sit with the air con on in the living room, so it was with some relief that I commandeered the sofa chair directly below the cooling unit, countering Mum's warning look with what I hoped was a winning smile before swiping up a slice of homemade apple and walnut strudel and pouring myself a large glass of ice tea from the jug on the coffee table. Despite the cool of the previous night, the heat was creeping up again today, and I sighed as I felt the air con hit the back of my neck and shoulders.

Tetka Sabinka and Renata were the first members outside our household to arrive.

When they came into the living room, Renata took one look at me and mouthed, 'Big night?'

I shrugged in a worldly way and accepted a one-armed hug, twisting my fingers away from her T-shirt as they were sticky with strudel filling. It was a relief to see Tetka Sabinka and Renata, though it wasn't surprising: idle threats were the most common kind exchanged in our family. Clearly, Tetka Sabinka had taken my mum's disinvitation last week as seriously as it had been meant (which was to say, not very).

When Elizabeta arrived – separate from Tetka Mojca, which was the new norm as she'd moved out at the beginning of the year – she made a beeline for me, crouching down beside my chair and whispering, 'Who's the cutie in the pic?'

I made a face that I hoped conveyed my confusion. Elizabeta took out her phone and opened our group chat, glancing over her shoulder to make sure there was no one of our parents' generation nearby before showing me her screen. The moment I saw the picture I had taken of the monstrous alcohol concoction and Kasun's smiling face, Renata's lines of messages below it, I felt my own face bloom with heat.

Elizabeta, spurred on by my reaction, mouthed, 'Boyfriend?'

I shook my head, hoping I didn't look ... sick? Sad? Jealous?

'Mae's, almost,' I whispered back, hoping I had landed convincingly on a mixture of supportive and conspiratorial even though the words left a sour taste in my mouth.

Elizabeta nodded, winking at me. I tried to wink back, found I could only blink, and took another bite of strudel.

Once Tetka Mojca had arrived, the coffee table had been filled with baked goods, and my dad had delivered everyone a black coffee brewed from beans roasted in Slovenia – he got a regular supply from his cousin who lived in Trbovlje, in exchange for I wasn't sure what, exactly – book club began.

All eyes turned to Tetka Sabinka, who was already on the edge of her seat and clearly ready to express her thoughts.

'I still think we should have read about the whale,' she said. '*But* I will say I enjoyed this Mr Knightley, though I did not care for Emma.'

Not one to leave a strike unparried, Mum said smoothly, '*I* liked Emma. She could be headstrong, but she had the strength of character to admit when she was wrong.'

Tetka Sabinka opened her mouth to reply—

'It reminds me,' Tetka Mojca said, pausing to take a sip of her coffee, 'of Josipina Turnograjska.'

Tetka Sabinka scooted forwards on her seat, frowning at her sister. 'We are talking about books, not authors. We talk about authors at the *end*, Mojca.'

'Who made this rule? I didn't make this rule,' Tetka Mojca said. 'I would like to talk about Jane Austen and I would like to talk about Josipina Turnograjska. They are both women who wrote at a time women were not expected – or encouraged – to write. They both died young. They lived not so far apart from each other in time. I think there is a lot to talk about.'

'We are talking about *Emma*,' Tetka Sabinka insisted.

'We are talking,' Tetka Mojca said, 'about literature and about history.'

'*I'd* like to hear about Josipina Turnograjska, Tetka Mojca,' Kamilia said.

And on it went.

I was brought back from the brink of dozing off to the sounds of my family arguing over whether or not Emma should have realised she was in love with Mr Knightley sooner by the buzz of my phone against my stomach. Fishing it out of my jacket pocket and angling my body to make my movements less noticeable, I squinted at a text.

> Mae
> **NEED WINGWOMAN.**

> Amalia
> Find another bird. At book club.

'I'm just saying, maybe she should have realised she at least had feelings for him, in, I don't know, chapter eighteen,' someone was saying.

'If she had realised then it would be a completely different book,' someone else snapped back.

> Mae
> Soo funny. But also EMERGENCY

A cup went BANG against the coffee table. I winced, then glared at my sister, who shot me a sly smile, clearly aware of my hangover.

I looked around the circle, looked at my watch, and made a quick estimate.

> Amalia
> **Give me 30 mins.**

The moment conversation began to wane enough that I could see my mum's attention turn to the post-session clean-up, I leaned over to her and whispered, 'Can I go to Mae's? She says it's an emergency.'

'You are too young for emergencies,' Mum murmured, but she followed that with a hand wave, saying: 'Yes, fine. Make sure you're back for dinner. Don't let her parents feed you rubbish.'

'They bought us burgers *once*, Mum,' I said, adding a swift: 'Thank you!' when her eyes began to narrow.

When I got to Mae's, she ushered me straight up the stairs and into her room. Once I had plopped down onto the end of her bed, she frantically resumed curling her hair into ringlets.

I couldn't help rolling my eyes after I finally got the 'emergency' out of Mae.

'Mum was right,' I said, then frowned at myself. 'Wow, never let her hear me say that. Seriously though, Mae. How is going to the movies an emergency?'

Mae's reflection widened its eyes at me.

'It's a *date*,' she said.

'It's a group hangout,' I corrected, glancing down at the message from Kasun on Mae's phone.

Mae's phone was a cheap little thing with a fuzzy pink case and almost no storage space, which meant she was a diligent text deleter. This meant I had no other correspondence to nosey poke my way through – which, I told myself, was for the best.

'You know I'm not allowed to date,' Mae said. 'If my parents thought boys were involved, let alone that a boy had *invited* me, I wouldn't be allowed out of the house. So yes, right now I am treating it like a date.'

I watched her as she let go of her final curl, plumping her hair with her fingers. Her eyes were bright in a way that was almost feverish. In normal circumstances I would have said she looked excited, but her expression was too tight for that. She looked determined, but determined like she was about to eat something nasty yet necessary, not like she was about to score alone time with our crush.

'Are you sure you want to go out?' I asked.

Mae frowned a little, twisting so she could look at me properly.

'Definitely,' she confirmed, then widened her eyes, popping her lower lip out ever so slightly. 'Be my alibi? Please?'

I sighed, then nodded. 'I'm there.'

Mae nodded back.

'You should bring a jacket this time,' I added. 'You'll get cold in the cinema otherwise.'

That reminded me, Kasun's bright orange jacket was still hanging over the back of my desk chair. I shifted in my seat, feeling a jolt of guilt and hoping that it wouldn't show up on my face. Mae gave me a once-over, then put out her hand.

'Can I borrow your jumper?' she asked.

I looked down at the oversized navy jumper I was wearing, then back up at her.

'Black jeans, and I bet you're wearing a black T-shirt under that,' Mae said, a smile playing at the corners of her lips. 'You need a black jacket to top it off.'

Before I could say anything or even try to contradict her (though she wasn't wrong), Mae was opening her wardrobe, grabbing her leather jacket and holding it out towards me. I eyed it. I was a bit bigger than Mae in all measures, but she liked her jackets oversized, so I knew it would fit. It was a nice jacket, too – heavy yet soft, with a minimal number of buckles and no complex detailing.

Sure. I wasn't going to complain.

✶ ✶ ✶

When Mae and I arrived – fashionably late – the group wasn't hard to spot due to its size, and there seemed to be an argument going on. As Mae said her hellos and gamely jumped into the fray so she could work out what was happening, I drifted towards the counter, eyeing the food available.

I was trying to drown out my hangover headache by focusing very hard on the popcorn machine when someone said from across the counter, 'Hey, Book Club. Long-time no see.'

I looked over to see Jake, who was wearing the cinema's work uniform of a black polo and black slacks. He grinned lazily when we made eye contact.

'You're joking,' I said.

Jake looked thoughtful.

'Don't like Book Club either?' he asked. 'I know you hated Eyebrows. Thought I'd diversify.'

'Did you steal someone's uniform to get back there?' I asked.

Jake snorted. 'Some of us have jobs, Book Club.'

'I—' I began, then stopped myself.

It was more than a little self-centred of me to think that Jake had got behind the counter just to mess with me. Beyond rudely (and, unfortunately, correctly) assuming I had a crush on his best friend, and being cryptic to me last night, I shouldn't assume he thought about me at all.

'Sorry,' I said. 'So. I guess you won't be watching the movie with us?'

Jake's grin relaxed into something smaller, his eyes crinkling. 'I don't even think they've decided on a movie yet. Last I heard it was a three-way split.' He leaned his forearms against the counter, the fabric of his shirt pulling tight against his biceps. 'Nice that you'll miss me, though.'

Despite the fact we'd talked enough in the last week that I didn't get flustered whenever he said something like *that*, it was still startling. I reminded myself that he was just a teasing person. Still, my stomach and head were feeling funny. I consoled myself that it was probably hangover related.

Oblivious to my strange stomach, Jake nodded towards the group. 'I reckon the council has made its decision.'

I turned to see a much-reduced selection of people walking towards the ticket counter. Mae broke off, trotting over to me and pulling me a few steps away from the group. I shot one last look at Jake, but he didn't notice, back in work mode as he served a group of movie patrons who had come up after me.

'Okay, so, a couple of people ended up going to the food court,' Mae said under her breath, oblivious to my split focus, 'and everyone else is stuck between a gory horror movie and one of those big budget, bad CGI action movies.'

I narrowed my eyes at Mae, already guessing where this was going. 'I'm bad with gore.'

'But Kasun—'

'And *you're* bad with horror,' I interrupted.

'Guys love comforting damsels in distress,' Mae said, wiggling her shoulders.

As I was no great expert on what guys did or did not love, I frowned and stayed silent.

'There are only going to be four of us for the horror movie, too,' Mae said. 'Kasun, you, me, and two other guys.'

Great. I was going to be the third wheel: stuck in a dark theatre with my crush, my best friend with the same crush and way better chances, and two boys I didn't know, watching a movie I wasn't interested in that would make me feel sick. My stomach-ache was getting worse, too.

'Mae, I ...' I began. Then, starting again: 'Your parents saw us leave together. They'll think we were both here. If anyone asks, I'll say I was. I don't really need to be here, though.' My voice shook on 'here', and I realised with horror that I was on the verge of tears.

I took a breath, trying to make the inhale as subtle as possible.

'I'm really hungover,' I said, once I was sure my tears had retreated, 'and I'm really happy you're going to get some time with Kasun, but I'm like ... already way out of my comfort zone.'

Mae was frowning. She reached out and grasped my hand, and I gave hers a quick squeeze in response.

'I want you to have fun,' I said. 'But *I* want to go home.'

Mae nodded. She squeezed my hand again, then let it go, turning and walking back to the group. I felt my eyes swim, and tilted my head back, blinking. The lack of goodbye was a bit like a kick in the chest, but whatever. She was allowed to be focused on other things.

I was turning to go when I felt someone grasp my

hand. Mae had come back, and was watching me with both eyebrows raised.

'Not even going to let me say goodbye?' she asked.

Oh.

'Bye, Mae,' I said, feeling the tightness in my chest ease.

Mae snorted. 'I meant to the group.'

Oh?

'You've got to give me the rundown on book club, and what you told Tetka Mojca you were going to study,' Mae said, steering us towards the exit. 'And we're going to get you some electrolytes and maybe some ginger lollies, because after I mentioned gore you started looking *really* peaky. I don't want you to throw up on the way back to mine.'

I felt like I'd missed a step somewhere. 'What about Kasun?'

Mae focused her gaze on me, waiting for me to meet her eyes.

'You already came out with me last night,' she said, once she was sure she had my attention, 'even though I know you didn't really want to. And you were so brave about it. So now we're doing what *you* want to do.'

'I *was* brave,' I murmured, as we turned to the entrance and headed back into the shopping centre proper. 'And I do want electrolytes. And ginger. My stomach feels bad.'

'Mine too,' Mae said, letting go of my hand only to hook her arm through mine, bumping our hips.

'Also Tetka Mojca totally forgot to ask me about uni,' I said.

'What were you going to say?' Mae asked.

'I was thinking of making a joke about getting inspired by *Emma* and deciding to go into professional matchmaking, just to see what she would say.'

Mae snorted at that and, spurred on by her, I started to giggle.

Sniggering like kids who had been shushed by their teacher, we left the theatre – and Kasun – behind.

9

The next two weeks passed quickly. I studied, I read roughly a paragraph of *Moby-Dick* a night, and I studied some more. (I technically had a new book club pick to be reading – we were doing an Agatha Christie this month – but I didn't want to give up on the whale just yet.) We were cresting the wave of midterm exams, which I assumed was why Mae had gone quiet on Kasun. I almost started to convince myself that I had imagined the earlier weeks of the term except every now and then I'd catch Mae biting her lip when she stared at her phone and, more strangely, Jake had started walking me from maths to geography every time the classes ran back-to-back.

This meant that twice a week he'd fall into step next to me and, for the roughly four-minute walk between classes, engage me in conversation about topics including the plots of very bad crime procedurals he had watched recently, a Wikipedia spiral that had left him knowing a lot about Archimedes of Syracuse but not improved his differential calculus and, most recently, why beluga whales looked 'like that'.

Then we'd get to class, he'd nod a farewell, and that would be that until the next time.

Mae had picked up on it, of course, and never failed to jiggle her eyebrows at me when we'd leave the classroom to find Jake waiting in the hall for me (he was consistently faster at getting out the door than us, which I attributed to his lack of stationery – I had noticed that he seemed to need to borrow a pen from Kasun every class). I didn't think Mae's eyebrow jiggle had the right idea – Jake, I had observed, was a casually warm person, and I suspected he just liked having the company between classes.

After our maths midterm, I was expecting to dive right into a debrief about the exam with Jake. Instead, he opened our conversation with, 'I have a surprise.'

I frowned as I fell into step beside him. 'I don't know how to react to that.'

'Well,' Jake amended, 'there's a surprise. It didn't need to be a surprise, except Laeli—'

Something in my chest did a lurching flutter at her name. Did I definitely, absolutely still have a crush on Kasun? Yes, unfortunately for me. Still, I had thought about Laeli on and off over the past couple of weeks, the memory of our beach interaction slipping into my thoughts whenever my brain decided it had had enough of focusing on exams.

Had we been flirting? I still wasn't sure. We had never *said* so. Then again, I was pretty sure those things were more ... vibes-based. Had there been a vibe? Had I *wanted* there to be a vibe?

'I've lost you,' Jake said, breaking me out of my thoughts.

'You did,' I admitted. 'Sorry. I was thinking about ... exams.'

'Okay,' Jake said, in a tone that suggested he knew I was lying but that, in the grand scheme of lies, this one wasn't worth unpacking. 'Well, she told me not to tell you, so maybe look surprised. Not too surprised, though. She doesn't want it to be a big deal.'

'Sure,' I said.

Jake and I stepped into the stairwell that led to our geography classroom, walking up the first round of stairs in silence.

'You have no idea what I'm talking about,' Jake said finally.

'I do not,' I agreed.

We were out of the stairwell now, and coming up on the classroom.

'So are you going to tell me the surprise?' I asked, lingering in the doorway.

Jake shot me a crooked grin. 'Nah. Maybe next time wear your listening ears, Book Club.'

My mouth got mixed up between the words 'Jake!' and 'Rude!' and I ended up making a frustrated noise instead.

Jake's grin widened, but he only slid around me, heading into the classroom while I glared at the back of his head.

✻ ✻ ✻

The surprise, and its connection to Laeli, revealed itself the next day.

Laeli was in my visual arts classroom.

Laeli.

In my visual arts classroom.

Sitting next to Kasun and a few of his other friends, cheeks cupped in her palms, legs crossed at the ankle, smiling and laughing like this was her hundredth time in the classroom and not her first. I blinked, knowing my brain was short circuiting.

It was then that Laeli looked towards the doorway and saw me.

I wondered if she wouldn't recognise me. We'd only met twice, and both places had been dimly lit.

I didn't have to wonder for long – it only took a moment for her eyes to crinkle, her mouth tugging up into a small smile. I felt my own expression open in response, and before I could overthink it I was walking to her table. For once I wasn't hyperaware of Kasun. In that moment, I wasn't even regular aware of him. My attention was all on Laeli.

'Hi,' she mouthed, when I was a few steps away.

'Hey,' I replied, hoping I sounded normal as I came to a stop beside her desk.

Laeli sat up, folding her arms on the table and turning her face towards mine. I blinked down at her and wondered if I had managed to summon her through the power of my anxious thoughts.

'Amalia,' I said suddenly. 'Sorry. If you didn't remember.'

Laeli's smile widened, her dimple deepening. 'I remember.' Then she tapped a finger to her chest, pursing her lips to contain her smile. 'Laeli.'

'I remember,' I echoed.

We looked at each other, smiling, and then the teacher cleared their throat from the front of the room and I realised with a jolt that I was the only person not sitting down.

'I'm going to—' I began, and Laeli nodded.

Managing one more smile, I slipped past her, hurrying to my usual seat. Over the course of the class I took in no information and made zero progress on my major work, my brain refusing to move past the fact that Laeli was right there, in my classroom, sitting only two rows in front of me.

Sitting next to Kasun.

Kasun, who Mae was almost certainly still texting, though she had stopped giving me updates. Was that good? Was I glad? I didn't think so. It felt more like I was waiting in the calm before the storm.

At the end of class, Laeli turned and waved at me as she and Kasun headed out the door. Kasun glanced at her as she did so, then at me, smiling when he caught sight of me and mimicking Laeli's wave. My heart gave a heavy thump in response.

I was still rubbing my chest when I reached Mae at our usual lunch spot. Mae had beaten me there, and grabbed my arm when I sat down next to her, her eyes wide.

'There's a new girl!' she said. 'In our year!'

I processed that. 'Yeah. Laeli.'

Mae's eyes widened further. 'You know her?'

'I mean …' I raised one shoulder. 'Kind of. We've met before, at Jake's house then at the beach.'

'I knew it, I knew she seemed familiar,' she said. 'Of course she's friends with Jake and Kasun. Every time I see her she's with one of them.'

'Yeah, they're childhood friends.' I pulled my bag into my lap and rummaged around inside for my sandwich.

'She's so pretty,' Mae said. 'Like, influencer pretty. Her hair is so perfect and shiny. How does she make it so shiny?'

I touched the side of my own hair as I took a bite of my food, watching Mae. Her expression was caught somewhere between wistful and annoyed.

'Do you know why she started so late in the year? We're practically halfway through Year Twelve already,' Mae said. '*And* we're literally in the middle of an exam week.'

'It's only the first exam block of the year,' I retorted. 'We haven't done any exams that are heavily weighted yet; we still have literal *months* until trials.'

'Yeah, but it's Term Two for us even if it's Term One for everyone else,' Mae said.

'Still not halfway,' I mumbled, taking another bite of my sandwich.

Mae side eyed me. 'Okay, technically. It's still a weird time to change schools, though. Why is she here?'

I shrugged. I didn't think Mae noticed. She looked as stuck in her head as I had felt during visual arts.

'You excited for the zoo on Friday?' I asked, trying for a change of subject. 'I feel like our teachers keep talking about it like it's some kind of reward, and now I'm worried about how hard the bio exam is going to be this week.'

'Sure,' Mae said, in a tone of voice that suggested I could have said anything and got the same response.

I left her to her thoughts.

Mae's focus on Laeli didn't waver as we progressed through the week – an impressive feat, considering we were inundated with exams. Every conversation we had contained at least one Laeli observation. Wasn't Laeli just *so* pretty? And wasn't she just *such* close friends with Kasun? And *why* would she start at our school so late in Year Twelve? Did I think she was *actually* a model, like *actually actually*? Because she *so* could be.

To which my standard array of responses ran: yes; yes; I have no idea; Mae, I really have no idea, *please* can we go back to studying? These flashcards on chromosomal mutations aren't going to write themselves.

Which brought us to the zoo trip.

I still didn't understand why we had to go to the zoo – not that I was complaining, but also. Yeah, I was kind of complaining. I liked the zoo. I didn't like the zoo with a hundred other kids, and I also didn't like being herded by a handful of tired science teachers.

Luckily, the coursework part of the day – a rehash of our biotechnology content with a focus on zoo animals – was over, and we had been allowed to move more slowly through the exhibits.

I found myself lingering in the marsupial exhibit. The noise of my classmates aside, the dim light was a relief. I stood in front of one of the enclosures and let myself be soothed by the sight of a furry creature wriggling around in its bed of leaves.

'Hey, Book Club,' Jake said, from over my shoulder.

'Check out that bilby,' I replied, pointing as one shot across its enclosure.

When Jake didn't answer, I turned towards him, tucking my fingers into the straps of my backpack. 'Where are your friends?'

'Reptile exhibit,' Jake said, which I already knew – embarrassingly for me, I'd been keeping tabs on Kasun for most of the visit.

I turned my attention back to the bilby. From my peripheral vision, I saw Jake get comfortable against the glass.

'So Mae's been pretty focused on Laeli,' Jake said.

'What?' I glanced over at him, feeling my eyes go wide. 'Are you eavesdropping on my conversations?'

'I resent that,' Jake said pleasantly. 'Can't a guy talk to a girl and have the girl say, *Hey, who is that other girl and why has she been looking at me funny all week?*' He paused. 'And by "guy" I mean me. And by "girl" I mean Laeli. And by "other girl" I mean—'

'Mae, yeah, thanks,' I said.

I felt a groan of embarrassment well up from somewhere deep inside me, like a whale emerging from the depths. Managing to divert the sound into a huff, I leaned back against the glass next to Jake, crossing my arms.

'So … Laeli noticed that,' I said.

Jake nodded. I realised we were standing close enough for our sleeves to brush. In the dim light, his eyes looked all pupil.

'People normally notice when they're being stared at,' Jake said.

I pushed away from the glass, refocusing on the bilby and feeling glad the dim lighting cloaked my expression. I wasn't sure what to say. *Thanks for letting me know that my friend made Laeli uncomfortable, that's super embarrassing?* I wished I could make like one of the bilbies in the enclosure and crawl into a sensibly sized log.

'I'm just letting you know,' Jake said, finally, 'because if your friend is keeping tabs on Laeli for Kasun reasons, she doesn't need to worry. Kasun's not Laeli's … *type*.'

I stared at Jake and wondered if that comment was meant for both Mae *and* me. He knew about my crush on Kasun, after all.

'But maybe, y'know, tell Mae to stare other places,' he added.

I cleared my throat, wishing the bilby would come out of its log and help me face this situation.

'And you should talk to her, too,' Jake said, like I wasn't in the process of melting into the ground from second-hand embarrassment. 'Laeli, I mean. I think you two would get along.'

'We've talked before,' I said.

The bilby stuck its nose out into the open, giving it a wiggle.

'I know,' Jake said. 'I meant, like, talk more.'

'Are you … ordering me to talk to Laeli?' I asked slowly.

'Just a suggestion, Book Club,' Jake said, then nodded at me, stepping back. 'Okay. Good talk.'

I rolled my eyes at Jake, though I couldn't suppress a smile. 'Thanks, coach.'

Jake grinned, and for some reason that made me feel … less melty and embarrassed. I realised, with some amount of wonder, that it was hard to hold onto embarrassment when Jake was just … so … Jake.

As I contemplated that, he pushed himself off the glass, rolling his shoulders in a stretch before ambling back towards the reptile exhibit. I felt his hands on my shoulders for a moment, but when I turned he had already passed me.

The rest of the trip passed quickly after that. I tried to soften the blow of my conversation with Jake to Mae by relaying it through the mouth of a gift shop lion plushy. Did that make things better or worse? Unclear. Either way, Mae left the gift shop with both a keyring for her mum and the knowledge that Laeli had picked up on what she was (unintentionally) putting down.

Still, the conversation didn't seem to have hit her too hard, because as the class was piling back into the charter bus she turned to me with a twinkle in her eye that I didn't trust.

'So,' she said.

I groaned. 'No.'

'It's not even at night this time!' Mae said, in something approaching a whine.

When I didn't say anything, she said, 'It's right after this, actually. And it'll be so chill.'

She stared at me expectantly.

'What's so chill?' I asked finally, taking the bait.

We were on the bus now. Mae gestured for me to take the window seat.

'A bunch of people are going back to MacKenzies this arvo,' she said, once she'd sat down.

I groaned loudly. 'Why MacKenzies? Have you already forgotten our last trip there? It's so hard to get to.'

'Nope,' she said. 'There's a bus that goes directly there from school until six, so it'll be easy. We'll get off at school, get on that bus with everyone, and then be home before our parents start wondering where we are.'

'I don't have swimmers,' I countered.

'I brought two pairs,' Mae said. 'One of them I'm like ninety per cent sure is yours.'

I glared at Mae. 'You've been plotting this.'

'I wouldn't say plotting,' Mae said, prim.

'Scheming,' I insisted, as the bus pulled away from the kerb.

Mae didn't say anything, only smiled at me.

'Yes, fine,' I snapped.

Mae's smile widened into a grin, and she wiggled happily in her seat.

✱ ✱ ✱

The spare pair of swimmers Mae had brought were a little too small, so I found myself as the designated bag wench for the afternoon (title self-appointed), which was a fancy way of saying I hung out with people's school supplies while they swam.

That suited me fine. I had the latest book club pick to keep me company.

I was lying on the sand with a floppy black sunhat half over my face, book in hand, when I felt rather than saw someone sit down next to me. A few people had come back this way, but nobody had actually sat down, so I felt a jolt of surprise when I peeped over my book to see Laeli kneeling in the sand beside me.

'Hi,' she said, with a smile.

I lowered my book.

'Hi, Laeli,' I said, a little shyly.

Laeli's hair was dark with water and slicked back off her face. This close, I could see that she had a patch of freckles on her nose. Her long eyelashes, which had clumped together in little 'v's, were her only visible imperfection.

'Would you mind putting sunscreen on my back?' she asked. 'I can't reach.'

I sat up, putting my book down and adjusting my sunhat. Laeli smiled, and I realised that I had been so distracted by her face that I hadn't noticed she was holding a bottle of coconut-scented sunscreen out to me.

When I took it, she turned her back to me, sweeping her hair out of the way. I was glad she wasn't facing me – I could feel myself going red.

'I kept wanting to sit down and talk to you properly this week,' Laeli said, as I put a dollop of sunscreen on my hand. 'But, I … honestly, I chickened out.'

I blinked at Laeli's back, not sure what to say to that.

'You're probably wondering why I'm even at your school,' she continued, as I started to rub the sunscreen into her shoulders.

'I … was,' I confirmed, searching for something else to say and coming up blank.

I was too distracted by her back. Were my hands lingering? No, I needed to rub in the sunscreen. Was I pressing too hard? Was I pressing too *lightly*? Was I accidentally tickling her? It was just sunscreen. God. It was *just* sunscreen.

'I was having a pretty bad time at my old school,' Laeli said. 'Things were *not* great there, and then I went through a ... a rough break-up, and I ... my parents thought ... *I* thought ... the school was good — top-ranking for the HSC — but it wasn't good for *me* anymore. It made sense to go somewhere I had ... friends. People I trusted.'

Laeli lapsed into silence.

After the silence had stretched for long enough that I was sure Laeli wasn't going to start speaking again, I said, 'I'm sorry, Laeli, that sucks.'

'It did,' was all she said. Then she pushed her shoulders back, shaking her head a little. 'Anyway, I wanted to come say hi. Properly. I liked talking to you, and Jake said you were cool, so ... you have the best friend seal of approval.'

I felt myself blush at her words. My face became even hotter when I slid my hands under the straps of her bikini to cover the skin there. Laeli pulled the straps aside, leaving them hanging over her shoulders, and I gave her shoulders a quick splash of sunscreen, eager to get this done.

'Why was Jake talking about me?' I asked — *almost done, almost done.*

'Oh,' Laeli said, and I realised with a start that I might have just forced her to admit that she had noticed Mae staring at her and had a quiet word with Jake about it.

'I asked about you,' Laeli said, and left it at that — I appreciated the simple but kind lie.

'And Jake said I was … cool,' I said, adding, as I scooted back, 'All done.'

Laeli turned to face me, leaning against one hand and fixing a bikini strap with the other.

'Are you going to come swim?' she asked.

I glanced down at my book, and she followed my gaze.

'Jake also said you like to read.' A smile played on Laeli's lips. 'What have you got there?'

'Oh, it's an Agatha Christie,' I replied, flashing the cover of the book in a way I hoped wasn't too awkward. *'The Murder of Roger Ackroyd.'*

'Oh! My dad loves old-school murder mysteries,' Laeli said. 'He made me read that one. It's got a good twist.'

'Yeah?' I said.

'Yep,' she said, still smiling, a little sly now. 'It keeps you guessing. It's not clear at all who it's going to be at the end.'

Then Laeli was pushing herself up, brushing her hair out of her face.

'Thanks for your help, Amalia,' she said. 'Let me know what you think of the end.'

10

I didn't have the sense that I'd knocked the conversation with Laeli out of the park, so I was surprised when, upon entering my visual arts classroom the next week, she not only smiled at me but beckoned me towards her.

Kasun was sitting opposite her. When I walked over, she took her bag off the seat next to her and gestured for me to sit. I did so, returning the politely confused smiles and nods of her companions and forcing my heart to *chill out* when Kasun put out a hand for a fist bump.

'How's the book?' Laeli asked, once I had finished the mortifying ordeal of being acknowledged.

'The Agatha Christie?' I said, as though there were another book we had discussed. 'I finished it.'

Laeli leaned her elbow against the desk, resting her cheek on her palm and turning the full force of her attention on me.

'What did you think of the end?' she asked.

'Oh, I didn't see it coming. I kind of love books with unreliable narrators.'

Laeli nodded, then tilted her head a little, still watching me attentively. 'If you were a narrator, do you think you would be reliable?'

I blinked at her, feeling myself frown as I turned the question over in my mind.

'I'd like to think so,' I said slowly.

'Maybe that's kind of too existential for a Monday.' Laeli squinted one eye closed and offered me an apologetic smile.

'I wouldn't be,' Kasun said, before I could think of a reply.

We both looked over at him – the interruption was almost startling. Kasun looked back, nonplussed.

'Sometimes when I'm reading something I really don't get it's like I become self-aware,' Kasun said. 'Like for a bit I realise that I don't know what I don't know. You know?'

'I get that, I think,' I said, even as Laeli snorted.

Kasun directed a smile at me that was so sunny I had to tell my heart to settle down in my chest.

When the teacher arrived we quietened down, but Laeli kept chatting to me over the course of the class, asking me questions and drawing conversation out of me. At a few points I was surprised to find myself deep in conversation with her, Kasun and other people at the table. When the bell rang at the end of class, I actually felt disappointed.

'I'm having a party,' Laeli said to me, as we put our sketchbooks in our bags. 'My house, this Saturday. I'd really like it if you came by.'

She smiled at me, and I smiled back, dazzled but thankfully not blushing.

'That'd be cool,' I said.

It was like all she had to do was smile at me and I was convinced that I liked sneaking out and going to parties.

As I walked to my next class, my head clearing the further I got from Laeli's presence, I realised that this could be my chance to encourage some progression in Mae and Kasun's relationship. I was sure Kasun would be attending, and if I plus-one'd Mae she'd have another chance to get some one-on-one time with him. Then, if they got together, I could finally convince my feelings that I had zero chance, and that it was time to give up already.

I tried not to think too hard about the way my stomach dropped at the thought of Mae and Kasun … *progressing*.

It wasn't like he was going to go for *me*. Even today, when he had talked to me and smiled at me, I hadn't got the feeling that he was being anything other than friendly.

But Mae. Beautiful, confident Mae. Loyal, considerate Mae. Mae, who had given up her chance to sit next to Kasun in a dark cinema because I wanted to go home. Mae had a fighting chance – and, more importantly, regardless of whatever nasty feelings were wriggling around in my stomach, Mae was good and kind and deserved a happy ending.

Which meant I was going to channel all my energy into being the best wingwoman ever.

✯ ✯ ✯

Mae was making it hard for me to be the best wingwoman ever.

'I don't know,' Mae said, her voice sounding tinny through my phone's speakers. 'My parents are getting at me to focus more on my major work for Extension Two because I've been second-guessing my concept and they're worried I'm going to end up behind on it.'

I stared at my phone. It was afternoon now, and my plan to surprise Mae with the invitation had backfired. Between the two of us, I was currently the most surprised.

'Okay, but ... you can do that *and* go to a party,' I said. 'And it's *Laeli*'s party. I'm sure Kasun's going to be there. Are you worried he's *not* going to be there?'

Are you worried that Laeli won't want you there? was what went unspoken. Maybe me breaking the news via a lion plushy hadn't softened the blow of that conversation as much as I had hoped.

'We *just* went to a party,' Mae said, 'and I hung out with Kasun at the beach.'

'Yeah, how was that?' I asked.

We hadn't had a proper debrief after the beach, because my mum had called not long after Laeli and I had talked. After that phone call, it was a matter of me getting on the soonest bus home. If I hadn't, I would have had to suffer the embarrassment of my dad and his ludicrous moustache arriving at the beach ready to interrogate me in front of my peers as to why I hadn't told my parents where I was or who I was out with.

Mae sighed, and there was rustling from her end, which I figured meant she was getting comfortable on her bed.

'It was good,' Mae said. 'We talked. We played like … a group game. Volleyball, sort of. Um. Yeah.'

There was a stretch of silence.

'Did something happen?' I asked.

'Like what? Something bad? No. I just … don't feel like I'm getting anywhere.'

I blinked at my phone. Was Mae … giving up? Was it because of Laeli?

'You know that Jake said Laeli isn't Kasun's type,' I reminded her.

'I don't *care* about Laeli.' There was enough of a snap in Mae's tone that I pulled the phone further away from me, blinking at the call screen like it was going to solve the mystery of her mood.

After a beat, I said, 'I think we should go to this party. I think we've got this sneaking out thing down, and I bet you'll end up enjoying yourself. And … Kasun will be there.'

Mae didn't say anything.

'Let me wingwoman you,' I said.

I knew, even as I spoke, that I was getting pushy.

So what if Mae didn't want to go to this party? What did I care? I should be glad. One less party meant one less chance to get caught.

But then I thought of Laeli smiling at me as she put her visual arts book in her bag. And Kasun's jacket, draped over my desk chair under Mae's leather jacket.

'Bleh, okay, let's go,' Mae said finally, and I felt both a twinge of guilt and a swoop of relief.

My stomach had been a battleground lately.

'I'm going to be the best wingwoman,' I promised.

'I know,' Mae said, sounding resigned.

✱ ✱ ✱

Later in the week, I got a message request from Laeli, and once I accepted it she sent through her address and the date and time of the party. She ended the message with a pink heart emoji, which I spent longer than I would have liked to admit staring at, trying to decide if it was friendly or flirty – and, if it *was* flirty, how that made me feel.

Pink-cheeked, bewildered and a little giddy was the answer. Maybe this was the antidote to my Kasun crush? Laeli was cute and friendly and her attention was, honestly, a little thrilling. Why not lean into it? For once I wouldn't be at risk of sharing a crush with Mae, too, and that felt like a positive, especially right now.

After checking that Kamilia would cover for me (she only waved me off with a 'Have fun, little rebel', which filled me with unexpected warmth – I had officially graduated from 'baby rebel'!), getting permission from my parents to 'sleep over at Mae's', and checking and rechecking the route on the maps app until I could recite the directions by heart, I was ready to party.

When we got to Laeli's house on Saturday night, my first observation was that it was big. My second observation, once we had tentatively knocked on and then pushed open the door, which was already cracked to allow entry, was that it had a pool (a big pool!) that far outclassed the piddling kidney in my own backyard. I had a feeling Laeli's was also superior in that it wasn't a hack job done mostly by her dad and uncle, with mates rates playing into its choice of tiling.

We found Laeli quickly: she was in the kitchen pouring a drink, and was quick to put down the vodka so she could pull me into a hug. It was an overwhelming experience that rendered me frozen and limp for a moment, before I managed to convince one of my arms to wrap around her in response. She smelled like sugar. Her hair, when it brushed against my cheek, was soft as silk.

'So glad you could come,' she said. Then, to both of us: 'Welcome!'

'I'm sorry if I was staring at you,' Mae said, in a rush.

I watched Laeli's eyes widen, though her smile stayed untroubled.

'I just love your ... hair,' Mae continued. 'It always looks professionally done. And I know that my thinking face can be, like ... intense. I was just trying to work out your ... hair secrets.'

Mae laughed then, like, *what a silly situation, huh?* Laeli laughed too, with a little, 'oh!' There was a beat of silence, and then Mae smiled in a determined way.

'So, just wanted to clear the air,' she said. 'Sorry if it was weird. Um, thank you for having me!'

'No problem,' Laeli said. 'I love your shirt, by the way.'

Mae looked down at her chest, which was emphasised by a silver sequinned crop top. She hadn't liked it when I had called her outfit 'sexy disco ball chic', but I had meant it as a compliment. She was stunning – though right now she looked more stunned.

'Thanks,' she said, a moment too late, adding, 'Your dress is *gorgeous*.'

It was. Laeli was wearing a velvety maroon dress that made her look like she had strolled off the set of a photoshoot.

'Thanks, Mae,' Laeli said. 'I've got a drink to deliver,' she raised it towards us, 'but I'll see you two later, okay?'

As she passed, she pressed her free hand to my arm.

Once she was gone, Mae said, 'I think I blacked out when we got into the kitchen. How did I go?'

'You got right into it,' I said, after a moment's thought.

Mae nodded, looking grim. I pointed at the assortment of alcohol and mixers spread out on the counter.

'Your consolation prize,' I said.

'My consolation prize will be kissing Kasun directly on the mouth,' Mae said, which made my gut twinge.

'Monster concoction?' I asked, pushing through the feeling as we surveyed the drinks.

'*No*, thank you,' Mae said. 'Let's try—'

She stepped forwards, picked up a bottle of vodka, and then gestured at a bottle of cranberry juice nearby that had been left out, shooting me a questioning eyebrow raise. I shrugged. I had about as much of an idea as she did about combining the liquids in front of us in a way that would taste nice.

There was a stack of paper cups on the counter, so we grabbed one each. I watched as Mae sloshed some vodka into each cup, paused, and then sloshed some more.

'Is that too much?' I asked.

'I have no clue,' Mae said, topping both cups up with cranberry juice.

I eyed the cup as she handed it over, then thought of my tasks for the night ahead. The looming spectre of having to get Mae and Kasun together so they could *get together* made the drink in my hand a lot more appetising.

'Na zdravje,' I said, tapping my cup to Mae's.

'Na zdravje,' Mae echoed, looking oddly grave.

We drank.

Despite knowing that I had given myself a job for the night, I found that, when it came to follow-through, I couldn't find the motivation because I was having too much fun hanging out with Mae.

I should have expected it. We had been friends since before we could easily distinguish between Slovenian and English. Yes, we lived around the corner from each other, and yes, we had grown up in the same community, but the friendship wouldn't have worked for this long if we didn't genuinely like spending time with each other.

It was easy to surrender and let myself float around the party on Mae's arm, starting conversations with strangers and acquaintances alike. At one point, Mae and I ended up in the backyard, Mae drawing us into a game that involved bouncing ping-pong balls into empty cups. The loser had to drink from one of the cups in the centre of the table, which were filled with a selection of mysterious, no doubt alcoholic fluids.

Mae slotted us into the game in such a way that she managed to prod me into place beside Jake, wiggling her eyebrows at me when I looked at her suspiciously. She nudged me with just enough force that I jostled Jake, who glanced over at me as I knocked against him, frowning at first. Then his expression warmed.

'Hey, Book Club,' Jake said. 'How's the whale? Or should I be asking about *Emma* instead?'

'*Emma*'s done. I'm all about Agatha Christie right now,' I sniffed. 'I have less time for whales.'

Jake's eyes crinkled. 'That bad, huh?'

'I think it's your turn.' I tilted my head towards the table.

'Smooth escape,' Jake commented, but he turned his attention back to the game, picking up the ping-pong ball being held out to him.

It didn't take long to work out I was very bad at the game. My hand-eye coordination had never been good, and the combination of alcohol and yelling people didn't make it any better. At some point, when I found myself staring down the barrel of yet another mystery cup, I felt the drink gently but firmly pried from my hand.

I looked over in time to see Jake drink the alcohol meant for me, throwing up a middle finger at the sound of boos. Then he leaned in towards me, his breath warm against the side of my neck, smelling faintly of cider.

'You want to take a break, Book Club?' he asked quietly.

I took a moment to rotate the thought in my mind a few times, then nodded.

'Want company?'

I shook my head. Jake leaned back, nodding once and squeezing my shoulder. Mae, who had clocked the interaction, mouthed, *Want me to come?* I shook my head, then stepped back from the table, feeling unmoored from myself as I walked back into the house.

Somewhere quiet, that's what I needed. I just needed to sit down until the world stopped ringing. I walked further into the house, passing through the noise and keeping my eye out for quiet.

'I knew it was too early.'

I paused.

'I knew we weren't ready for this.'

Laeli.

Sober me would have hurried on, but I found myself lingering by the nearest doorway, resting one hand on the wall. My head dropped to the side, waiting for the next words.

'Why did you come?'

Laeli again, softer this time.

And then another voice, throatier, with a harsh edge: 'Why did you invite me?'

There was a pause.

Then Laeli said, still quiet, 'I don't know.'

My sense of propriety snapped into place, and I hurried away before I heard anything else not meant for my ears.

✳ ✳ ✳

Sometime later, the alcohol *really* hit.

This was my second time drinking literally ever, so I hadn't yet got good at judging the line between 'wow this is a *fun* amount of drinks' and 'I think I'm going to die'. I hadn't even realised there *was* a line.

I realised it now. I realised it and I realised I had skydived over the edge of it and *oh*, I had so many regrets.

I felt so bad that I almost felt sober – except that if I *was* sober, I wouldn't feel so bad. The bad hit me hard when I got into the bathroom. Sitting down on the toilet had never required so much coordination, and the wall in front of me was swimming and swaying like I was on the world's worst cruise.

I had hoped that by the time I got to the washing-my-hands part I would feel better, but my hands were numb under the water, and I found myself losing focus, squeezing my fingers under the flow of the tap. I looked at my reflection, feeling my face and my throat heat and spasm – ah, vomit.

Chunky, too, and so much of it that I thought I was going to choke. Just the sight of it in the sink made me heave. I turned on the tap, checking around the sink for any – ugh – splatter damage and wiping it down with my fingers. Once everything seemed appropriately washed and clean, I rinsed my mouth and slapped some water on my face, smoothing back my hair. The baby hairs that normally curled around my forehead were stuck to my skin, twirled and wet with sweat. I stared at my reflection, aiming to give myself a pep talk, but my reflection wasn't holding still and my stomach was really, *really* angry. I turned and tilted towards the door.

Had the lights been this bright before?

I made my way down the hallway, feeling like I was in a house of mirrors and that the wall was going to peel away from beneath my fingers any moment, a mirage of stability in a world that doubled in on itself and wouldn't stay still.

Despite not knowing where I was going, I managed to end up on the front porch. This was better. The music from inside was dulled, and the air was cool and fresh. My pocket was also moving.

'I did it,' Mae was saying, before I had properly matched the phone to my ear.

'What?' I asked.

'I did it,' Mae repeated. 'I kissed Kasun.'

My head was ringing.

'You did it,' I echoed.

The darkness and the quiet of the street wasn't soothing. The world was singing, and I wished it would stop.

'Are you okay?' Mae asked.

For a wild moment, I thought she was talking about my thoughts on her and Kasun.

'I feel really bad,' I said. 'I need to go home.'

'Okay,' Mae said, 'okay, where are you? We can go.'

I could feel my eyes pricking. Sweet Mae, ready to drop the boy she'd been chasing to help.

'It's fine; I already called a ride,' I lied. 'I was just going to call you to let you know. I feel really bad, and I need to go right now.'

My voice cracked. I swallowed.

'What kind of ride?' Mae asked.

'My sister,' I lied.

There was a pause.

'Okay,' Mae said. 'Tell me when you get home, all right? Text me. Call me. Promise?'

'I will.'

'I love you,' Mae said. 'Get home safe.'

'Love you,' I said. 'You too.'

I hung up before Mae could change her mind. Then, walking out onto the street, I sat down on the kerb. I could feel the gravel sliding under my sneakers, and I pushed my feet backwards and forwards, kneading the stones. I didn't look up. I knew the stars would be spinning in the sky above me.

Well.

That was that.

11

If I were the main character, my night would have ended differently.

I wouldn't be so drunk that I couldn't see straight. I'd be inside, still having fun.

I'd be kissing Kasun.

Instead I was outside, I was getting cold, and I was calling my sister.

'Amalia?' Kamilia said.

'Can you pick me up, please?'

There was a pause.

'If Mum notices I've left the house, she's going to kill me,' Kamilia said finally. 'I agreed to help you sneak in, not to *also* sneak out.'

'Pleeease,' I wheedled. 'I'm really drunk.'

'Mum and Dad will absolutely hear me start the car,' Kamilia shot back.

'Okay,' I said, 'well, if they do, just tell them you forgot something at your boyfriend's house.'

My sister was silent. I knew she was narrowing her eyes. 'If you tell Mum and Dad I have a boyfriend—'

'Oh, my bad,' I said. 'I'm so drunk, I'm saying anything. Actually, y'know what, don't worry, I'll call Dad instead—'

'You're conniving when you're drunk,' Kamilia commented. 'Okay, you bastard. What's the address?'

✱ ✱ ✱

Home wasn't far from Laeli's, luckily, especially by car. Kamilia was there sooner than expected – or maybe time was just slipping through my drunk little fingers and I couldn't judge how long I'd been sitting on the kerb. She thrust a bucket at me before I could get in the car.

That was a good move, because once the car started, all bets were off.

'What's up with you?' Kamilia asked when we pulled up in front of our house.

'What?' I lifted my head from the bucket.

'You're hungover one week, throwing up another.' Kamilia pointed at me. 'This better not start being a pattern. Next time I might not be able to pick you up.'

'There's not going to be a next time,' I said, closing my eyes – and then opening them again when I became overcome by the dizzy darkness behind them. 'I've had a weird, like, month. It's done now.'

Mae had kissed Kasun. My job as a wingwoman was over. It was in her hands now.

Mae, with her beautiful disco ball wiles.

Me, with my bucket.

'You're being really depressing,' Kamilia commented.

I realised she was out of the car and peering at me through the passenger side window.

'I have a prac first thing in the morning,' Kamilia said, tapping on the glass. 'C'mon. I gotta sleep. Get out of there.'

My bucket and I made our way out of the car, plodding after Kamilia and then bumping into her back. She had stopped quite suddenly in the doorway.

'Hey, Mum,' Kamilia said.

Oh, no.

'Girls,' Mum said.

Oh, no.

✳ ✳ ✳

I was grounded. Luckily, Kamilia was not, which was good. Being forced to stay at home holed up in my own, cosy room, I could handle – being harangued by a resentful sibling, I could not. Of course, my parents knew that telling me I had to stay home wasn't going to be an effective punishment, as I only voluntarily left the house to go to school and hang out with Mae.

Instead, Mum had me do community service.

My parents' South Slavic Catholic church of choice (the only one in a thirty-kilometre radius) had just got a bright-eyed, bushy-tailed new priest who did services for the Slovenian and Croatian Roman Catholic communities. He was also pushing a series of initiatives that involved trying to better the community. Because most of the people at the church were of the World War II generation, with only some smatterings of post-nineties migration attendance (like my parents – mostly my mother), the manual labour had a low take-up.

That was why I found myself being roused early on Sunday by my mother, who ignored my groaning, allowed me a brief grace period of vomiting in the toilet, and then bundled me, sweaty and pale, into the passenger seat of the car.

She didn't talk to me for the whole drive, which worked well because I spent it focused on keeping my remaining stomach contents (negligible) where I preferred them and checking my phone notifications when I could convince myself to engage with the screen without throwing up.

I had meant to send Mae a warning text when I got in the previous night, knowing that if I had been caught it probably meant Mum had contacted Mae's parents when it became obvious I – and by extension we – weren't where we'd said we'd be. When I checked my phone on the drive to church, however, my texts read:

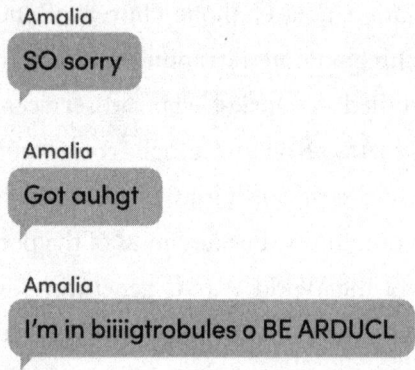

Luckily it seemed I'd made just enough sense to get my point across, because Mae had given my last message a thumbs up. I still hadn't received a morning update, but I clung to that thumbs up like a lifeline. Although her parents were strict, she'd never actually pushed boundaries or broken any of their rules, so it wasn't clear what the consequences would be for her. Would they ground her too? Take her phone? Make her clean the house from top to bottom?

I also had a series of notifications from the family group chat that I'd somehow managed to miss the previous night. I blinked down at my phone, then felt my expression crystallise into a glare. Kamilia had managed to snap a candid of me hunched over the bucket in the back of the car, and she had sent it to the chat moments after we had been caught by Mum.

> **Kamilia**
> guess who blackmailed me into getting rescued AND was trashed when I got there ANDDDD got us caught by mum??

> **Kamilia**
> dead to me

Elizabeta, who was the earliest riser of the group of us, had replied a few minutes ago.

> **Elizabeta**
> rip to a good one. Gone too soon

> **Elizabeta**
> her rebellious ways will be missed x

> **Amalia**
> i'm not dead

> **Amalia**
> mum's just making me go to church

> **Elizabeta**
> whoa who said that

> **Elizabeta**
> seriously tho, now that youre dead to ur sister does that mean this chat is technically a seance

> **Elizabeta**
> SERIOUSLY tho. Say hello to father Danijel from me

> **Elizabeta**
> ur mum showed me a pic of him last book club and if I wasn't already a taken woman and he wasn't a man of the cloth I would, respectfully—

I closed my phone.

When we arrived at the church, my mother ignored my pleas to stay in the car and hustled me inside, allowing me the one concession of a seat at the back. The moment we entered, the musty air and smell of incense and wood polish made me feel like a child again. I sat, I stood, I crossed myself, I mumbled along, I tried not to throw up.

When it was time to consume a bit of Jesus, Mum nudged me to get up after her.

'But I didn't do confession,' I tried.

I wasn't sure why I felt the need to highlight that fact – it wasn't going to come as a surprise to my mother. She hadn't managed to get me into a confession booth since I had gone through the sacraments of initiation as a child. At the time I had also been encouraged to do my confession in Slovenian, which had been an incredibly optimistic suggestion on my mother's part, considering my parents' focus on Slovenian language education had been directed more at my older sister than me. The highlight of the experience had been when, via a grammatical slip, while trying to describe a scene at dinner I had accidentally implied to the priest that I ate mice.

My mother was undeterred by my argument.

'He's very modern,' she said grimly, directing me by the elbow up the aisle.

As I approached, Father Danijel beamed at me. He was a little taller than me, with a dark flop of hair that made him look younger than he probably was.

'You must be Malka,' he said. 'Dobrodošli.'

'Dobrodošli,' I mumbled back, which was super embarrassing for me, because saying 'welcome' was not a call-and-response activity.

I took the wafer, had my sip of 'wine' (the church was out of non-alcoholic grape juice and seemed to be using cranberry juice in the interim), and slunk back to my seat, kneeling down and resisting the urge to rest my forehead against the pew in front of me.

When the service was over, Mum marched me up to the priest, waiting for a break in the flow of congregants to push me forwards.

'Father Danijel, Malka wants to take part in the rubbish collection service,' she said.

'Yeah,' I agreed, miserably.

The priest beamed.

'Wonderful. It's a new project, so we don't have many volunteers. It runs from four to five in the afternoon,' he said. 'At the moment, Mondays, Wednesdays and Fridays are the days. Do any of those sound good?'

I looked at Mum. She looked back.

'I'll do all three,' I said.

Lord help me.

✶ ✶ ✶

When we got home from the service, I clearly looked as bad as I felt, because my dad brought me a sliced apple and a cup of coffee within minutes of me slumping down at the kitchen table.

'Now you're making me look like the bad guy,' Mum complained, as he set the plate in front of me.

Dad looked at her, looked at me, then very lightly tapped the back of my head with his palm.

'Shame, Malka,' he said gravely. Then: 'Eat your apple.'

'Thanks, Dad,' I said, adding meekly, 'Could I have some more milk for my coffee, please?'

Mum rolled her eyes.

Later that morning, a text came in from Mae:

Mae

> They were both waiting for me when I got home, but told me to go to bed

> Mae
> They werent happy but not really super mad either? So

I nibbled on my thumb as I waited for Mae's next message to come in. After a moment, my phone pinged:

> Mae
> About to family roundtable now. Wish me luck

I sent back a fingers crossed emoji.

Come Monday, I still hadn't heard from Mae, which made me think phone confiscation had been part of her punishment.

Sure enough, when I met her in the morning at the bus stop, she said, 'I'm *so* sorry I left you on that cliffhanger yesterday, my parents took my phone like immediately after.'

'I figured,' I said, adding, 'For how long? And was that all?'

Mae shrugged, kneading the straps of her backpack as she checked the road for our bus before looking back at me. 'No phone for a week, which also means I have to borrow my dad's personal laptop if I want to do anything. They've told me I'm not allowed to message anyone and—' Mae raised a hand, pointing one finger at me and saying, in tones of mock strictness, '—they *will* be checking the browser history to make sure.'

'Do they know that you can delete browser history?' I asked.

'If they do, I'm not going to remind them,' Mae said. 'I also have to do, like, two hours of admin work for my uncle's law firm every day after school this week because Dad's helping them at the moment with some stuff. So my punishment is unpaid child labour.'

'We're eighteen,' I pointed out. 'I think that's just regular unpaid labour.'

Mae groaned, then sighed. 'Yeah, I guess so. Anyway, I feel like it could have been way worse, but I think they kind of didn't know what do with me?'

'Same,' I admitted.

After my punishment had been doled out and I had come back from church, Mum sniffed at me whenever I entered a room but, apart from making me do the dishes without Kamilia's help that night, treated me normally. My dad was even more chill: as the apples and coffee episode suggested, he seemed to feel that, now that my punishment had been laid out for me, all was forgiven.

All in all, it had been a bit anticlimactic.

'So,' Mae said after a moment, 'what about you?'

As I laid out my grounding and my job as unpaid garbage collector in service of the church, Mae frowned. The expression deepened when I told her I wasn't sure for how long I'd have to do it.

'I'm sorry,' she said, when I finished.

'Not your fault.' I stuck out a hand to flag down the bus. 'Actually, I'd say this time was pretty clearly my fault, because neither of us would have been at the party if it wasn't for me. I did the crime and now I'm servin' the time in the jail of Mum and Dad. Or church jail? I'm doing church jail.'

The bus pulled up to the kerb and we piled on, scoping out the back (full) before wedging ourselves in the centre aisle.

'Well, I'm glad you made me come out,' Mae said. 'I had fun.'

The words *Was kissing Kasun fun?* were on the tip of my tongue, but I couldn't quite make myself say them. Mae hadn't brought him up either, so it could be argued I was just following her lead. Maybe she was saving it for a private hangout, away from prying ears.

Either way, it didn't matter. What was done was done, and now I had a community to clean.

✷ ✷ ✷

Honestly, the cleaning wasn't bad.

After school that day, Mum had taken me straight from home to the church, loading me into the church's minivan after extracting a promise from me to 'be good' (did she think I was going to 'be evil' while picking up street debris?). My only companions were an older man and a middle-aged woman, and they spent the hour chatting after failing to engage me in Slovenian. My big, noise-cancelling headphones helped. I figured my companions both had kids or grandkids who, like me, used them to signal they weren't in the mood for talking, because once I put them on I was left alone.

Even better, Mum seemed to be feeling guilty about the severity of my punishment. Helped, probably, by the fact that I hadn't kicked and screamed about it – and that I'd made a point to bring up with great frequency how stressed I was getting about the final exam block of the term next week (with heavy emphasis on the *next week* part). She even bought me a chocolate milkshake on the drive home as a reward for my hard work.

'Don't get used to this,' she said, taking a hand off the wheel to point it at me. Then she crooked a finger towards her to gesture that she wanted me to put the straw in her mouth.

Dutiful daughter that I was, I let her have a sip.

'And,' she said, 'you only have to do this for this week and next week. Father Danijel only needs to get this started. Having some young blood around, helping, will make him happy. Make him feel like he's succeeding. He's already stretched between services. Did you know he does German and Polish services too?'

'Okay,' I said. 'So I'm a tool in your silent war against other congregations?'

'Don't be rude, Malka,' Mum said. 'I'm a good Catholic. I love my neighbours.'

I could see the corner of her mouth tick up, despite her tone, and I grinned around my next sip of milkshake.

Over the next week, Mae and I continued to not talk about the Kasun kiss. When discussing the rubbish-collecting with Mae I'd leaned into the drama of it, insinuating that my garbage-picking afternoons were endless, arbitrary, and subject to the cruel whims of my mother (I omitted mention of the milkshake), but I had conceded that I could probably swing a Friday movie night. This, I thought, would be it. We'd finally talk about the kiss, and it would hurt, and maybe then I could convince my heart to move on.

I was still grounded, and Mae was still phone-less, so it was a little different than usual, with Mae borrowing her dad's laptop to video call me in secret after we'd both finished dinner.

All afternoon I'd been psyching myself up for the 'kissing' conversation, but I clearly hadn't done a good enough job preparing my expression because when Mae picked up the video call she took one look at me and said, 'Who died?'

'Nobody,' I replied, rearranging my face into something I hoped was more neutral. 'I'm just bummed we can't do this in person.'

'Yeah,' Mae hummed, carrying the laptop to her bed. 'But we can soon, right? I'll have my phone back by next week and I bet your parents will un-ground you soon too.'

'Maybe,' I said, which felt like an understatement.

I had a feeling if I asked my mother now she would just wave her hand and say, 'Fine,' because it was clear to all of us by this point that the grounding had had precisely zero effect on me, though asking to go to Mae's for a movie night was probably still a step too far.

'So,' I said, and Mae must have caught something in my voice, because she tilted her head at me, the slightest of frowns creasing her forehead.

'So?' she repeated.

'Oh my god!' I adjusted my laptop on my lap so my hands were free, then waved my hands. 'Mae! You kissed Kasun! And you haven't said *anything* about it!'

'Oh.' She got up from her bed and walked to her desk, sitting down on her desk chair.

The sudden distance, which was exacerbated by the fact that I was looking at her through a screen, disoriented me. I was immediately worried I had said the wrong thing.

'You don't have to tell me anything,' I said, backtracking. 'If he was ... did he ... do ... something?'

'Oh, no,' Mae said. 'No, don't worry.' She started twirling from side to side, gaze focused on her knees now instead of the screen. 'I just didn't want to be gross, or bore you with all the details.'

'Okay.' There was a weird, twisting feeling in my stomach, and I hunched forwards, resting my forearms on my knees.

'It's okay if you want to keep it private,' I said, though even as I said it I felt an ache; as though, in that moment, there was nothing I needed more than for Mae to lay out every gory detail.

Like I needed to know there really wasn't any chance for me.

A smile ghosted across Mae's mouth. 'Well, it was nice.'

'How did it happen?' I asked, managing to ignore the fact that I had just told Mae she had a right to privacy.

'You know how we dropped our bags off in Laeli's room? Well, after you left the game outside, I played for a bit longer then realised I didn't have my phone with me. I went to go get it from my bag, and Kasun came in a little bit after me.'

'Do you think he did that on purpose?' I felt a pang as I said it, sharp enough to hurt. 'Do you think he was waiting for the chance to kiss you? Keeping track of you so he could get you somewhere private?'

Mae shrugged one shoulder, her mouth still pressed into a faint smile.

'I don't think so,' she said, 'it seemed like a coincidence. Anyway, we talked a little bit, and then he was standing super close, and I thought ... *this is it*. And I put my hand on his arm.'

The pang was still there in my stomach, sharp-edged, digging in. I hunched further forwards.

'Wow,' I said, surprised by how normal I sounded. 'So did he ...'

'I think we both sort of leaned into each other,' Mae said.

'Wow,' I said, again.

Mae was still swinging side to side on her chair, wide swings, pushing herself off and then braking with her feet.

'What was it like?' I asked.

Mae wasn't looking at her knees anymore, but she wasn't looking at me, either. Her gaze was unfocused, cast over the laptop towards something – some object, some thought – I couldn't see.

'He's a good kisser, I think,' Mae said, finally.

I had run out of questions. I didn't need to know any more. It was like I could see it, the scene vivid behind my eyes. Mae, oblivious, checking her phone. Kasun, coming in behind her. An exchange of words. Mae, getting up, moving back towards the door. Kasun, stepping aside but not stepping away. The feeling of his body heat making Mae step a little closer, cold in her little disco ball shirt. Kasun smiling down at her. The touch. The lean in.

I closed my eyes, like that would make the images in my mind fade to black.

'Anyway,' Mae said, 'should we start the movie?'

'Oh. Yeah,' I managed, thrown by the conversational change but also glad for it.

'You got your snacks?' Mae leaned towards her desk and picked up a pack of chips, which she brandished at me.

'Yep,' I said, patting the pack of biscuits on the bed beside me.

I didn't think I'd be able to eat, though. My stomach was killing me.

12

My grounding was ended on Sunday by my mother, just in time for book club. Very little of the discussion was dedicated to *The Murder of Roger Ackroyd* or even Agatha Christie herself, apart from a digression initiated by Tetka Mojca about Christie's disappearance, which led to twenty minutes of theorising about whether or not she'd done it on purpose and faked the amnesia.

That discussion devolved somewhat when Renata described the on-purpose theory as queen behaviour, as she was then made to explain 'what she meant by that'. This focus on the younger members of the book club was turned on me in short order. My mother, apparently spurred on by our discussion about crimes and deceit, decided it was time to tell everyone about the terrible crimes *I* had committed the previous weekend, by not only lying about my whereabouts but then also convincing my sister to 'steal' the family car, and coming home drunk on top of it all.

I sat slumped in my seat, doing my best not to glare, as my aunts gasped and tutted and had a great time at my expense. My mother's description of what a wreck I'd been when I'd got home was a crowd pleaser, apparently, because even my traitorous cousins had a giggle at my expense when Mum described the state I'd been in at church the next morning.

By the end of the session, Mum was in the best mood I'd seen her in a long time. She didn't even complain when Tetka Sabinka suggested *Wuthering Heights* as our next book club pick, even though when I'd been assigned the book by my Year Nine English teacher my mother had told him it was 'bitterly depressing and a waste of my time' during the parent-teacher conference.

It meant that it gave me an easy choice of listening during garbage-picking the following week: I had the *Wuthering Heights* audiobook locked and loaded for my fourth session, and was hopeful I could get through it by the end of my rubbish penance.

Other than some new listening material, session four also offered a change of scenery. Father Danijel joined us, taking the wheel of the church minivan (which I think was actually Marta's, the older woman who had proved as much of a garbage-picking regular as me), and drove us down to the beach. I kept my headphones on and watched the scenery go by, content in the knowledge that I would be left alone for the whole afternoon. After all, to this crowd, how could I compete with a priest?

It was the nicest rubbish collection session I'd had so far. I fell into a meditative state, *Wuthering Heights* humming in my ears, the sound of the waves a distant crash. The sand was warm between my toes as I cleared out the garbage that had gathered between the dunes. The beach was busy, so I made sure not to pick up anything that seemed to be part of a purposeful pile of towels, thongs and bags.

As I was skirting around one such collection, something closed around my ankle.

I yelped, my garbage-picking stick flailing in the air like a flag of surrender. My wobble turned into a topple, and I found myself falling towards a pile of towels, realising as I fell that it wasn't *just* a pile of towels, but was in fact a pile of towels that contained a partially covered, familiar *boy*, whose laugh froze on his face as I bore down on him.

Somehow, my catlike reflexes kicked into gear, and I managed to catch myself before dropping straight onto him, my hands thudding into the sand on either side of his head. We eyed each other. Then his upside-down face grinned.

'Are you actually trying to murder me, Jake?' I snapped, adding, 'What the hell!'

'I didn't think you'd fall,' he said, as though that made it better.

'Oh, *well* then.' I sat back on my heels and brushed my hands off, doing nothing to stop the spray of sand falling from my palms towards his face.

Jake rewarded me with a splutter, sitting up and half-twisting in my direction.

'Oh *sorry*,' I said, sour, 'I didn't think any of that sand would actually get on your face.'

Jake didn't say anything, his eyes scrunched. I felt a jolt of guilt, and eased forwards on my knees.

'Okay, that was mean of me.' I hesitated and then gave his knee a pat. 'Just blink really fast. You have to make yourself cry a bit, to get the sand out.'

Jake let out half a laugh, though he followed my advice. After a moment, his expression relaxed.

'Truce?' he said.

'Truce,' I agreed, and tried to smile. I was mortified to feel my lip wobble.

Even worse, he seemed to notice. Reaching forward, he pressed a hand to my cheek, fingers tucking under my chin, thumb hot on my cheekbone. The touch lasted only a second.

'Not a mean bone in your body, huh, Ames?' he said.

I blinked at him, frazzled by the double whammy of his touch and the nickname. Jake didn't seem to know what to do with my silence, because he frowned.

'Didn't like Eyebrows, didn't like Book Club,' he prompted. 'I thought I'd use one I know you've vetted.'

'Only Mae calls me Ames.'

'Reckon she can share?' he asked.

I didn't say anything, and the double meaning of his words seemed to dawn on Jake a moment later, because he let out a short laugh, looking away. I looked away too, willing the heat out of my face. Why was my face hot, anyway? He hadn't meant anything by it. Did it suck that he was so obviously embarrassed to have insinuated ... something? No, it didn't. It was fine, and I was fine, because I had a crush on *Kasun*. I didn't need Jake of all people to validate me. *Really. Jake! Of all people!*

My spiralling thoughts were interrupted when I noticed someone picking their way across the beach towards us – Father Danijel. Thank god. I was saved.

'Malka,' Father Danijel said, once he reached us, 'good to find you. Is this young man your boyfriend?'

My relieved smile died on my lips. Not saved. Betrayed. Betrayed absolutely by my local priest, who was looking like an awkward dad in rolled-up jeans, his clerical collar on full display.

'No, Father,' Jake said, politeness itself.

'Well,' Father Danijel said, with the hint of a smile, 'Malka, I wanted to let you know we'll be driving back soon. But if you want to spend more time with your friend, I'm happy to take your rubbish bag and—'

'No, that's fine,' I said in a rush, standing up.

Jake stood too, for some reason, wiggling his eyebrows at me when I shot him a look.

'Good to meet you,' Father Danijel said, pausing in a meaningful way.

'Jacob,' Jake offered, stretching his hand out to shake.

'Oh! Yaʻaqov,' Father Danijel said, and I swallowed a groan at his *I'm a cool Catholic because I know some of the Hebrew* act. 'You don't happen to be a twin, do you?'

Oh, no. He was cracking out the Catholic dad jokes.

'No, sorry,' Jake said, with a polite laugh to show that he had no idea what Father Danijel was getting at, but could assume it was a biblical thing. (Good guess, Jake.)

Before Father Danijel could ask any other particularly Catholic questions, I trilled, 'Okay, bye Jake. See you at school!'

Father Danijel got the hint. We began the trudge back through the sand dunes.

'Bye, Amalia,' Jake called.

I waved over my shoulder without looking back.

That night, I got a message request from Jake.

Jake

Sup, Sunday School?

I accepted the request, then typed back:

Amalia

Catholics don't do Sunday School.

I was settling back on my bed, phone in hand, audiobook in my ears, when another message from Jake appeared.

Jake
Catholic, huh?

Amalia
Non-practising.

Jake
Still doing church events, tho?

I squinted at my phone, wondering how much to reveal, and also wondering why Jake cared. I finally typed back:

Amalia
Punishment for going to Laeli's party. Technically wasn't meant to be there. Got caught.

Jake
Rough.

Then:

Jake
Malka?

I felt myself flush at the sight of the name on my phone. It wasn't something people outside my community called me. Seeing it there – even typed – felt weirdly intimate.

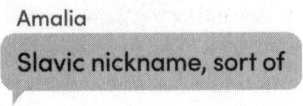

Amalia
Slavic nickname, sort of

He sent back a thumbs up. A text bubble appeared, then disappeared. Finally:

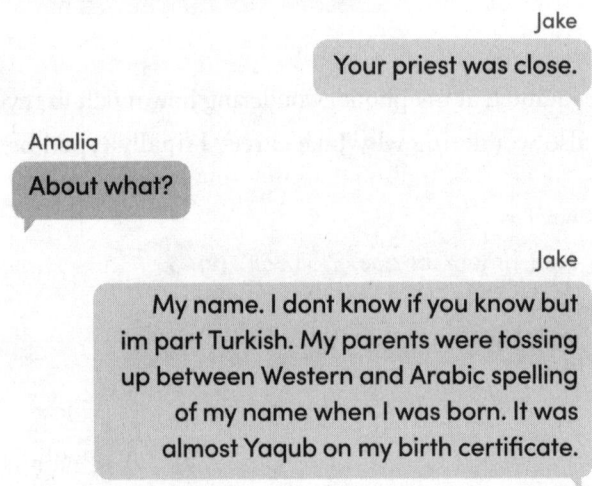

Jake
Your priest was close.

Amalia
About what?

Jake
My name. I dont know if you know but im part Turkish. My parents were tossing up between Western and Arabic spelling of my name when I was born. It was almost Yaqub on my birth certificate.

I paused before typing my next question.

Amalia
Why not Yaqub?

The text bubble appeared and disappeared a few times. Finally, Jake typed:

> **Jake**
> they watched what my sister went through as a kid and I think they got spooked. went the other way with my name

> **Amalia**
> Damn. That's ... sorry.

Jake sent me another thumbs up.

I stared at my phone, waiting for his typing bubble to pop back up. Was that where we were going to finish? It seemed like it, because five minutes later there still weren't any new messages.

I squinted at my phone for a moment then thought, *to hell with it,* and typed:

> **Amalia:**
> So do I need to beat up some kids or what

A reply popped up almost immediately:

> **Jake**
> well my sister is older than me by like seven years so you'd be throwing hands w some racist ass adults. Also their parents. But appreciate the thought

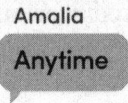

Amalia

Anytime

Then, before I could second guess it:

Amalia

so why were u at the beach.

Jake

Hanging out

Jake

w Laeli and Kasun.

My heart gave a single, painful thud as I read Kasun's name on my phone. I focused on Laeli's name instead. Kasun was out of bounds now, for real this time, but Laeli – Laeli was safe.

Or, well … she was meant to be.

I was still sitting with her in visual arts, and in our first class after the party she had asked if I'd had fun, apologising that she hadn't had a chance to talk to me much. I had waved that off and given her a vaguely positive response, because she seemed like the kind of person who'd feel guilty if she knew I'd got in trouble because I'd gone to her party. I wasn't about to say, *Actually, I was so drunk I couldn't feel my hands and then my best friend kissed my crush and now I'm in church jail.*

I also wasn't going to say: *I overheard you talking to someone and it seemed intense. Was that your ex? Not that I'd know, but it sounded like the kind of conversation you'd have with an ex you're trying to stay friends with. By the way, are you over your ex? It's just that I'm currently trying to stop crushing on your best friend because it seems like* my *best friend might start dating him soon, and I know I don't actually have a chance with you, but if I'm going to let myself have a crush on you it would be great to know if you're definitely, for real single. I'm sick of giving myself stomach-aches whenever I think about Mae and Kasun kissing and I don't want to go through that with you, too.*

I realised I'd zoned out for long enough that two more messages had come in from Jake without me noticing.

> Jake
> **You missed them by like 5 mins**
>
> Jake
> **Laeli thought it was cool you were 'choosing to go out and help clean up the community'**

I stared at my screen, mulling that over. Had Kasun and Laeli seen me talking to Jake, and asked what I had been doing there? Or did he just ... bring me up in conversation?

Either way, it didn't make sense. Why would any of them bother talking about *me*?

> Amalia
> **Is that what u said I was doing?**

> **Jake**
> you were, right?

I squirmed down against my pillow.

> **Amalia**
> maybe not choosing

What I really wanted to ask was, *did you say I was doing it as part of a church group?*

The more I thought about it, the worse I felt. Had they been getting a laugh out of the good little church girl?

I was startled out of my thoughts by my phone buzzing.

> **Jake**
> How much longer do you have to do it?

> **Amalia**
> Two more sessions this week then I'm free

> **Jake**
> Bet you're counting it down

I looked at the ceiling. While today had been okay …

> **Amalia**
> yeah i'm excited to have my afternoons back

> **Amalia**
> Not that i'll be doing much else besides more studying

I followed that message with a string of crying emojis, just in case my thoughts on that weren't clear.

> **Jake**
> Oh yeah school is kicking my ass rn

> **Jake**
> maybe you can come out with us next time

I blinked at the message. Jake was still typing.

> **Jake**
> Laeli was sorry to miss u

I blinked again. What was I supposed to say to that? I played it safe and polite:

> **Amalia**
> Sorry to miss her too

Why would Laeli miss me? Yeah, maybe I had got a bit of a flirty vibe once, and we were hanging out in class, and yeah, she *had* invited me to her party, but I struggled to imagine her actually *missing* my company. And why was Jake telling me? Why was Jake inviting me places?

Jake didn't send anything else after that, and neither did I. I tried to get some studying done that night, but my brain wouldn't settle down.

Jake wanted me to come to the beach. Laeli wanted me to come to the beach.

They wanted me to come because they … liked me?

Laeli liked me?

Jake liked me?

Did *Kasun* like me?

What did Kasun think about me volunteering to clean the beach? Did he just think I was a boring, hyper-religious kid with nothing better to do than hang out with people his parents' and grandparents' age?

Did he think about me at all?

Why would he, when there was Mae?

God, I was *so* sick of this crush.

✷ ✷ ✷

My swirl of thoughts from the night before came back into focus when Laeli caught me between classes.

'Hey! I saw you yesterday,' she said, falling into step beside me. 'I only realised it was you when you were leaving.'

'Oh.' I smiled automatically because Laeli's smile was infectious.

'I think it's really cool that you're going out during your free time to clean the beach,' Laeli said.

'Oh,' I said, again (*more words, Amalia, c'mon*). 'I mean, I kind of have to right now.'

Laeli cocked her head, and I realised I had walked myself into a conversational corner, and would have to explain what I meant by that.

'I sort of wasn't meant to be at your party,' I explained. 'So I got in some trouble.'

'Oh, no!' Laeli breathed, reaching out and clasping my wrist.

Her hand was soft, and I got a waft of sweet citrus. She squeezed my wrist, which, lacking any better ideas, stayed limp under her touch.

'I'm sorry if I got you in trouble,' she said, contrite, as though she had forced me at knifepoint to attend her house party. 'Are your parents super strict?'

'Not *super* strict,' I hazarded, 'just … a bit … *old school*. They don't want me going places where there might be drugs, which is, like, every party to them. They don't like the idea of me drinking either, even though I'm eighteen already so they can't really stop me.'

We were closing in on my classroom, which I knew for a fact was not Laeli's. I was surprised Laeli hadn't broken away from me yet.

'I'm sorry again that I didn't get much of a chance to say hi,' she said. 'It would have been nice to hang out a bit more.'

I nodded. For a moment I put away the question of to-crush-or-not-to-crush and tried to imagine just ... hanging out with Laeli. My brain struggled to form a picture. What would we talk about? What would we do? Maybe it was reductive of me, but I couldn't imagine this beautiful person sitting next to me in wrinkled pyjamas for a movie marathon, groaning as we tried to get through the snacks we had bought when we were too hungry to be sensible about our choices.

But maybe that wasn't a Laeli problem. Maybe I just needed to get better at making friends, because at this point the only person I could imagine sitting down with for that marathon was Mae.

'I'm glad you had fun, at least,' Laeli said, snapping me out of my thoughts.

'Oh, yeah,' I lied, hoping I hadn't been quiet for too long. 'Your pool is really nice, by the way.'

'I love it,' Laeli said, eyes lighting up. 'You should come over some time, actually try it out.'

I tried to imagine that. I could picture Laeli lying on a towel in the sun, feet dangling in the water while I floated on my back nearby. I found it easier to imagine than joining her for a movie marathon. Maybe the trick wasn't to try to slot her into a pre-approved friend activity. Maybe I needed to try more new things and feeling comfortable with new people would follow.

'That would be cool,' I said, surprised to find I meant it. As Laeli still didn't show any sign of branching off from me, I asked, 'Do you like swimming?'

'I love the water,' she enthused. 'I'm not a great swimmer or anything, but even when I was little I loved the water, and the beach. I still remember going to a beach in Indonesia near where my nenek lives, and it had *the* clearest water, and sand that was, like, almost pink. I think I really fell in love with the ... the whole *event* swimming could be, when I went there.'

'That sounds beautiful.'

'I was also obsessed with baths when I was little,' Laeli added, with a laugh. 'So my love of water definitely predated beaches.'

'Well, a bath is basically an ocean to a baby,' I said.

Laeli nodded, expression turning thoughtful. 'Yeah, I guess so.'

On that note of profundity, we came up to the door of my classroom.

'This is me,' I said.

Laeli nodded. Before she left, she pressed a hand to my shoulder.

I didn't read into it. (I absolutely did.)

13

'My butthole is killing me,' Mae groaned, flopping against my side during lunch. 'Why are periods like this? Also, how *dare* my period start during exam week.'

'Sorry about your butt and its bad timing,' I said, patting her shoulder. 'Truly. My deepest condolences.'

'Oh, also, news!' Mae propped herself up, readying herself for an announcement. 'You know how I was helping my uncle's firm do some admin while I was grounded?'

I nodded. Mae grinned at me.

'Guess who got a job there?' she singsonged.

I slapped at Mae's shoulder, and she knocked into my palm, laughing.

'Congratulations!' I exclaimed. 'Does this mean you want to do law now?'

'No, it's just, like, an admin assistant thing,' Mae said. 'I'll get to keep working with one of the new lawyers I was helping out when I was doing it unpaid, too, and she's kind of the coolest, so … I feel like I'm kind of being rewarded for rule-breaking now?'

'Sounds about right,' I said. 'Are your parents okay with it, though? I thought they were worried you weren't spending enough time studying. Surely they wouldn't say yes to you starting a new job during exams?'

'No, I'll start after the Easter long weekend. My parents love it, they think it solves all their problems.' Mae glanced down at her phone and then back at me with a smile and an eye roll. 'Since my "big rebellion" they've started worrying I'm *up to no good* every time I'm not directly in front of them. A job with family, where I'm being paid by someone who's going to report back to my parents about me? Their dream. *And* Dad made my uncle promise he'd let me take time off when I have exams or really need to study or whatever, so it's pretty flexible. I think they're excited about it, honestly. The fact my uncle offered me the job at all has totally gone to their heads. Now they're talking about how this will be a great "introduction" to law, though I'm literally only doing, like, filing and coffees and stuff at the firm and I'm still pretty set on studying communications, which they *know*. Oh!' Mae pulled back from her rant, widening her eyes at me. 'Speaking of communications … what did Jake message you?'

I resisted the urge to say, *are you actually going to listen to me this time?* because Mae had been fiddling with her phone all lunch – all day, really, and it had felt like her attention on our conversations had been fading in and out.

On cue, Mae glanced down at her phone again then back at me.

'Distracted?' I asked.

Mae smiled a little guiltily, slipping it into her pocket and giving it a pat as though to prove it was really in there. 'Okay. I promise I'm one hundred per cent focused. Tell me about the Jake messages.'

I opened my mouth and my phone, ready to embark on an analysis of my messaging spree with Jake, when Mae's gaze snapped away from me, red creeping along her throat. I followed her gaze, and my heart lurched.

Kasun – *Kasun* – was standing there, holding two blocks of chocolate. He was looking at Mae with a smile that made my heart hurt.

'You didn't say what kind of chocolate you liked,' Kasun said to her.

Glancing at Mae, I watched her fingers glide over the pocket where her phone was. Ah. So *he* was the phone distraction. It made sense. I felt my mouth tick up in a smile I couldn't control, and had to fight the urge to let that smile split into a grin, because I knew it was going to be an off-putting one. Of course. *Of course* this was happening.

'Are these ... okay?' Kasun said.

I realised that neither Mae nor I had said anything, both opting to stare instead. I kicked her ankle with great subtlety. She jumped like I had shocked her, but then stuck her hand out towards Kasun.

'Thanks,' she said, mechanical.

Oh, the poor thing. Her expression was tight, distant. She was probably overwhelmed by the moment. The feeling of all my – *her, her, her* – dreams coming true had to be too much.

'She loves chocolate.' I smiled at Kasun, hoping my heartbreak wasn't visible on my face. 'That's so sweet of you.'

'Oh,' Kasun said, glancing at me, 'yeah, I mean. I know you're ...' he looked back at Mae, like he had already forgotten that it was me and not her who had spoken, 'surfing the crimson wave. So.'

Mae didn't say anything, gaze focused on the chocolate.

'Periods,' he added, in case we hadn't got it.

I stared at Mae. What kind of messages were they exchanging? Mae only ever complained about her period to me. How far had their relationship progressed since their kiss?

I felt unbalanced, like I'd missed a step. I focused on my breathing.

'That's sweet of you,' Mae said finally, her expression smoothing into something more relaxed, though she still seemed tense. 'That's ... really sweet of you.'

'Well, you know,' Kasun said, scratching the back of his neck, 'I have one sister who's going through it. I get that it sucks. Hopefully those'll make it ... nicer.'

'Definitely,' Mae said.

I looked at Mae. I looked at Kasun. I knew, without a doubt, that if Mae continued like this, she wasn't going to get anywhere with him. I steeled myself, even though my stomach sank. Time to be noble and selfless.

I was her set-up girl, after all.

'Hey, about that horror movie you wanted to see on Saturday,' I said.

Mae stared at me. I widened my eyes. *Come on, Mae. First rule of improv: just say yes.*

'*Making a Killing*?' Kasun asked, clearly more on top of the rules of improv than Mae.

'Yep,' I lied.

'I want to see that,' Kasun said. 'It looks like it'll be fun.'

'Uh-huh,' I said, smiling and nodding at Kasun and then smiling and nodding, eyes widening, at Mae.

Mae nodded back at me.

'Oh, yeah,' she said, more like her usual chipper self.

'Well,' I said, feeling both frustrated and relieved that Mae seemed to be catching on, 'I was just about to tell you that I can't actually make it on Saturday.'

'I'll go with you, Mae,' Kasun said, barely a moment after the words had crossed my lips.

Mae smiled at Kasun. 'That would be really nice.'

I zoned out as they exchanged a few more pleasantries, biting into my sandwich without tasting it. My eyes closed, and I must have spaced out, because it felt like suddenly Mae was saying, 'Are you okay?'

I opened my eyes. Kasun was gone. Mae, leaning back against her palms like she didn't have a care in the world, was focused back on me, her head cocked to the side.

'That was exhausting,' I said, meaning for the words to come out light.

Mae frowned, so it seemed like I had missed the mark on that one.

'I can't set up all your dates, you know,' I said, trying, and once again failing, to muster up a light tone.

Mae glanced down, her usual armour of confidence faltering. 'Sorry. I guess I got stuck in my own head.'

I tilted my head at her, feeling a stirring of concern. 'That's *my* line.'

'You're not the only one who feels uncertain sometimes,' Mae shot back.

Her tone was sharp enough that my concern shrivelled up in response.

'Obviously I know that,' I snapped. 'I was just … It doesn't matter. You're welcome, anyway.'

Mae looked out over the schoolyard.

'I hate horror,' she said.

'Suck it up,' I said.

✱ ✱ ✱

Friday night found me lying on my bed, my Bluetooth speaker on low where it sat next to my pillow. Kamilia would be banging on my door if my music got loud enough for her to hear it across the hall. I figured some big deadline was coming up, because she was holed up in her room listening to whale song, which was always a sign that her stress levels were peaking. Whenever Kamilia got stressed, it was in my best interests to be extra quiet.

My phone chose that moment to let out a shrill hiccup of sound. I snatched it up and pressed answer to stop it going any further.

'Is tomorrow happening?' Mae asked.

I frowned. 'You tell me. *We're* not going on a date.'

'Yeah,' Mae said, which wasn't much of a response. After a pause, she said, 'It just doesn't feel real.'

'Mae, you're beautiful and kind and smart. Of *course* Kasun was going to fall for you.'

'No, *you're* beautiful and kind and smart—' Mae began.

'Hello, beautiful and kind and smart, I'm waiting for you to get to the point,' I interrupted.

Mae made a sound that I knew would have been accompanied by a shove if we were talking in person.

'It just doesn't feel real,' Mae repeated.

'Let's make it feel real, then,' I said, turning onto my side and tucking my knees up against my stomach. 'What session time have you decided on?'

'Five-thirty,' Mae said.

'Early enough that you won't have time for dinner before,' I said, 'so you can eat together after. Smart.'

'He suggested it,' Mae mumbled, like she wanted to throw off any suspicion I might have that she wanted to maximise time with the guy she'd been gushing about off-and-on for years.

'That's a good sign,' I said, instead of calling her out on her weirdness. 'That means he wants to spend more time with you.'

It was getting easier to say stuff like that – the pang I felt every time I referred to Kasun was easing. Now it was just a twinge. I was proud of myself for not being a sore loser.

Not that I had ever been in the running.

I got out of bed, sitting down on my desk chair and twirling myself back and forth. As I leaned back, I realised both Mae's and Kasun's jackets were still hanging over the back of it. I tried not to think about how that offered a parallel to my life right now.

Mae and Kasun, together.

Me, also there.

'Ames,' Mae said.

There was something about her tone that made me narrow my eyes.

'Mae?' I asked.

'I don't think I can do this,' she said.

I sat up straight. 'What?'

There was a stretch of silence, and then Mae said, 'I don't think my parents will let me.'

'You didn't *tell* them you're going on a date, did you?'

I had never understood Mae's parents' blanket ban on dating. My parents were also anti-dating in a general sense, which was why Kamilia had kept all her boyfriends a secret, but I had never got the sense that they'd actually try to stop us if we were open about being in a relationship, just that we'd get an earful about it. Mae's parents were a step more intense. Once she hit puberty, they'd sat her down and told her point blank that, as long as she was studying and living under their roof, she wasn't allowed to date.

'Of course not,' Mae said, 'I told them we were going out to a cafe to study.'

'Okay,' I said. 'That makes sense.'

'Except that we literally *just* got caught for using each other as alibis,' Mae added.

I digested that.

'You're not wrong,' I said slowly.

'They're probably going to check with your parents,' Mae said. 'And when they find out you're at home they're going to wonder who I'm out with and I'll get in trouble all over again.'

I wasn't liking where this was going.

'I see your point,' I managed.

'So …'

I closed my eyes.

'Mae,' I said, as gently as I could, 'I'm not going to come on your date with you.'

'You don't need to come *on* the date,' Mae said with a huff, like I was being absurd – like that hadn't been what she was hinting at. 'We'll leave together and then you can … do something else nearby.'

I saw the logic of Mae's request. I did. There was also *no way* I could tell Mae why I was so anti-this.

'What if I have plans?' I asked.

'With who?'

Her tone – the implication, though true – raised my hackles. I snapped, 'I *might* have other plans, Mae.'

'Okay,' Mae said, placating. 'Well, then … I think I'd have to cancel the date.'

I groaned softly, mashing my face into my palm.

'Don't cancel,' I said finally.

'You're the reason I'm going on the date in the first place,' Mae said. 'You kind of owe me.'

I felt a surge of frustration. 'You're making it sound like I'm *forcing* you to date Kasun.'

Mae didn't say anything. I cycled through the stages of grief, then let out a loud sigh.

'Fine,' I said. 'Fine! I'll come with you. But you owe me a milkshake.'

14

At least I had my promised chocolate milkshake.

Mae had even thrown in a toasted sandwich, which I appreciated. I had staked out a two-seat table at a cafe just outside the shopping centre, a stretch of study materials relevant to subjects Mae and I shared spread out in front of me. Combined, they were there to act as a cover story in the unlikely event that a member of my or Mae's family happened to stumble on me while I was here sans Mae.

Why no, family member, I am not here alone. Can you not see the shared study materials in front of me? Can you not see the second chair?

Not that much studying was happening. I was doing my best, but between it being both the first day of school holidays and the day after I had turned in my last assignment of the term (an essay on *The Tempest* that made me wonder what reaction I'd get if I suggested Shakespeare for book club), I was finding it hard to convince myself that studying was a priority. After long minutes of staring into space and flicking a highlighter between my fingers so vigorously that they were lined with streaks of blue, I roused myself, pulling out my phone and googling *hobbies*.

If Mae and Kasun were an item now, I was going to have to find something other than Mae and book club to fill my time.

'I guess I *could* legally invest … I don't really have money though,' I muttered to myself, as I scrolled through one of the first articles that appeared in my search results.

A message popped up at the top of my screen, catching my eye.

> Jake
> **Sup Catechism**

Then:

> Jake
> **what are you glaring at?**

I looked up and around, gaze sweeping the cafe. And there was Jake, standing near the counter. He waved at me when I caught sight of him. I stared at him, then refocused on my phone. Hobbies. Jake was walking over now. *Hobbies*.

'This seat taken?' Jake asked.

'Catechism?' I countered, putting my phone down.

Jake shrugged, pulling out the seat opposite me with his foot and slouching into it. I tried to ignore how broad his shoulders were when he had his elbows propped up on the armrests like that.

'I was trying to work out what Catholics did instead of Sunday school,' Jake said.

'Catechism and Sunday school aren't exactly one-to-one.'

'Yeah,' Jake said, like that was obvious. 'I *can* use a search engine, Amalia.'

'Good for you,' I said, patronising, then flipped my phone back up like I had something important to do on there.

That was a mistake. Jake leaned forwards until his forehead was almost touching mine, peering down at my phone. I didn't bother pulling it away, leaning back with a sigh instead while he cocked his head and his eyes skimmed across the screen.

'Hobbies, huh?' he said. 'Book club not stimulating enough anymore? Brenda's divorce drama running dry?'

'Brenda?' I asked, and he fixed me with a bright-eyed stare.

'Book club,' he repeated, and all at once I was thrown back to our very first conversation.

Oh. Oops. He had caught me in an old lie and, by the way his eyebrows ticked up, he knew it.

'So I embellished.' I knew that I sounded defensive rather than casual. Giving up and leaning into the defensive tone,

I continued, 'I didn't know I was going to talk to you ever again, so what did it matter what I told you?'

'Wow,' Jake said, drawing out the word. 'Not gonna lie, the betrayal cuts deep.'

I stared at him. He grinned. After a moment, his gaze flicked down to his coffee cup, and he took a sip.

'*I* wanted to talk to you again,' he said.

I stared at him harder. Had I misheard? Jake was looking at me, expression relaxed.

As though saying he liked spending time with me wasn't a super intimate, embarrassing thing to admit that could open him up to rejection.

'It's fun talking to you,' he said, taking another sip of coffee while I reeled. 'Even if it turns out you're a dirty liar.'

'I embellished!' I huffed.

It was half-hearted. I hoped I wasn't visibly red.

The thing was, despite doing my best to convince myself every conversation with Jake was a chore, I … had fun too. I *liked* talking to him. It was easier to act like I was annoyed with him existing near me than it was to admit I was a snappy bastard around him because I was scared that every time he decided to talk to me would be the last.

I knew the emotionally mature thing for me to do now was to say, *I like talking to you too*, but emotional maturity was for fools and chumps.

'Why are you here anyway?' I asked. 'Did you just come off shift?'

Jake raised his eyebrows at me over his drink.

Was he really going to make me say it?

'Yeah,' he said, finally (thank god). 'I'm tired as hell. There was this one patron, rude bastard—'

And then Jake was off. Talking to me. Relaxed, gesturing every now and then. Like we were mates.

Were Jake and I mates?

Huh.

'And how's the Agatha Christie?' Jake asked, once he had finished his story. '*Murder of Roger Ackroyd*, right?'

'That's the one,' I said. 'Laeli was right. I didn't guess the ending – though the clues were there, when I thought about it after.'

Jake nodded. 'You have a new book yet?'

'*Wuthering Heights*.' I sat back and pulled a face.

'Wow, that's an expression,' Jake said, a smile playing on his lips. 'Not excited?'

'It's ... not a favourite.'

Jake nodded, then took out his phone. I leaned over the table, feeling confident in my nosiness – I was only following Jake's lead, after all.

'I'm just looking it up,' he said, shooting me an amused glance. 'I'm guessing you're not reading the song *Wuthering Heights*?'

'No,' I agreed.

'So why are *you* here?' he asked, pointedly tucking his phone back into his pocket. 'Scouting out a new study spot?'

Jake's relaxed conversation had, in turn, had a relaxing effect on me, because instead of nodding, I sighed and said,

'That'd be very normal of me, but no. I'm actually here because I'm the best wingwoman in the world.'

Jake peered around the cafe, turning in his seat to get a full view of the space, before refocusing on me.

'For who?' he asked.

'Mae, still,' I said, looking down at the table. 'You probably know already, but she's on a date with Kasun right now.'

'So your job is done,' Jake said, nice enough not to mention my crush.

'Yeah, not … exactly.' I fiddled with a length of bread crust left on my plate. 'Mae's parents are super against her dating, so I'm her alibi and – it's a whole thing, basically. But I'm here so she can go on the date. And it's not all bad – she got me some food. So.'

'Free food's not bad,' Jake said.

I looked up, watching him scratch at his jaw. He seemed like he was turning something over in his mind.

'So, what?' he said, finally. 'You sit here, wait for them to go in, then …'

'Wait for them to come out again,' I finished. 'And get work done while I wait. Theoretically.'

Jake waved that off. 'Have they gone in yet?'

'Yeah, like, twenty minutes ago.'

Jake was squinting at the wall behind my head. *'Making a Killing*, five-thirty?'

I nodded. He looked at me, focusing back on my face. For a moment I could see the guy I had met that first night, who had set up an illegal fireworks display to celebrate his sister's promotion. There was something puckish in his expression.

'Do *you* like horror movies?' he asked.

✳ ✳ ✳

Was this illegal? I didn't know. It definitely wasn't allowed.

Still, for some reason, I hadn't put up any resistance. When Jake disappeared to the bathroom and reappeared in his work shirt, I was confused. When he passed over his work jacket – replete with a little logo from the cinema over the right breast – I stayed confused, but put it on. When I did, I got a whiff of something like rosewater and, under it, something else that was just Jake. I resisted the urge to duck my head into the collar of the jacket to get a proper sniff, because that was weird. Friends didn't smell friends, probably. I wasn't sure. Mae and I didn't have many boundaries with each other, so my frame of reference wasn't great.

As I put on the jacket, Jake had started closing my textbooks and shoving my highlighters into my pencil case, so everything was ready to put inside my bag by the time I had collected myself.

When Jake got up, I followed.

The cinema was right next door, and Jake walked us past the ticket collector with nothing more than a nod. Because I was the kind of person who got nervous bringing food from outside the cinema in with me, I gripped the straps of my bags and felt myself break out in a cold sweat as we passed (sorry, Jake's jacket). The ticket collector didn't even look at me, though, and suddenly we were in the belly of the cinema.

It was as Jake led us towards one of the cinema doors that I dug my heels in.

'We can't go in,' I said.

Jake smiled at me from the doorway, amused, and I stared back, hoping I didn't look as sweaty and nervous as I felt. I imagined walking into the cinema while the ads were still playing, the lights bright enough to identify us. I then imagined locking eyes with a shocked Mae and Kasun as staff swarmed us, shining torches in our faces and then frogmarching us out of the theatre.

'I can't do this,' I said.

'Okay,' Jake said, after a stretch of silence. 'Can I show you something else, then?'

I squinted at him, then waved my hand in a *go on* gesture.

'Trust me?' he said, a question and a request all in one.

I narrowed my eyes, but nodded.

He grinned. 'Follow me.'

That was how I found myself in the projectionist booth – Jake called it the 'bio box' – peering through the projection window at the theatre beyond. I always imagined the projection space as cosy and dark, a small room with a reel of film being projected out onto the screen. This was not that.

'It's all digital now,' Jake explained. 'We don't have a projectionist or anything. We get the film in these cases,' he pointed at an orange case sitting on the floor, 'and the hard drive is in there. We just load it up and let the films run.'

Rival to Jake's voice was the sound of white noise coming from the surrounding equipment. The space was full of tech, bulky stacks of processing power that were in charge of getting the movie from here to the screen. The picture was still being projected by a beam of light. That, at least, fit with my mental image.

I turned away from the viewing hole, taking in the room before looking back at Jake.

'Not what you were expecting?' he guessed.

'Being inside this room kind of feels like you just told me the Easter bunny isn't real,' I said.

Jake's mouth tugged up in half a grin, even as he tried to school his expression into a look of regret.

'While we're here, I've got some bad news about the Easter bunny,' he said.

I rolled my eyes, turning back to the projection window. Again, not an ideal way to view the movie, but I was getting the gist. The cinema beyond had darkened, the opening scene underway. I watched the woman on screen with a mixture of trepidation and expectation. She was going to be dead by the end of the opening credits.

I was so focused that it made me jump when I felt Jake's hand on my arm. I whipped towards him, eyes wide – and my heart stuttered at the sight of the door to the projection booth starting to swing open. As I stood frozen, Jake wrapped his hand around my arm, pulling me *towards* the door.

I let out a moan of fear. Was this some kind of set-up? Was Jake trying to get me caught? The door was opening – Jake guided me behind it, catching it with his hand as it swung so it didn't hit me. I wedged myself into the gap, closing my eyes. My heart was thudding hard enough that I was glad for the white noise of the room, sure my heartbeat would be audible otherwise.

'What are you doing in here?' the person on the other side of the door asked. 'Your shift is over.'

'I forgot my bag,' Jake said, apologetic, nodding down at my backpack – thankfully clear of any marks that would identify it as mine – where it sat on the floor beside the door.

'You shouldn't keep your bag in here,' the person said, though the statement sounded more cursory than annoyed.

'I know,' Jake said. 'Sorry. I was just picking it up.'

Finally, finally, the door closed. I didn't open my eyes.

'Okay, she's gone,' Jake said. 'That was my manager. She's chill – I think she's mostly worried I'll accidentally break something and it won't be covered by insurance because I'm off shift.'

I took a deep breath, still pressed against the wall.

'Amalia?' Jake asked.

'That was scary,' I said, my voice cracking.

When I opened my eyes, I was embarrassed to find my vision swimming, Jake a blur in front of me.

'It's okay,' he said, moving to my side. 'Seriously, she's chill.'

'We could have got in so much trouble,' I said, the crack in my voice now a full wobble.

Jake was close, head bending towards me. His hands were on my cheeks, thumbs brushing under my eyes.

'I promise the worst thing that would happen is that I'd be yelled at,' he said, then paused and added, 'Maybe fired.'

I burst into tears.

Jake pulled me into a hug. I gripped the back of his shirt and cried.

'Ames,' he said, his voice a low hum, 'it's okay.'

'I don't want to get you fired,' I said, muffled and wet.

'I'm too charming to fire,' Jake said. 'Have you met me?'

'Bit overconfident,' I said, still sniffling.

My face was pressed into Jake's chest, and I felt him laugh as he gave me a squeeze. 'There you are.'

He used one hand to guide my face away from his chest, and once he had coaxed me into making eye contact, he grinned.

'All right, Miss Goody-Two-Shoes?'

I nodded, my fingers relaxing against his shirt. One of Jake's arms stayed wound around me for a moment longer, and then he stepped back.

'Want to wash your face? I can let you into the staff bathroom for extra privacy,' he said.

I shook my head, pressing my palms against my cheeks. 'Absolutely not. I've been in enough places I shouldn't be for one day.'

Jake laughed, loud enough that I glanced at the door, worried that his manager might burst back in.

'Ames, nothing would have happened if my manager had found us, I promise. She's chill, she straight up would not care,' he said. 'We gotta get you out more.'

I thought of standing in my doorway late at night, clutching a bucket and avoiding my mother's gaze as she stared at me disapprovingly. I had been out enough lately.

'Whatever,' I said, instead of verbalising that particular memory, 'but I'm not going into the cinema.'

Jake opened the projection room door, checked outside, and then nodded at me. Picking up my bag, I followed him out. He paused near the cinema doors, and I was worried he was going to push the issue.

Instead, he said, 'Want to go somewhere else?'

15

Jake directed me to a car, letting me connect my phone to the Bluetooth once I was bundled inside. By the time I had chosen music for us, we were on the road. Jake glanced at me sideways when it started playing, and I frowned back.

'Not what I thought you'd like,' Jake said.

'What did you think I'd like?'

Jake shrugged. We were at a traffic light, and he had one hand on the wheel, the other drumming on his thigh. I resisted the urge to lift the drumming hand up and mould it back to the wheel. He seemed to catch the direction of my gaze, though, because he smiled slightly, putting both hands on the wheel as the light turned green.

'Well, you're in a book club where you read stuff like *Moby-Dick*,' Jake said. 'Ergo, you probably also listen to fancy stuff.'

'Don't know how you're calling me fancy when you're the one using words like "ergo",' I shot back.

'Okay,' Jake said. 'What do you like, then?'

I fiddled with my phone, changing the music to something more relaxed. I let the question hang between us, because what was I meant to say? I was an open book. A boring one. I liked reading the classics, although most of the time I didn't understand them. I liked hanging out with Mae. I liked bad horror movies. I liked … well, I liked Kasun. And maybe, if my heart deemed it safe, I was on my way to liking Laeli.

'I'm not exactly mysterious,' I said eventually, knowing I sounded annoyed. 'Anyway, what kind of question is that?' I snorted. 'What do I *like*.'

Jake didn't say anything for a moment, and I glanced over at him. His mouth was tight. I felt a swoop in my stomach, a pang too close to guilt. Squinting out the window, I ran back over our conversation. Maybe, in my heart of hearts, I could concede that I had reacted with unnecessary negativity to the question.

So I told Jake what I liked, sans Laeli. My sad little tally. I kept my gaze directed away from him as I spoke, not looking over even when I felt him staring at me.

'You still like Kasun?' Jake asked. 'But …'

'Yeah. Bummer, right?' I said, trying for light. 'You'd think watching my best friend go on a date with him would kill those feelings. I'm working on it, though.'

It felt almost good to admit that to someone. Jake was nodding, too.

'It's normal,' he said, finally, 'to … I know it's normal to …'

We were at another traffic light, this one near the park where the firework fiasco had taken place. Jake was frowning. He looked like he was thinking very, very hard.

'You know,' he said, 'Kasun is popular, and good-looking, and … lots of girls have crushes on him. So it makes sense you have a crush on him.'

'Okay?' I said, not adding that Kasun being popular hadn't really been a contributing factor to the crush forming.

Jake's expression had turned both serious and sympathetic.

It was … odd.

'I bet it felt … inevitable,' he continued, 'like you *had* to have a crush on him. Like it was compulsory.'

I squinted at Jake's profile. 'Absolutely what in the world are you talking about, Jacob?'

Jake pulled up to the kerb.

'Doesn't matter,' he mumbled. He added, more clearly, 'We're here.'

Jake hopped out of the car before I could say anything. I sat back against my seat, blinking at the windscreen and trying to make sense of the bizarre turn the conversation had taken.

Jake, despite his hasty exit from the car, was waiting for me nearby. He started walking when I drew level with him.

'So was that your car?' I asked, mostly to fill the silence.

'Technically it's my sister's,' he said, letting me guide the conversation in a less bizarre direction, 'but she only uses it sometimes. Most of the time her girlfriend drives her around.'

I tried not to let my interest show at this new detail about Jake's life, slotting *sister has a girlfriend and a car* into my little mental Jake box. It was filed beside *sister got a promotion* and *Jake likes fireworks, bad crime procedurals and Wikipedia spirals*. Also present were: *Jake is my friend?* and *Jake smells nice*, both of which I could unpack at a later date.

'So, one sibling?' I asked.

'Yeah. You?'

'Also youngest,' I said. 'Also only one sister. My cousins Renata and Elizabeta are around a lot, though—'

'Book club?'

'Book club is a big one, especially now that they're in uni and sort of ... building their own lives outside family,' I said, trying to keep my tone upbeat. I don't think I was totally successful, as Jake shot me a sympathetic smile. 'But we basically grew up at each other's houses. My mum and her sisters all migrated to Australia within a couple of years of each other, so I think they really like ... leaned on each other, especially at the beginning. Elizabeta – she's twenty-three, the oldest of us cousins – was actually born in Slovenia. The rest of us were born here, though.'

We walked further in silence, though this one was less awkward.

'I'm the younger one by seven years,' Jake said eventually, 'so I'm the only one still living at home. My sister still comes home all the time for free dinner and laundry, though. Both of us were born here – so was my mum, though my dad wasn't.'

Jake turned off to the side then, leaning over what I assumed was his gate to unlatch it. I took in the unassuming one-storey brick house in front of me: its outside facade was painted a dark salmon with red accents around the windows and door, a tangle of flowering shrubbery blooming beside the short path that ran from gate to door. Jake headed up the path. After giving the house another once-over, I followed him to the door, waiting behind him as he started riffling through his pockets for his keys.

'So … what now?' I asked.

'Thought we could watch a movie,' Jake said.

Retrieving his keys from his pocket, he let us in, pausing to take his shoes off by the door. After doing the same, I followed him further into the house, looking around as I did. Jake led me to a living room lit gold by the late afternoon light, switching on a lamp near the couch. Once lit, the lamp glowed a few shades brighter than the last rays of the sun.

The most attention-grabbing object in the room was a large painting of a white cat, which stared back at me through imperious, two-toned eyes from the nearest wall.

'Family pet?' I queried.

Jake observed the painting. 'Nope. My dad just really likes cats.'

'Do you have cats then?'

He shook his head. 'Nah, Mum's allergic. She can take a million antihistamines and will still start wheezing and crying when she's near one.'

'Rough.'

'That's love,' Jake said, almost absently, starting to root around for the TV remote.

'What, cat allergies?'

Jake paused for long enough to squint at me before resuming his search. 'No, Book Club. I mean it's – not what you expect. You don't choose the person. Or – you do, but feelings aren't always for the most … *convenient* person.'

I nodded, maybe a little too vigorously, because Jake shot me a wry smile, probably remembering our conversation in the car like I was. As he retrieved the TV remote, my phone pulsed in my pocket.

I fished it out, frowning at Elizabeta's name on my screen, and then let out a soft groan.

'Why the noise, Book Club?' Jake asked.

'It's one of my cousins,' I explained. 'She said her mum – my aunt – just remembered she wants to ask me about what I'm planning to study at uni.'

Jake nodded, flicking the TV on. His attention was on me, though.

'And you don't want to answer that question?' he guessed.

I flopped down on the opposite side of the sofa. 'I do not.'

'Why?' Jake was looking at me with a patient sort of interest.

So far this conversation was nothing like talking about my future with my family, or even with Mae, and I felt the stress that had tightened my shoulders at seeing Elizabeta's text begin to unwind.

'I get frustrated when people ask me what I'm going to do at uni,' I found myself saying, 'because I get … freaked out. I'm not one of those people who have a perfect plan. I'm not super passionate about one single thing; I don't have a dream job. I'm like … what's the rush? Yeah, we're halfway through Year Twelve – but we don't have to lock in our final UAC preferences for ages.' Jake was nodding as I spoke, expression thoughtful. 'And even once we do … my sister says that once you're in uni it's not actually that hard to change what you're studying. So why does it matter? Why do people *keep* asking? All it does is make me feel bad for not being totally sure.'

When I finished speaking, slightly embarrassed by my own rant, Jake said, 'I get it. Having best friends like Laeli and Kasun, who know exactly what they want to study, is like … that's cool for them, but that's not me. I think uni sounds like it could be interesting, but I don't know if I'll like it, and I guess I'll just … find out. And if it's not for me, I'll do something else.'

I tried not to stare at Jake. How did we have such similar feelings about uni and yet such different ways of thinking about it?

'How are you so laidback about this?' I asked. 'You don't ... feel any pressure?'

'I guess there's pressure, but ... what other people expect me to do isn't really my problem. If someone is really intense about thinking I need to know *exactly* what I want to do with my life, that's more about them than it is about me. Their priorities don't have to be mine. You can only be you, right?'

I was definitely staring at Jake now. 'How are you so wise?'

Jake shrugged in a worldly way. 'So if your aunt called you right now, what would you tell her?'

I sat back on the sofa, taking a moment to actually think about my answer. No deflections, no last-minute inventions of possible degrees to throw my aunt off the scent of my own uncertainty.

'I guess ...' I said slowly, '... I'd say I'm not one hundred per cent, but I'm thinking about biology at the moment, because I like doing it in school, and I know enough about what it looks like at a uni level from Kamilia that I think I'd enjoy it.'

'That's a solid answer,' Jake said, and my cheeks warmed.

I willed the heat away, irritated at myself. It hadn't even been a compliment.

'What would you say?' I asked him.

Jake relaxed against the sofa, gaze turning up towards the ceiling as he thought. 'I'd say ... probably an arts degree, because there's lots of things I could try, and it sounds pretty flexible. Maybe I'd do a history major – it's my favourite subject at the moment. I'm kind of bummed that I didn't do history extension this year, to be honest.'

I perked up, my mental Jake box reopening to accept this new scrap of information. 'You like history?'

'Yeah.' Jake scratched at the back of his neck, seeming self-conscious now. 'It's not, like, a hobby – not like Kasun with philosophy – but it's been cool learning about, um … we've been doing the nuclear age, so learning about the Manhattan Project and the Trinity Test and stuff. It's actually pretty interesting.'

I opened my mouth to ask another question, but my phone pulsed again. I frowned when I saw Mae was calling me. Shooting an apologetic look at Jake, I picked up.

'You're at the cafe, right?' Mae said.

My stomach dipped.

'Shouldn't you be in the movie?' I asked.

Jake and I hadn't been talking for that long, had we? The movie couldn't be over yet.

'You know I don't like horror movies,' Mae said.

There was a sound in the background, a shushing spray of white noise.

'Are you in the bathroom?' I asked.

'I told Kasun I felt nauseous.'

I made a face. 'Did you throw up?'

Mae didn't love horror movies, but throwing up would be a new reaction for her. Normally they only made her scream and flinch. She also made me sleep within grabbing distance if we watched them together during a sleepover, so that if she noticed any threatening shadows she could wake me up to go and investigate them.

'It wasn't what I expected,' Mae said. 'Or maybe it … was, and I … I had hoped …'

I wasn't sure if we were talking about the movie anymore.

There was a pause. I heard the blare of a hand dryer, the sound receding as Mae walked away to somewhere quieter.

'Are you in the cafe?' she asked again.

'Not exactly.' I felt that swoop in my stomach again. 'I … went out for a bit.'

'How far away are you?' There was something in Mae's voice that made my gut twist.

'Like fifteen minutes, tops,' I said. 'What do you need me to do?'

'I'm so embarrassed,' Mae said, the words coming out on a soft groan. 'I just … Come? Please?'

'Okay,' I said. 'Of course. I'm coming.'

When I hung up, I realised that Jake was standing beside me. Had he been close enough to hear Mae's side of things?

'I know we just got here,' I said, 'but can we go back? Sorry.'

'Sure. Everything all right?' He cocked his head. 'Mae … threw up?'

'Um.' I flipped my phone against my palm a few times, staring at the cat painting before putting my phone back into my pocket. 'I don't think so. She's feeling … I don't know. I think she's fine, mostly, but she needs me.'

Jake nodded like any of that made sense, the pucker of worry between his eyes easing. He didn't tell me I was overreacting, or push me for more.

All he said was: 'Let's go.'

✳ ✳ ✳

Jake was efficient. He got us back to the cinema in record time, and had his hand on the car door a moment after switching the car off. Before he could get out, I reached over and grabbed at the hand he had braced against his seat. Jake froze in response, then settled back, turning his gaze towards me.

'I know Kasun's your best friend, but don't tell him that Mae had me waiting on standby,' I said. 'Or that she called me in for … support.'

Jake looked at me. His fingers flexed under mine, just once.

'Wasn't planning to,' he said, finally.

Then he looked at where my hand was still clasped over his.

I let go of him, pulling my hands back towards my chest and turning for the door. I scrabbled at the door handle, needing desperately to remove myself from the situation, and swung out of the car as fast as I could.

As I rounded the car, I wiped my hands on my legs.

I hoped my fingers hadn't been sweaty. Next time, I'd be normal and stick to using my words. No more hand grabs for me, no siree.

I hoped Jake wasn't regretting telling me he liked my company. That simple declaration – and he probably said that kind of thing all the time, because he was a friendly guy! – had made me get too comfortable too quickly.

Grabbing his *hand*. What had I been thinking?

As I beelined for the cinema, Jake appeared beside me.

'You could slow down, Book Club,' he said.

I looked at him and he looked back, eyebrows raised.

'Aren't you …' I started, glancing ahead and then back at Jake. 'I thought you'd go home. Or … somewhere else.'

'Nah,' Jake said.

When my expression stayed confused, he smiled slightly.

'We didn't get to see a movie,' he said. 'I figure this might be more entertaining than going home.'

I blinked at him, starting to frown. Before I could say anything, though, my phone started to ring.

When I picked up, Mae said, 'Oh, hey Ames!' with surprise that almost sounded genuine.

'*You* called *me*?' I said, then nodded to myself. 'Oh, you're with Kasun. Okay. Well, I'm here. I'll be there in, like, a minute.'

'Dinner?' Mae said. 'Oh, I'm out with Kasun, remember?'

'Is that the excuse you want to go with? Yeah, sure then. I want to eat. I'm asking about your dinner plans.'

'Yeah, the movie was fine,' Mae said. 'But look, I don't know—'

I stayed quiet, letting Mae act out whatever her planned half of this 'conversation' was.

'Oh, the food court?' she said. 'We could totally swing by there.'

I imagined her shooting a bright, half-apologetic smile at Kasun, and felt my worry for Mae's wellbeing begin to dwindle.

'Before you plan out the evening in too much detail,' I said, 'I've got company.'

There was silence on Mae's end.

'Company?' she repeated.

'I'm with Jake,' I said. 'Or, Jake's with me.'

I resisted the urge to say: *Jake is with me because he gave me a lift and seemed really understanding about all of this, but just now he said something that made me feel a bit weird. I think he thinks this is funny?*

Should I feel hurt by that?

I think I'm feeling hurt by that.

'*Jake?*' Mae repeated.

I could hear Kasun say something. I couldn't make out the words, but his tone sounded cheerful enough.

'So, are Jake and I meeting you at the food court?' I asked, studiously not looking at Jake in case my expression was as wounded as I felt.

'Yeah,' Mae said. 'Food court.'

I hung up.

I was feeling a lot less guilty and a lot more annoyed now, my annoyance shot through with hurt.

Jake thought of me as 'some entertainment'.

Mae sounded fine, and not at all like someone who needed rescuing.

And Kasun was going to think I was some kind of obsessive weirdo who couldn't handle her best friend going on a date without trying to crash it.

'You look pissed,' Jake commented.

I didn't answer. What was there to say?

No, Jake, this is my happy scowl. What could I possibly be upset about?

We went to the food court.

16

Kasun and Mae were already at the food court when we arrived. Mae waved. I lifted a hand.

After greetings had been made, I launched into the spiel I had been mentally rehearsing since I had got off the phone.

'Totally forgot you had a date tonight, sorry,' I said, pushing my tone towards something that approximated cheerful. 'I was studying nearby and wanted some food. I thought I'd see if you were around.'

Kasun and Mae nodded, then turned their attention to Jake.

'Just got off shift,' he said, with a shrug, adding, 'I'm hungry.'

'Okay, so, great!' I said, trying to tamp down the rush of frustration I felt at the absolute non-emergency this situation was turning out to be. 'I'm going to go and get a drink now.'

I turned and stalked – *walked*, walked calmly and normally – to the counter of the nearby bubble tea stand, focusing on the drinks menu with a calm and normal expression. When I turned towards the counter to order, Jake stepped up beside me, adding his own order and tapping his card to the card reader before I could.

'On me,' he said.

I wondered if he had picked up that some of my annoyance seemed to be directed at him too.

I walked back to join Kasun and Mae. Mae was looking at a nearby menu with the unfocused stare of someone who hadn't taken in a single item. Kasun kept glancing at his phone. I watched them standing together, not touching or talking, and felt a flutter of hope in my chest.

No. Nope!

I took a mental mallet to the flutter, banging it down. No hope. Not allowed! Even if this date didn't pan out (*I bet it won't,* the mean little voice in my head said, *they're being so awkward with each other*), it wasn't like I could swoop in and take Mae's place. I didn't suddenly have a chance. And it would be disloyal of me to want one.

I gave the flutter in my chest a few more tamping blows, then walked over to Mae, who shot me a look. I shrugged back. If she wanted someone to break the silence, it wasn't going to be me. I was here for a getaway only. If she wanted someone to drop some icebreakers, she needed a different best friend.

'Do you work at the cinema too?' Kasun asked. My heart lurched when I realised the question was directed at me.

I followed the direction of his gaze. I was still wearing Jake's jacket.

'Oh,' I said. 'No.'

We lapsed back into silence.

Jake, who had dawdled his way back to us, said, 'How was the movie?'

I glared at him. Mae started fiddling with the ends of her hair.

'Oh,' Kasun said, half-laughing, 'nah, we didn't even finish it, did we?'

He elbowed Mae gently like they were in on a joke, and Mae smiled back at him, close-lipped.

'This one couldn't take the blood,' Kasun continued. 'We're, like, thirty minutes in and she leans over like "I'm going to vom".'

'I didn't say *vom*,' Mae protested, though she was keeping her tone light, as though she was totally fine with the joke being at her expense.

Nobody said anything to that, and we lapsed back into silence. Mae cracked her knuckles. I tried to catch her eye, but she seemed intent on not looking at anyone at all.

Someone touched my arm, then. Jake was holding out my tea, which I accepted with a tight smile.

I tried – and failed – to catch Mae's eye again, and the failure triggered a surge of annoyance so strong that, if I was being honest with myself, it wasn't annoyance anymore. I was in anger territory now.

'Well, it was so great to see you both,' I said, giving up on cheer and trying instead to keep the anger out of my voice. 'Sorry for crashing your date. I need to get back to studying.'

'Need a lift somewhere?' Jake asked.

'Thanks, but I'll be fine,' I said, voice shaking a little on the 'fine'.

Without another glance at any of them – especially not Mae – I left.

I spent the bus ride home choking back tears, finding myself wishing I had never intervened to help set up Mae and Kasun's date.

✳ ✳ ✳

I spent Sunday in a state of mortification that verged on hysterics. It didn't help that every time I checked my phone, it remained bare of notifications. Oh, sure, there was a message from Jake, but I ignored that, still hurt by his grinning presence in the food court. I had thought – it was just …

We had talked. We had had fun. He had been …

I thought of his hands on my face, of the way he had coaxed me out of a crying panic without making a big deal out of it. He had been kind. And then suddenly he was talking about how I was *entertainment*. A replacement for a missed movie.

It made me rethink all of our interactions.

He had said he liked my company, but was it my company he liked, or my mess?

What did he say after he had witnessed me attempt to set up Mae and Kasun at his sister's house?

Oh, yeah.

Thanks for being entertaining.

I had thought he had meant our conversations. I had thought he had meant it had been … fun. That *we'd* had fun. Maybe I had got it all wrong. Maybe it had only been fun to see me try to set my best friend up with my crush. Maybe I was only fun when I was a slow-motion emotional train wreck.

And then I would start thinking about Mae's failed cinema date with Kasun. And I would get angrier.

After dinner on Sunday, Mae came knocking. Mum called me downstairs without telling me it was Mae outside, so I didn't get a chance to pretend I wasn't home. I had just enough dignity not to turn away with my hands over my ears when I saw her standing in my doorway.

Mae was wearing the navy jumper I had loaned her for her first – and even shorter-lived – movie excursion with Kasun, the sleeves bunched over her hands. She waved at me with one stumpy fist.

'Come for a walk?' she asked.

'You know Mum gets strict about me going places at night.'

'I know. But it's only seven, and it's me,' Mae said. 'And we're not going far. And you have your phone.'

I looked at her, not saying anything – not ready to admit she was right. Mae raised her eyebrows, offered me a tentative smile, and then headed for the gate. Instead of leaving, she stopped there, leaning against the fence and gazing out into the street like she had all the time in the world.

I put on my shoes and went to join her.

We walked to Mill Hill Park in silence.

It was a good park to walk through at this hour of the night, lit by floodlights thanks to the regularly used sports field – technically a cricket field – in its centre. Mae and I had done two loops of the path before she spoke.

'Did your family do church things this weekend?' she asked.

'Just Mum,' I said. 'This morning.'

Mae nodded. 'Did I tell you? Babica said she wouldn't have alcohol or meat during Lent but we went to dinner at hers last Wednesday and she made a whole roast chicken for all of us. She was actually shocked when I asked if that meant she wasn't giving up meat anymore. Can you imagine trying to explain vegetarianism to her?'

I snorted. 'She wouldn't have dared eat it on Friday though, right?'

Mae's lips turned up in a cheeky smile. 'Oh, for sure not. Not even the Pope can convince her that's allowed.'

I managed a smile in return, but didn't say anything else.

'So, what were you doing with Jake yesterday?' Mae asked finally, tilting her head towards me with a smirk.

I stopped walking. Putting my hands on my hips, I took a deep breath.

'No,' I said. 'We are not going to pretend that the weirdest part of yesterday was Jake.'

Mae cast her gaze towards the sports field. I saw her swallow, and watched her bite down on her lip and then let go. My anger wilted.

'The only explanation I can think of,' I said, 'was that ... that Kasun did something. Did he do something to you?'

Mae looked at me and shook her head.

'No,' she said. 'No, he was totally friendly, and ...' She laughed. 'He wanted to hold my hand.'

I absorbed that.

'Like ... forcefully?' I asked. 'He wanted to force you to hold his hand?'

'No. He just ... put his hand on the armrest. Palm up.'

I stared up at the sky, squeezing my eyes shut for a moment.

'I don't get it,' I confessed.

'I felt nauseous. I had to go. I freaked out so I called you,' Mae said, matter-of-fact.

I shut my eyes again. The back of my eyelids didn't provide me with any clarity. 'What does that have to do with putting his hand on the armrest?'

'It doesn't,' Mae said, 'it doesn't matter. I felt sick—'

'But it wasn't even a gory movie,' I muttered, pressing my fingers to the skin between my eyebrows.

'—and now I've messed up my chances with Kasun,' Mae continued, voice winding up in pitch.

I mulled over what to say next.

'Mae,' I said, finally, 'do you think ... maybe you and Kasun aren't ... maybe dating him is ...'

Mae was looking at me with an expression that was so blank it was stony. My words were shrivelling in my mouth. I pushed on anyway.

'Maybe,' I said, 'maybe you panicked because you liked the *idea* of going on a date with Kasun, but you weren't ... ready, maybe, to *actually* go on a date with him.'

Mae kept staring at me.

'Are you going to say something?' I asked.

Mae stared a moment longer, than shook her head, looking at her feet.

'I don't know,' she said.

'Well, that's something.' This whole exchange had given me a headache. 'It sounds like ... like you were so worried the date was going to go wrong that you tanked it sort of ... on purpose?'

I squinted at Mae, waiting for any reaction to that theory. She was focused on her shoes, but she nodded slowly.

'I don't really want to think about it,' she said, after it had been long enough that I was wondering what about the tops of her shoes was so fascinating.

I felt a twinge of irritation.

'I'm still annoyed with you,' I said.

Mae looked up then, face full of woe.

'Not super annoyed,' I relented. 'I'm just ... embarrassed. I looked like a huge weirdo and that sucked.'

Mae threaded her arm through mine and rested her head on my shoulder.

'*I* was the huge weirdo,' she said. 'You were fine. I promise. I won't call you like that again unless I really definitely need saving.'

'Okay,' I said, feeling the remaining tension drain from my shoulders.

'Why was Jake there, though?' Mae asked. 'And why were you wearing his jacket?'

'Not going there right now,' I said.

'Do you still have it?'

'*Not* going there right now, Mae.'

17

It was officially the first week of school holidays, but I was finding it hard to relax, because I couldn't stop thinking about Easter. About Jake. I spent more time than I wanted to admit lying facedown on my bed replaying the weekend's events, my stomach squeezing with embarrassment and hurt.

The weather matched my mood: it was getting cooler now as the year slid into autumn. Monday brought the wettest weather we'd experienced in a months, which at least meant that nobody bothered me about spending the entire day in my room.

Jake had sent me a message around an hour after I'd stormed off from the food court on my own:

Jake

Get home safe, Ames?

When I finally looked at the message after dinner on Monday, I gave myself a moment to stew and then wrote back.

Amalia

yeah.

I went to put my phone away, but it buzzed with a notification before I could.

Jake

You okay?

Then, before I could process what was happening, Jake was calling me.

I watched my phone buzz against my palm, blinking at Jake's name on the screen. Against sense, against my own wishes, I found myself picking up the call, folding my knees into my chest as I did so.

'I'm hurt,' Jake said, not sounding hurt.

The words straightened my spine and flattened my voice as I said, 'Oh?'

There was a pause from Jake's end.

'You full-stopped me,' he said, after a moment, the lightness in his voice sounding a little forced, like I'd pulled his punchline out from under him.

'I guess I did,' I said.

Another pause.

Then, in a tone that meant business: 'Okay, I was trying to keep things light, but something's up. What's happening, Ames?'

I blinked, shocked for a moment by his directness, though I supposed I shouldn't be anymore. Then I took a deep breath.

All right. Two could play at that.

'I've decided,' I said, 'that I can't be friends with someone who thinks the fact that I'm crushing on the same guy as my best friend is funny.'

There was silence from Jake's end.

Then Jake said, '*What?*'

'It's not funny,' I said, 'it's … it's sucked. It's not entertainment; it's my life. It's been my life all year, and believe me, I want it to be different, but it's *not*.'

The longest silence so far ensued.

'Amalia,' Jake said slowly, 'I'm going to need you to explain how you came to … all this.'

I blinked at my window, feeling, for the first time, the first blushes of doubt.

'In the car park,' I said, 'when I asked why you were coming with me to the food court.'

Jake made a *go on* noise.

'You said – you said that because you'd missed a movie, you'd come with me. For some *entertainment*.'

'I didn't say that,' Jake said.

I looked at the rain, biting at the corner of my mouth hard enough that it hurt.

'I didn't go with you because I missed a movie,' Jake said.

'Why would you say it like that, then?' My voice came out small.

Jake made a noise that sounded like the start of a sentence, then sighed.

'I don't know,' Jake said. 'I don't – I didn't mean—'

'Saturday night wasn't entertaining,' I said, my voice firmer now as I found my footing again; as I put words to what I had been feeling. 'I thought we were hanging out and having fun. And then it's like, oh, you're coming with me to crash the date between my best friend and my crush because you want to be entertained? That—'

'I didn't mean it like that!' Jake said, words tumbling over mine. 'I – Amalia—'

A creak of wood. The shifting of feet outside my door. My heart leaped to my throat. If anyone other than my sister found out Mae had been on a date, they'd tell her parents and then we'd be in trouble all over again—

'I've got to go,' I said, my voice distant to my own ears.

I hung up, then crept to the door, opening it slowly.

No one was there. I crept further so I could see the staircase – as a head of red hair disappeared out of sight. A moment later, I heard the front door open and then slam closed.

My heart dropped from my throat to my toes.

No one in my family had red hair.

There was only one person in my life who had red hair.

I blinked down at my phone, seeing I had missed notifications – not from Jake, though. From Mae. It looked like the notifications had come in when I picked up Jake's call.

> **Mae**
> Still feel weird and a bit awful about Sat so I made u some cookies and I'm bringing them over now

> **Mae**
> Cookies make everything better

> **Mae**
> Consider them my second sorry

I felt like I was melting. Like my world was tilting on its axis. She had heard. She had heard. She had—

I walked downstairs to find my dad in the hallway, holding a plate of cookies and wearing a lightly disgruntled expression.

'Your friend is a bit strange, you know,' he said, holding the plate out. 'I have just let her in and now she's running off.'

He glanced down at the cookies suspiciously before looking back at me. 'Is she that bad at cooking?'

I just looked at Dad, feeling a nauseous tug in my gut, like I'd taken a step expecting ground and only found air.

She knew.

Mae knew.

* * *

I took the cookies from Dad and walked to the kitchen. The plate had been covered in cling wrap to protect the cookies from the rain, the surface of the wrap still dappled with water droplets.

Mae had felt so bad about Saturday that she had not only made me cookies, but walked them over to me in the rain. And I had rewarded her with – with—

'Mum?' I called, my voice cracking in the middle of the word.

'Yes?' she called back.

'Where are you?' I asked, voice properly wobbling now.

'In the living room, Malka.'

I upped my pace, traversing the kitchen in a few quick strides and rounding my way into the living room. All I wanted to do in that moment was throw myself into my mum's arms and have her tell me everything was going to be okay.

But, as I entered the room, I found to my dismay that the position was already taken.

My mum and sister were on the sofa opposite the TV, Kamilia lying with her face buried in Mum's stomach. Mum patted Kamilia's shoulder, half her attention on the tennis, which she'd turned down but not muted. That was something of a relief, because a muted tennis match could only mean something catastrophic had happened.

Mum looked up, reaching out a hand for me to take.

'Kamilica's boyfriend broke up with her,' she told me.

Kamilia turned her face away from my mum's shirt long enough for me to see her face was drawn tight in a sob. She also threw up a hand towards me. I stepped forwards, balanced the plate of cookies on the back of the sofa, and took both of their hands.

'How did you know she was dating someone?' I asked, my curiosity momentarily able to override the sense that my world was crashing down around me.

'Do you think I know nothing?' Mum said, flat.

Kamilia, face still pressed into Mum's stomach, began to sob again. Something about that, combined with the grunts coming from the TV, and the bland expression on my mother's face, made a hysterical giggle rise up in my throat. I let go of Kamilia's hand to clap my palm over my mouth, but not before a burst of laughter slipped out. Kamilia raised her head and shot me a tragic look.

'Don't be a bitch!' she sobbed.

'You are not too old for me to wash your mouth out with soap,' Mum told her.

I came and sat down on Mum's other side. After a beat, Kamilia reached her hand back towards me.

'I'm not laughing at *you*,' I said, gripping her hand firmly. 'It's just … um. Timing. Everything's gone a bit … I dunno.'

My voice wobbled on the 'dunno', and both my mum and my sister looked at me. It was enough. The floodgates opened, and, moments after I had laughed, I found myself crying. Both Mum and Kamilia offered murmured consolations, and when I could control my voice again, I found myself telling them what had happened (censoring and generalising where needed).

'What a mess,' Mum sighed once I was done, though I knew she was happy to be included in the gossip.

My sister had also perked up, my misfortune distracting her from her own woes. When Mum followed her statement up with, 'I hope this day will teach you girls that boys are not worth your time,' Kamilia rolled her eyes rather than bursting into tears.

She had also peeled back the wrap covering the cookies Mae had made, ignoring my woeful stare as she bit into one.

'I was too good for him anyway,' Kamilia said. 'But *why* have you been trying to set Mae up with the boy you're into?'

'Because she's a good girl and knows she shouldn't be dating,' Mum said.

Clearly, she felt that Kamilia had made it over the *must be coddled* hill and was now back in *emotionally secure enough to endure a lecture* territory.

'You can't tell Mae's parents that she's – erm – that she has a crush, though, okay?'

I had omitted mention of the fact that Mae had actually gone on a date with Kasun, and instead framed it more as a case of me suggesting Mae talk to him at school.

'Do you think I have nothing better to do than this?' Mum snorted, which I knew was the best I would get.

To Kamilia, I said: 'Because she's my best friend.'

Kamilia rolled her eyes again, sitting up from Mum's lap and putting one hand on her hip, a cookie in the other.

'It's because you've got low self-esteem,' Kamilia said.

'Thanks,' I mumbled.

'It's not an insult,' she said, matter-of-fact. 'It's something to work on.'

'Okay, well ... sorry,' I said.

'If you had better self-esteem, you wouldn't be apologising.'

I glared at my sister. She shrugged back at me, then leaned into our mum.

'Can we watch something else?' she asked – half simper, half whimper. 'I just need to be distracted.'

'These girls, always coming in during my time off and telling me what to do,' my mum sighed, though she passed the remote over.

I folded myself against Mum's other side, snuggling under her arm as Kamilia did. Before I turned my attention to the TV, I opened up my message chain with Mae.

With my heart in my throat, I wrote:

Amalia

When you're ready, we should talk.

18

Mae didn't reply. I didn't push it.

Jake also hadn't sent me any further messages after I had abruptly hung up on him. I felt a twinge of guilt when I thought about it, but it was nothing compared to the chasm of guilt that seemed to grow ever deeper as hours and then days passed without any word from Mae.

I tried focusing on *Wuthering Heights*, thinking it would suit both my mood (anguished) and the weather (still rainy). Reading about the nasty romantic dynamics between the characters managed to cast my own romance-adjacent dramas in a gloomier light, however, so I found no consolation there. Though I supposed I should be glad that I wasn't a character in *that* particular book, rather than let its bleak mood overtake me.

Kamilia was schlepping around the house in a state of emotional disarray too, and was being unusually clingy, which offered another – and perhaps more effective – distraction from my woes. She was always like this after a break-up, moping around at home, commandeering the TV and clinging onto the nearest family member like a limpet.

Her clinginess had extended to the group chat: an update would pop up from her in the cousins chat every few hours, either to let us know she didn't think a contestant on whatever miserable reality dating show she was watching was 'there for the right reasons' or to give us an update on the 'glow-up' she was subjecting herself to (which mostly seemed to consist of her sending pictures of various exercise routines and hairstyles, followed by: *thoughts???*).

Renata was doing her best to cheer up Kamilia by sending us screenshots of bizarre exchanges she was having on dating apps, while Elizabeta was choosing the tough love approach.

In response to a rant from Kamilia about a contestant on something or other, she only wrote:

> Elizabeta
> I love you but please leave ur house.

On Thursday, while I was lounging around in my room feeling particularly woeful and scrolling through my phone without taking in any of the content, I heard nails running over the wooden surface of my door. Before

I could acknowledge the sound, Kamilia poked her head around the door. We locked eyes, which she took as an invitation to slink inside and fold up on the bed beside me. She watched me scroll for at least a minute before saying, 'Why are *you* moping?'

I glared over at her. 'I'm literally just hanging out.'

'Yeah, you're doing it in a mopey way though.' She grabbed my phone before I could say anything about *her* mopey ways.

'I want to show you a video,' she said, in response to my squeak of resistance – then squinted at my open tabs. 'Why does one of these just say "hobbies"?'

I made a grab for my phone, but Kamilia was faster, holding it out to the side so I couldn't reach it.

'Maybe I was looking for new hobbies,' I said.

'By searching *hobbies*?'

'I was drawing a blank!'

Kamilia gave me my phone back, frowning thoughtfully. 'There's this girl in one of my labs who always comes in wearing these cute crop tops made out of these, like, multi-coloured doilies, and when I complimented her, she was like "thanks, I make them myself".'

I gave my sister a look like, *can you get to the point?* She gave me a look in response: *that* was *the point*.

Then she sighed. 'There's a hobby for you. Make stuff with your hands. Crochet or knit or whatever. Make cute crop tops.'

'Why don't *you* make cute crop tops?' I shot back.

My sister didn't take that in the spirit it was meant, turning to face me with a serious expression.

'Why don't *we* make cute crop tops? Like a sister activity.' To punctuate this, she reached over and squeezed my hand.

I looked down at our hands dubiously.

'I'm not a crop top kind of person,' I said.

My sister smiled in a way that let me know she thought she had won this round. 'Just think about it, Malka.'

✺ ✺ ✺

By Friday, the isolation was starting to get to me. I had to talk to Mae. I had to try to explain. What exactly, and how exactly, I was going to explain, was still something I was working out.

Baby steps, though.

With this in mind, I texted her:

Amalia

> I want to talk soon, if you're okay w that

Almost immediately, she texted back:

Mae

> I think we should talk too

I blinked at my phone, surprised by the swiftness of her response compared to the days of radio silence. My fingers hovered over the phone's surface for a beat, then I typed:

I spent the rest of my morning doing my best not to think about any of it, scrolling through pictures of knit and crochet designs until eleven-thirty, at which time I was so full of nerves that I got dressed, put on my shoes and went to sit on the fence to wait.

When I saw Mae round the corner of my street, I tried to take deep breaths, but I was feeling light-headed by the time she reached me.

We looked at each other for a long moment. Then, like the first sun after a storm, Mae offered me a tentative smile. I felt my throat tense and my eyes well up. I managed to avoid bursting into full-on tears as I hopped off the fence and fell into step beside her.

After we'd walked a few blocks, Mae said, 'I'm sorry for not responding sooner. I've just been … thinking about things.'

I nodded, not ready to trust my voice yet.

We reached Mill Hill Park.

When we stepped onto the path, my throat had relaxed enough that I could say, 'About what you heard—'

'I think I just want to know,' Mae interrupted me, 'that like … when we were talking about the date – when we were talking about *how* the date went – and you said that maybe I wasn't ready, or that I liked the *idea* of Kasun more than I liked actually dating him …'

Mae trailed off and swallowed. She wouldn't look at me. We had barely started on the path, but now we were stopping, Mae stepping to the side to let a bike pass.

'Were you glad?' she finished.

Her voice was soft, but the words were a blade, and I felt a sharp curl of pain in my gut as she spoke.

'No,' I choked out.

It sounded like the lie it was.

How could I not be? In my secret heart of hearts, how could I not be glad?

'I wanted it to work,' Mae said.

'I did too.' These words were true.

'I thought it might,' she said, drawing in a shaking breath, eyes distant. 'For a bit there. I thought it might actually work.'

I in turn thought of sitting on the side of the road, watching the stars spin above me. Of the devastation one kiss could cause. It wasn't fair, that I could be … upset for Mae, and glad all at once. It felt cruel. It made me *feel* cruel.

'If I had never talked to Kasun, maybe I wouldn't have known for sure,' Mae said, and she was still distant, staring through me even as I tried to catch her eyes.

'I'm sorry,' I said.

Mae didn't say anything. Her gaze wandered, landing anywhere but on me.

'Why didn't you tell me?' she said finally.

'It seems silly now,' I said. 'I just thought … I don't know. You saw him first. I didn't see the point talking about it when I knew I didn't have a chance. But you—'

Mae turned her face away then, her expression twisting into something like pain. I closed my mouth with a snap.

'I think I still need some space,' she said, 'and some time.'

I nodded. My throat had gone tight again.

'I need to think,' Mae said.

I nodded again.

And I let her go.

* * *

'Why do I feel like you're the one who had a recent break-up, not me?' Kamilia asked.

I didn't respond or move, keeping my face buried in my pillow. After a moment, the bed dipped, and I felt Kamilia's hand come to rest between my shoulder blades, rubbing gentle circles.

'Did you and Mae have another fight?'

'Same fight,' I mumbled into the pillow, turning my face to the side so my mouth wasn't directly pressed into the pillow. 'And it's not a fight, it's her being mad at me for really valid reasons. Because I'm a horrible friend, and a horrible person.'

'It's totally normal for girls to have crushes on the same guy,' Kamilia said, calm, with all the worldly wisdom of a second-year uni student. 'It's totally normal for *friends* to have crushes on the same guy. And it sounds like you were actually being pretty mature about it, and were really supportive.'

'No,' I said, pushing my face back into my pillow, 'I'm a horrible friend and a horrible person.'

Kamilia sighed. I felt the bed bounce as she stood up.

'You know, I came in here so *I* could be the one to mope,' she said. 'Now, though, I see your need is greater than mine. So, horrible person, want to go see a movie?'

I lifted my head towards her, just a little.

'What movie?'

✷ ✷ ✷

Kamilia agreed to see the evening session of *Making a Killing*, despite not being at all interested in that sort of horror. And, despite the fact that this movie had been the catalyst for … so many different things happening to me recently, it was good. Kamilia even bought us popcorn. For the first time that week, I found myself having fun.

It meant that, as we were leaving the theatre, Kamilia talking about the horror movies she *did* enjoy ('mostly I like it when creepy kids start crawling on the ceiling'), catching sight of Jake sweeping the main lobby didn't fill me with a mixed bag of bad feelings. When Kamilia excused herself to the bathroom, I walked over, pausing close enough that Jake could see me but also staying far enough away that he could pretend not to notice me.

To his credit, when he next happened to glance up he paused when he saw me, and leaned against the broom.

'Book Club,' he greeted, and something unclenched in my chest.

'Hey,' I said.

Jake looked down at his broom, then back at me. 'I'm going to finish soon.'

His gaze flickered to the side, and I realised my sister had come up beside me.

'Some of my friends are getting drinks nearby,' she said, glancing between me and Jake.

'You go, have fun,' I said.

'Okay.' Kamilia swept me into a side hug. 'If Mum and Dad ask, we went and got dinner together. Keep in touch. We'll coordinate our return.'

She smiled at me, then at Jake, and headed for the entrance. Jake pushed himself off the broom with the energy of an old man getting up from his recliner, continuing to sweep. I kept pace with him.

'Can I help?' I asked, after a moment.

Jake half-laughed. 'I'm not going to make you do my job, Amalia.'

A few moments passed. Jake leaned against his broom again.

'Speaking of sisters,' he said, 'I talked to mine. About Saturday. And about our call.' Jake squinted. 'You were … really upset.' He was still squinting, his jaw working. 'I was – I still am – kinda pissed off.'

I took a deep breath, feeling the discomfort of Jake's words wash over me, feeling my defensiveness fade into guilt. I had been hurt, yes, but I also hadn't let him explain himself properly. Now wasn't the time to snap back.

Jake seemed to realise he was tensing his jaw, and stopped, clenching and unclenching his fingers on the broom handle instead. I watched him do it, then watched him stop, and stand still. He squared his shoulders.

'It pissed me off,' he said, 'that you would think I'm the kind of person who only hangs out with someone to laugh at them.'

I blinked. 'That's not—'

'That's what you said,' Jake interrupted. 'That you think I only talked to you because I cared about a crush you had on my best mate. And yeah, maybe I was *curious* about why you were being a wingwoman for your best mate when you had a thing for Kasun, and maybe I thought it was kind of funny that you had to go save Mae from the tamest date in existence. I didn't think you being upset was funny, though. I could have chosen my words better, but I didn't mean that watching you … be uncomfortable or *sad* was entertaining. I was trying to say that … That I have fun when I'm with you. I don't care about watching relationship drama. I care about—'

Jake choked on the words, and subsided. His chest rose and fell hard, just once. He looked as shocked as I felt.

'Okay.' I took a step forwards. 'Okay.'

Jake laughed, rubbing his face with both hands. 'Why are you talking to me like I'm a spooked horse?'

'Because I was a horse girl,' I replied, keeping my tone level, 'obviously.'

Jake laughed again at that, a startled sound, and let his hands drop. I was standing right in front of him now. Before I could overthink it, I took a final step forwards, moving into him. I pressed my face into the hollow of his throat, and wrapped him up in the tightest hug I could muster.

It took a moment – a tense moment – but then Jake relaxed into me, hands curling around me in response.

'My sister told me I have self-esteem problems, which was rude,' I said, still holding on, feeling the bump of Jake's heart near mine. 'But maybe, I am willing to admit, in this case I might have done a bit of projecting, and assumed the worst. I'm sorry.'

'Okay.' Jake took in a breath that pressed him even closer to me for a moment. 'While we're being mature and whatever, can we agree that next time you feel like I'm … If I hurt your feelings, can you tell me?' He paused, and I shifted to pull away. Jake squeezed me and then let go. 'Just be like, *hey, you're being a dick*. Or something.'

'Got it.' I gripped my elbow, feeling a burst of awkwardness.

Jake eyed me, then smiled a slow smile. 'Regretting being so touchy-feely, huh, Book Club?'

I grumbled vaguely, but stepped back, letting Jake get back to his work and ghosting alongside him. He kept looking over at me, still half-smiling, and every time he did I felt a nervous little fizzle. No, not nervous. I wasn't nervous. So … what was the fizzle?

'What are you squinting at?' he asked.

I glanced over in time to see him stretch, and watched him put both hands behind his neck, his head dropping back.

'I'm so done with work,' he said, voice rough, head still thrown back.

I watched his throat bob, my gaze tracing the curve of his neck and then bouncing between the flex of his biceps.

I felt the fizzle again, and something else, too, a low, hot pulse that was unmistakable, and that made it impossible for me to stay in the dark about what, exactly, was the cause of the fizzle.

Well.

Damn.

19

'So, what do you want to do now?' Jake asked, then frowned. 'Amalia, you're very red.'

'I'm a normal colour,' I said, normally.

Jake narrowed his eyes, but didn't push it. 'Okay, well, I'm gonna clock out and then I'll meet you back here.'

I nodded, Jake nodded, and then it was just me and my thoughts. My awful, terrible thoughts. What treachery, what internal tomfoolery, had led to this? Sure, Jake was kind and he smelled nice and he was funny and he *cared* about me – but what right did I have to respond to all of that with a crush?

Jake hadn't even been in the *running*, for goodness sake. I already had my next unattainable crush lined up nice and neat for me, not to mention I was still dealing with the consequences of my last crush. And how was it fair that all of a sudden I was thinking about Kasun as my *last* crush, as a thing of the past, when the burning wreckage of those feelings, and their messy consequences, had been the main subject of my week? How could my emotional landscape alter so dramatically in the course of one evening?

Had it been over the course of one evening? Or had this been brewing in the background and I had been too busy angsting to notice?

When I thought of Kasun, my heart still gave a little stutter. The feeling was perfunctory, though, like every bit of emotional turmoil I had experienced over the last few months had officially drained my feelings for him dry.

And then there was Jake. Infuriating Jake, who toppled me on the beach. Sweet Jake, who had comforted me when I had panicked in the cinema. Jake, who I was only just starting to think of as a friend.

This wasn't fair. Why wasn't there an opt-out option?

Didn't I deserve a break?

'Now you look mad,' Jake said, coming back to stand beside me.

He had a black windbreaker on, and I was reminded of the fact that I still had his work jacket hanging over the chair in my room. Oh, I just *knew* I was going to do something obscene when I got home like put that jacket on and turn my face into the collar.

'You're probably hungry,' Jake decided.

Stepping up behind me, he put both hands on my shoulders, pushing me forwards. 'One foot after the other, Book Club. C'mon.'

Quietly seething, I let him direct me to the food court.

✱ ✱ ✱

Did I feel better after having some food? No. Now I was angry, and I also had bubble tea.

I gave my drink a hard pull, chewing at the pearls in my mouth like they were the physical manifestation of my new feelings and maybe, if I tore them into small enough pieces, I could swallow them down and never think about them again.

Annoyingly, Jake was the most calm and placid I had seen him maybe ever. We ate in silence, both of us in our own heads – between the two of us, Jake's seemed to be the better place to be. I imagined him mentally stretched out on a beach somewhere, drink in hand, hat tipped over his face. My own brain felt like a burning room.

I wanted to message Mae badly enough that the desire was a burning ache. She was my best friend. I needed her counsel. I got as far as taking out my phone, but a few moments of staring at its dark screen convinced me to put it back in my pocket.

I was giving her space.

As I slid it back into my pocket, I caught Jake's eye.

'Mae knows about my crush on Kasun,' I explained, still amazed that saying his name attracted only the smallest of pangs.

Was it that simple? Had the switch really been flicked? Sure, past crushes had been like that, with the feelings coming on hard and fast and then just as quickly disappearing, but … Kasun had been my longest crush. My most complicated by a mile, too. Surely that counted for something?

'When you and I were on the phone earlier this week, she sort of … heard me say it. That's why I hung up on you.' I refocused on the important part of that crush: Mae's hurt feelings. 'She's still upset.'

Jake nodded, taking a bite of his food and leaning back, gaze wandering as he chewed.

'Kinda silly,' he said finally.

I felt my hackles rise. 'Mae has every right to be upset. I should have – I should have told her. I should have told her months ago.'

'Okay,' Jake said, placating, 'but you weren't trying to sabotage her. You thought you had the same feelings, that's all.'

I looked at Jake suspiciously. I *thought* I had the same feelings? Did he …?

No. There was no way. *I* had only just been clued in to the fact that my emotions had decided to change targets. There was no way *he* knew. He couldn't. It was probably a slip of the tongue.

Anyway, he was right and he was also wrong, and what was the point in talking about it? Yes, I had helped Mae with Kasun. I also hadn't hesitated to suggest that maybe it was the fantasy of Kasun that she liked, and that she didn't really want to date him. Did I believe that? Yes. Had I been glad to say it? Also yes.

'I miss talking to her,' I said.

I went to sip my drink, realised I was done, and made a few listless stabs at the remaining ice cubes before leaning back with a sigh. Jake was smiling. When I narrowed my eyes at him, his smile widened. Resting his elbows on the table, he leaned forwards, shoulders looking unfairly broad.

'You need a distraction,' he said.

My mouth had gone dry. I swallowed, and managed to nod.

Jake directed us to the grocery store on the bottom floor of the shopping centre. At the entrance, he put his hands on my shoulders again, giving them a quick squeeze.

'I'll meet you in the party supplies section,' he said. 'Be right back.'

I had a lot of questions, but the pressure of his hands, and the way his thumbs rubbed gently, absently against my skin, was impeding the process of brain-to-mouth communication. I gave him a thumbs up.

I was looking at the themed paper plates when Jake moseyed back to my side a few minutes later, carrying a plastic bag jangling with cans.

'We need sparklers,' he said.

'Are you going to tell me why?' I asked, giving his bag an obvious once-over.

'She didn't want fireworks,' Jake said.

'She?'

'Did you eat enough?' Jake asked, countering with the old 'a question for a question'.

'Are you my mother?' I shot back.

'Am I?'

'*Are* you?'

Jake slung his arm over my shoulders. 'All right, Book Club. Places to be.'

✳ ✳ ✳

As a placating gesture to make up for his secrecy, when we got to Jake's car he gave me full control over the music. I ended up nosey-poking through his playlists, and it turned out he had a story for almost every song I played.

'First time I kissed a girl was during that song,' he said. 'Still not sure I managed to hit her mouth, though. I was so nervous I drank heaps before, and then when she went in for the kiss, I managed one touch before I had to throw up.'

'On her *face*?' I said, aghast.

'Her shoes,' Jake replied, solemn. 'They were sandals.'

During another song, Jake drummed his fingers on the wheel and said, 'Oh, yeah, I set off fireworks for the first time to this one.'

I leaned back in my seat, twisting so I could look at him. The streetlights cast his profile in gold and red and danced along the line of his knuckles. At every traffic light he would squeeze the wheel, letting his hands tense and relax as he waited.

'What was the occasion?' I asked.

'I dunno. I was mad. I was wired. I was, like, fourteen,' Jake said. 'My sister had some contraband fireworks. She saw me itching to do something, and the rest is history.'

'Are you two close?'

Jake lifted one shoulder, then nodded.

'After she came out,' he said, 'this was years ago, but – it was rough. Our parents didn't kick her out or anything, it was just ... weird. They were stuck in this limbo of denial and anger and ... and sadness, because her life wasn't going to turn out like they imagined and it took them a while to get okay with that. And they really struggled for a while. My sister and I weren't super close then, but I supported her and pushed back when our parents said things that were ... I dunno, passive aggressive. Mean? Yeah. Sometimes mean. We sort of got really close around then.'

'It's cool you're so loyal to each other,' I said, feeling the inadequacy of the words as I said them, yet not sure what else to add.

Jake tilted his head, and I sensed a deflection coming. 'What about you and your sister?' he asked.

'Nothing like that,' I said. 'She drives me up the wall, sometimes. But ... we've got each other's backs, too.'

Jake glanced over at me, and then said, 'I don't know if you two would get along, because my sister's loud as anything, and likes to push people out of their comfort zones. I think she'd like you, though.'

I felt my face go hot.

'Yeah?' I managed.

'Yeah. She's a pot-stirrer, though, so she'd probably do something like make you börek and then get you to swear it tastes better than our dad's.'

I tried to push past the implication that, in this scenario, I would have already met Jake's dad and tried his cooking, but my thoughts were going gooey around the edges.

Be normal, I told my brain.

He wants you to meet his family! my brain trilled back.

'Börek?' I said, instead.

'Flaky, greasy layers of pastry full of meat or cheese, or potatoes,' Jake said.

'Oh, yeah, burek!'

'Börek,' he corrected.

'We call it burek.'

'Okay, well, pretty sure it was ours first, and *we* call it börek,' Jake said.

I raised my hands, and he flicked his gaze towards me, shooting me a grin.

'Y'know,' he said, 'this isn't the first time I've had this conversation. I have a Tunisian mate who said they made a version, too. Called it brik.'

I nodded. 'I feel like most cultures get on the savoury pastry bandwagon at some point.'

The streets around us, which had been passing in an unfamiliar blur, had sharpened into something like familiarity. I leaned against the window, peering out, and then sat back as Jake pulled up to park in front of—

—Laeli's house.

I stared at it, and then looked at the kerb where I had experienced a lot of big, drunk emotions about Kasun. And then I thought about my big, sober emotions of that very moment and I turned towards Jake with some trepidation.

'What are we doing here?' I asked.

Jake was not to be so easily led.

'You want to come in, or you want to stay in the car?' he asked.

That depended on whether or not Jake intended to return rapidly, or if this was a leave-the-dog-in-the-car-while-we-do-the-shopping situation. When he swung himself out of the car, letting the door click closed behind him, I waited a moment and then, sighing, followed.

By the time I caught up, Jake was already at the door. As I mounted the stairs, he winked at me and then rang the doorbell. The door opened with an immediacy that startled me into stalling with one foot on the top step. Laeli was in the doorway, looking beautiful and faux pissed off. She pointed at Jake with an accusing finger.

'I knew it!' she said. 'I knew they weren't just "in the area". I knew this had your fingerprints all over it.'

'Happy birthday, Laeli,' Jake said, indulgent, like a parent to an overwrought toddler. 'I brought a plus one.'

'You can't have a plus one if there's no party,' she said, but her heart wasn't in it. She smiled at me, rolling her eyes like, *can you believe this guy?*

'In my defence, I wasn't told where we were going or what we were doing,' I said, replying with a half-eye roll of my own, like, *truly, I cannot.*

'Sounds about right,' Laeli said. Then: 'Okay, Jake, what's the plan?'

✳ ✳ ✳

The plan was pretty simple, it turned out, which was almost disappointing. Except that, based on Laeli's commentary, this was not the first time Jake had taken it upon himself to plan a birthday celebration for her, and past plans were *not* to be emulated – a statement even Jake agreed with. The plan was: surprise Laeli for her birthday (it had half-worked); take Laeli and friends to the beach; commence lowkey birthday celebrations. We were now in the midst of the birthday celebrations portion of the plan.

I didn't know many people at the beach, although Kasun was there. We managed a short, awkward conversation, the gist of which was:

'Oh, hey Amalia, what's up?'

'Nothing much, thanks.' (Why did I say *thanks???*)

'How's Mae?'

'Fine. Bad, actually. When she threw up during the date, turns out that was actually food poisoning – but she's way better now. So, she's fine.' (*Why* had I decided to make an excuse for Mae? Why didn't I pause to think about how long ago the date had been? Kill me, kill me, kill me. And I couldn't even text Mae to tell her I had given her a terrible, terrible backstory, because we still weren't talking!)

(I missed talking to Mae.)

'Oh, wow. Hope she's okay.' (He clearly hadn't been listening closely, thank goodness. Still, that rankled. If Jake had been the one listening to that same rambling mess, at the end he would have said something like, *You want to run that by me again, Book Club?*)

(Ugh. Stop thinking about Jake.)

So: everything was fine, and I was not cracking around the edges.

When everyone started singing Laeli happy birthday she covered her face and blushed in a cute way, so that was adorably distracting and helped remind me why she had been my top pick for next unattainable crush. Then we got to the cake-cutting. We were sitting in a circle, crowded tight, and someone had supplied Laeli with a butter knife, which she was using to cut through a cheap chocolate mud cake. A few drinks had been shared around already, so there was a lot of noise and some giggling. When the knife sunk straight through the cake at first cut, tearing at the paper lining beneath it, a few people went 'Oooh', and someone hollered, 'Now you've got to kiss the nearest girl!'

Laeli covered her face again, and then looked over at me with the same expression of commiseration she had used when Jake and I had appeared on her doorstep. I found myself unable to reply in kind, however, as my expression had frozen with the realisation that *I* was the nearest girl.

Laeli, seeing my face, leaned into my side and whispered, 'Don't even worry about it.' Before I could react or respond, she kissed me on the cheek.

Laeli's friends started clamouring for cake.

I stared at the cake and tried to make myself less obviously red.

Thankfully no one else was paying attention. The cake was a solid distraction and, soon after, Jake produced sparklers. I sat down in the sand and watched a dedicated group crowd around someone's phone, brainstorming how to take pictures where the sparklers created shapes and letters in the air. Then the sparklers were lit, their glow shining off the waves and painting the sand gold.

Jake had designated himself cameraman for some reason, and I watched him take a knee in the sand, positioning his phone near his face while he snapped pictures. As the birthday girl, Laeli got the most dedicated camera shots, and posed expertly for them. Then she was throwing herself down beside me, pulling Jake around with her. Before I realised what was happening, he had taken a handful of pictures of Laeli and me, the sparkler fizzing and bright between us.

After Jake's attention was turned back to the other partygoers, Laeli didn't get up. We watched her sparkler burn through its stem, the light flickering out.

'Are you having fun?' I asked her, blinking spots of light from my eyes.

As I re-acclimatised to the dark, Laeli stretched forwards, resting her chin on her knees and letting her spine relax into a curve.

'Yeah,' she said. 'I have good friends. They know I won't do anything for my birthday, so they're always finding new ways to trick me into celebrating.'

'Do you not like your birthday?' I asked.

Laeli turned her face towards me, leaning her cheek on her knee.

'I have some birthday baggage,' she said.

'Oh?' I said, not sure if I was about to open an unpleasant bag of worms for Laeli.

'I've had … some bad ones,' she said. 'I wasn't always the beautiful, unbothered, well-moisturised queen you see before you today.'

Laeli shot me a smile, and I smiled back.

'I didn't always have the friends I have now,' she continued, looking back out over the water. 'And even once I did … sometimes having two people you really care about turn up for your birthday feels worse than no one at all. If no one comes – no one has to know that …'

Laeli trailed off. I felt very, very guilty for setting us on this conversational path.

'Screw those other people,' I said, adding, 'Not Jake and Kasun, obviously. I assume they were …?'

'They always showed up for me,' Laeli confirmed, smiling again now, although it was still small. 'They *always* show up. Like today.'

I stared out at the water, blinked, and then said, 'I can't imagine it.'

Laeli tilted her head, eyeing me quizzically.

'People not showing up for you,' I elaborated. 'You're …'

I wasn't sure how to finish that sentence, but in the silence, in the words unsaid, Laeli's expression warmed, her dimple popping out in full force.

'You're sweet,' she said, 'but not everyone is accepting. Most of my life I haven't hidden who I am, which has … caused some problems, and I've since rethought that. Sometimes you have to be strategic, right? Not everyone deserves all of you.'

'Right,' I said, even as I felt myself prickle with awareness.

Was she confirming what I thought she was?

'Sorry about earlier, by the way,' Laeli said. 'I hope you weren't too uncomfortable.'

I shook my head, flushing at the memory.

'I don't like it when people pay too much attention to me,' I explained.

Laeli smiled. 'I used to be like that.'

'Any tips?'

Laeli's smile turned into a grin, and she rested her cheek on her knees again. 'Exposure therapy?'

'No thanks,' I said, though I smiled back at her.

We watched someone try and fail to cartwheel while holding a sparkler, Jake there to capture all stages of the train wreck.

'The kiss didn't make you uncomfortable?' Laeli asked finally.

'Huh?' I said, distracted by the sight of Jake wheezing with laughter. 'No.'

I looked back at Laeli. She had put one hand behind her, and had listed closer.

'Have you kissed anyone before?' she asked.

I nodded.

'Have you kissed girls?'

I shook my head. My thoughts were loud and clamouring. I was suddenly very sweaty.

'Do you want to?'

My brain emptied. My thoughts went quiet.

I felt myself nod. Laeli leaned in.

20

It was over so quickly. It was endless. Laeli's lips were soft, and up close she smelled like apricots and vanilla. I wove my fingers through her hair, pulling her face closer. In response, her lips parted against mine. She tasted like chocolate cake.

When we pulled apart, she smiled at me. I think I smiled back – I wasn't sure what my face looked like.

'Was that good?' I asked, breathlessly.

'I liked it,' Laeli said, still smiling.

That felt like code for *I've had better*, but she was leaning back in, so it couldn't have been terrible.

My phone started buzzing in my pocket. I ignored it. It stilled for a few seconds, and then—

I leaned away from Laeli with a sigh.

'What?' I snapped, once I had picked up.

'Sheesh,' Kamilia said, 'I was just calling to see if you were home or not.'

I looked at Laeli, and then back towards the waves. '... No. Not home.'

'Okay. Then we should start coordinating our rides home.'

'All right, all right,' I said, managing to soften my tone on the repetition – Kamilia didn't know I was *in the middle of something*. 'Give me a bit. I'll work something out and get back to you in a few.'

'You have to go?' Laeli asked, once I had hung up.

'Yeah,' I said. Then, bold, I leaned in and gave her a quick kiss. 'Happy birthday, Laeli.'

Laeli's smile was dazzling.

Trudging across the beach, I squatted down next to Jake, who was still acting as photographer.

'Did you have fun?' he asked, in a tone of voice that meant he knew exactly what I had just been doing.

'Yes,' I said, haughty, 'thanks. Lots.'

Jake laughed, shooting me a sideways look. 'Good to hear. So, what's up?'

It seemed hypocritical of me, considering I had been kissing someone else, but Jake's lack of reaction to that knowledge rankled. Obviously this was a silly reaction. It was pointless to expect someone who didn't have a crush on me to care about me kissing other people. And jealousy wasn't cute. I made myself take a few breaths before saying, 'I need to go. I'm meeting up with my sister so we can get home together. Stop my parents getting suspicious.'

'Sure,' Jake said. 'Do you need me to drop you somewhere?'

I blinked at him. 'I was going to find a route on my phone. Mostly I was coming to say goodbye—'

'I'm not sending you out into the wilderness alone,' Jake interrupted, calm.

I sat back on my heels. 'First of all, it's not the wilderness; there's a main road right behind the beach. I'm pretty sure they have buses there.'

'Let me rephrase,' Jake said. The group he had been photographing had grown bored and dispersed, so it was just us now, and he turned to face me. '*Can* I drop you somewhere? I'd like to drop you somewhere. Call it ... peace of mind.'

Well, when he put it like that. What was a girl with a crush to do?

✱ ✱ ✱

Kamilia and I decided we should meet at the bus stop closest to our house and walk from there. The walk would give us time to refine our story. My parents hadn't called so far, but I knew they would want to know where we had been once we got home.

In the car, I couldn't help saying to Jake, 'So, you're cool with me kissing Laeli?'

'Amalia,' Jake said, shooting me a look, 'have you already forgotten everything I said about my sister?'

'No,' I said, shuffling down in my seat and fiddling with the heating. 'I just ... wanted to check.'

'You're all good, Ames,' Jake said, more softly. 'Anyway, I was the one who told Laeli you might be, y'know. *Interested.*'

I stared at his profile.

'When?' I asked.

'A while ago.'

'A *while* ago?' I repeated. 'But I never—'

'My sister and one of my best friends are gay, Amalia,' he said. 'I like to think I know the signs.'

I snorted at that, even as I felt a thrill run through me.

Until now, having a sexual orientation that wasn't limited to one specific gender had been something private, a piece of self-knowledge that was new and precious and that I had kept close to my heart. I had kept it that way in large part because I had always been the type to keep romantic thoughts to myself (exhibit A: the Kasun mess). Announcing my sexuality – my bisexuality – had always felt strange to me. It wasn't like I tended to announce my romantic feelings anyway, so why would I announce the *potential* for romantic feelings? Why did people need to know?

Tonight, though, I felt like a different person. I had kissed a beautiful girl. I was talking about it, openly, with Jake. And suddenly I understood why people talked about this stuff.

There was a relief in acknowledging it out loud. There was anxiety, yes, because in speaking about it I was showing more of myself, and making myself more vulnerable in the process. But there was also joy. I was surprised by the force of it. A silly smile had been stuck on my face since Laeli had leaned in and kissed me.

'Define *a while ago*,' I said, still smiling as I forced myself back into the present.

Jake drummed the wheel. 'Remember MacKenzies, when you walked on the beach with Laeli and after I asked if you two had talked about anything fun?'

'Yes, when you were being weird,' I said, and Jake snorted.

It took me a moment. Then I was twisting in my seat to face him, mouth popping open. '*Oh my god*, you were trying to suss if we had been flirting!'

Jake lifted a hand from the wheel, palm up like, *you get it now*, though his gaze stayed focused on the road.

'Why weren't you *clearer*?' I said.

'Well, I only had a hunch about you, I didn't know for sure. And I'm not going to out my best mate if she hasn't said anything herself.'

'That makes sense.' I settled back against my seat. 'That's fair. But my god, Jake, you were so cryptic about it.'

'I … could have been smoother,' Jake admitted, grinning. 'Happy ending now, though, hey?'

We sat in silence for a moment, and then I blurted, 'Are you trying to *wingman* me?'

'I think it's fair to say I'm not just *trying* to be your wingman,' Jake said. 'You kissing Laeli means I set you up good. Give me some credit.'

'I don't think wingmen are meant to be secret.'

'I wasn't *trying* to be secret,' Jake replied, sounding amused. 'You're just oblivious.'

'Hey!' I squawked, which earned me a throaty laugh.

Jake nudged my hand away from the temperature setting — I'd been fretfully messing with the knobs — and flicked a finger towards his phone, like, *why don't you put that nervous energy towards choosing some music, huh?*

'So, Laeli is gay?' I asked, as I scrolled through his phone.

'Yep, she's been into girls for as long as I can remember,' Jake said.

'How long is that?'

'We've been friends since like Year Three,' Jake said, making a hand gesture at the song I had chosen — I skipped past it. 'So definitely since at least then.'

I contemplated my next words, decided *screw it*, and said, 'Laeli mentioned a … messy break-up?'

Jake shot me a sideways look. 'Don't be nosy, Book Club. Laeli can tell you all about it when she feels comfortable.'

When felt like a bold assumption.

'You're acting like a kiss means Laeli and I are a sure thing,' I said, feeling both uneasy and thrilled by the words — yeah, I had a crush on Jake, but this was *Laeli* we were talking about.

I had to be the first person in the world to view Laeli as a second choice.

Oh, god. I shouldn't have kissed her at all. She deserved so much better than that. Who was *I* to treat *Laeli* like second best? How dare I have a crush on Jake when Laeli was ... was *Laeli?*

None of this – absolutely none of this – was going to plan.

'Why shouldn't it mean that?' Jake asked.

His words took a moment to penetrate my sudden fog of panic, but when they did, I felt my eyebrows rise. 'Jake, are you a secret romantic?'

'Choose a different song, why don't you?' he said, obviously dodging the question.

I smiled in open-mouthed joy. 'Oh, you *are.*'

'You know, my mum used to say to me: *Jacob, you are so exasperating,* and I don't think I understood what she meant until right now.'

I grinned at that. It felt like something Mae would say to me. It also ... made sense that Jake took romance seriously. It was a strange revelation to have. When I actually thought about it, I couldn't recall a single instance of gossip that suggested Jake was anything but serious when it came to relationships.

After finding something more mellow to play, I said, 'I didn't mean to make you feel embarrassed. It's sweet.'

Jake groaned. 'You sound like Laeli.'

Laeli. Oh, Laeli. This would be so much easier if I had a crush on Laeli.

✳ ✳ ✳

At some point over the weekend, I checked Instagram and was stunned to see that Laeli had tagged me in a post. This made me think about the kiss (The Kiss!), and thinking about it inspired many conflicting feelings.

On the one hand, Laeli was so pretty, and so nice, and kissing was *so nice*. I couldn't believe that my ideas about kissing had been so warped by one awkward kiss in primary school. Thinking about kissing Laeli again thrilled me, but when I thought about kissing in *general*, I started thinking about Jake – and then I started thinking about kissing and touching and tongues, and the hot, heavy press of another body against mine – and it was always Jake. These thoughts made me feel hot and embarrassed, and also vaguely bitter, so I tried not to think too much about anything.

The Instagram post made it hard not to, though. It was captioned with a heart emoji, and displayed a series of pictures where party attendees brandished sparklers and slices of cake. I was tagged in a picture with Laeli, the sparkler between our faces, lighting the edges of our mouths in gold. She was smiling and lovely, and I had managed a surprised half-smile. The next photo was one of Jake, taken surreptitiously and capturing his role as photographer while also capturing him mid-laugh. Just looking at his unfairly cute face (unfairly cute face??? *Who was I?*) made my stomach erupt in butterflies.

I flicked between those two pictures for a while – Laeli and me, a laughing Jake, back and forth. Then I flopped facedown on my pillow and hoped I'd manage to accidentally smother myself.

The second week of school holidays, I got a text from Mae:

Mae

Mill Hill park take 2?

The weather had cleared, so I felt safe to once again sit on the front fence and wait for Mae, my heart doing a nervous tap-dance when I caught sight of her.

'Hey,' she said, once she'd drawn level with me.

'Hey,' I replied. 'I still need to give you your plate. Thanks for the cookies, by the way.'

Mae nodded. I pushed myself off the wall and we fell into step with each other.

'So, I saw Laeli's post,' Mae said. 'You were out with Laeli? And Kasun?'

I thought about all the ways I could over-explain the situation, and then settled for: 'Yes.'

Mae looked at me, and then, when I didn't give her anything else, said, 'Did Kasun say anything? About me?'

I admit the question made me a little … annoyed.

'Are you still mad at me?' I asked.

Mae blinked at me.

'Look,' I said, 'I don't have a crush on Kasun anymore. I promise. I'm over it. He's all yours – he always was, but, like, I mean—'

Mae stopped walking and took one of my hands between hers, her motions jerky enough that I paused mid-sentence.

'I shouldn't have brought up Kasun,' she said in a rush. 'I told myself I wouldn't and then I did and that was awful of me. Kasun doesn't matter. Can we forget Kasun?'

I put my other hand to the side of Mae's, giving her hands a gentle pat. 'Yes. Sure. And I wasn't lying when I said I'm over Kasun.'

With what looked like Herculean effort, Mae said, 'I'm over him, too.'

'You don't have to lie for me.'

Mae shook her head, appearing suddenly both sad and amused, like she was in on a joke I wasn't getting. 'I'm not. I've been thinking and, actually, I was … You know the lawyer at work who I said was cool? She's been really … Talking to someone with more romantic experience has helped me work out I … Anyway. I'm not lying, I promise. I'm really over Kasun.'

I wasn't sure what to do with that, so I said, 'I have a crush on Jake.'

That did the job. Mae's expression morphed into one of surprise, and then she grinned.

'Totally called it,' she said. 'He's so into you.'

She twisted so we were side by side, keeping a grip on my hand even once we started walking.

'He's not,' I said, 'he's a friendly, touchy-feely guy and …'

The words *and anyway, turns out he's been trying to set me up with Laeli this whole time*, died on my lips. I looked at the side of Mae's head. We hadn't talked about … this stuff before. Which, to be fair, was because I usually kept my crushes close to my chest. She would be fine with it, though. If I told her I'd kissed Laeli – that I'd liked it – she'd be *totally* fine with it.

'… and I know he doesn't see me like that,' I finished. 'He thinks I'm a pain in the arse.'

Mae would be fine with it. I was sure she would be fine with it. But … we were *just* coming off the back of a blow-up caused by romantic feelings I had hidden from her. Seeing as I'd been holding onto the secret of my sexuality for longer than my crush on Kasun, I didn't feel up to navigating the potential fallout if her feelings were hurt when she found out the Kasun-crush hadn't been the only secret I'd been keeping. Was I delaying the bandaid removal? Maybe. Still, I felt confident my coming out could wait until the wound of the Kasun-crush-secret was better healed.

'You *are* a pain in the arse,' Mae said, so affectionately that I couldn't take offence. Especially because she followed it up with, 'I really missed you. I'm sorry for …'

I squeezed her hand. 'Don't worry about it. I missed you too. I'm sorry too. And in case Kasun asks, you had really bad food poisoning at the movies. *Really* bad. You're fine now, though.'

Mae's expression flickered at the mention of Kasun, but she nodded, faux solemn. 'Got it. Pooping for days.'

21

Laeli and I hadn't talked since our beach kiss, so it was with some trepidation that I entered the visual arts classroom the first week back at school.

Had it been bad for her? Did she regret it?

I spent my morning preparing myself for averted eyes and awkwardness – or, worst-case scenario, direct rejection – but when I entered the classroom, she smiled at me like she always did, tilting her head towards the seat next to her in invitation.

I approached, doing my best to stay cool, calm and collected.

'We've been talking about going to Lotophage,' Laeli said, once I'd sat down.

Kasun, who was still unpacking his supplies from his bag, nodded. I looked at him for what was perhaps a beat too long, then back at Laeli, feeling my heart thud when

I did. Sitting this close to her, I could smell a faint hint of apricots and vanilla. I leaned closer without quite meaning to, convinced that I could smell salt on her too. Laeli's gaze flickered to my mouth, and my memory of the kiss rushed to the forefront of my mind.

'Cool,' I said, having forgotten what she had said.

Laeli leaned one elbow against the table, locking us into a more intimate formation.

I felt my stomach lurch – were we going to *talk*-talk? – but she just said, 'Are you going?'

'Maybe,' I hedged, trying to remember what she'd said. Something about lotuses?

'The line-up looks good,' Laeli said.

Oh. A music festival.

'I haven't checked it out yet.' I hoped my tone hadn't given away my *aha* moment, or that I'd never been to a music festival in my life.

Still leaning on one elbow, Laeli took out her phone, holding it under the desk in the space between our thighs as she pulled up the website for the festival. We both tilted our heads in, and I felt a thrill when our temples brushed.

Partway through Laeli laying out her thoughts on the artists playing, the bubble of *Laeli smells so nice and is sitting so close to me* popped, and I realised that there was no world in which my parents were going to let me go to a music festival. This wouldn't be a case of Mae and I being each other's alibis for an evening. This was going to be—

'How long is the festival?' I asked.

'Oh, it's just for a day,' Laeli said.

This was going to be a *whole day*—

'It's a bit of a trek, though,' Laeli continued, 'so some people will probably stay overnight nearby.'

This was going to be *a whole day and maybe a whole night* that I would need to be covered for. There was no way.

I opened my mouth to break the bad news, then, slowly, closed it. Laeli's enthusiasm was catching: I found that I actually *wanted* to go along. And why not? I was, technically, an adult. Also, I had recently graduated from the level of 'baby rebel' to the more prestigious level of 'little rebel'. I could do this. I was a card-carrying grown-up and second-level rebel. (The card in question was still a learner licence, because I got weepy when I had to drive over forty kilometres an hour.)

The world was my oyster.

I would just need a little help.

'Why do you want to go to a music festival?' was the first thing Kamilia asked, when I sprang my plan on her that afternoon.

The *you* and *music festival* felt unfairly emphasised.

'Maybe I'm feeling adventurous,' I said.

'It's going to be noisy and crowded and the toilets are going to be gross,' she said. 'Those are, like, three of your least favourite things.'

She narrowed her eyes at me, then pointed an accusing finger. 'Is your crush going to be there? Is that it?'

'Mae wants to go,' I said, because it was easier than saying, *A beautiful girl convinced me it would be fun. And while she's not technically my crush, I do think she's very beautiful and smart and kind and she could be, if I could just get over Jake. I got over Kasun, so surely I can get over Jake too. Right?*

And then I had to stop thinking about it, because thinking about Jake made my brain go a little dreamy, which was both annoying and counterproductive.

Saying Mae wanted to go wasn't a total lie. I had brought the idea up with her on the bus home, and her eyes had lit up for a moment before her expression dimmed and she had hit me with an, 'I love the idea, but …'

In fairness, she had done the same calculations in her head that I had re: the plausibility of us actually being able to attend, which I couldn't fault her for. However, while Mae's resources were limited, I had one last (potential) ace up my sleeve – though currently my ace wasn't being very helpful.

Kamilia's eyes narrowed. 'You made up with her, then?'

I nodded.

I was sitting cross-legged on Kamilia's bed while she did a series of complex stretches on the rug in front of me. I had caught her during a study break, and had initially buttered her up with a cup of chamomile tea ('Some kamilica for Kamilica,' I had sung, in what I thought was a perfectly charming imitation of our mother) and a plate of biscuits.

Their effects seemed to be waning, based on Kamilia's pursed lips.

'Did she apologise?' Kamilia asked.

'Basically.'

Kamilia rolled her eyes.

'She didn't have anything to say sorry for,' I said.

Kamilia stretched forwards so I couldn't see her expression, but I knew she was pulling a face.

'I'm not here to talk about Mae,' I snapped.

Kamilia's face reappeared, her eyebrows pulled down. 'No, you're here because you want me to help you go to a music festival.'

'And help *you* go to a music festival,' I said, starting to feel like a desperate used car salesman. 'If we work together, we could both go. I know you've never been to a festival.'

Kamilia sniffed, but didn't say anything. I gave into my role as the baby of the family and started bouncing on the bed like a toddler working up to a tantrum.

'I want to *go*,' I whined, 'please help me.'

Kamilia stood up. Stretching time was over, and so was my window to convince her. Putting her hands on her hips, she narrowed her eyes at me.

'I'll think about it,' she said.

It would have to be good enough.

The next day on the bus to school, I relayed my conversation with Kamilia to Mae.

'So I think we're in with a chance,' I concluded.

Mae bit her lip, listing into my side and then away as the bus took a turn. As usual, we had found ourselves standing in the crowded centre aisle, the crush of bodies working to counteract the mid-autumn chill.

'What can your sister do, though?' she asked, which was a fair question.

'We'll find out,' I said, because it sounded better than, *I don't know.*

Mae didn't seem heartened by that answer. I considered trying again, but got distracted by my phone. A message from Laeli had popped up on the screen:

I was already planning how I'd approach Kamilia with a request to cover me for the evening.

Laeli

Lovely!!!

The extra exclamation marks made my stomach fizz. Maybe there was hope yet for a proper crush to form.

'What are you smiling at?' Mae asked.

'Oh.' I looked at my phone then back at Mae. 'I think Laeli wants to hang out on Friday.'

Mae's expression did something I couldn't interpret.

'Sounds fun,' she said.

'Do you want to come?'

Mae was already shaking her head. 'I have work at my uncle's law firm. And I wouldn't want to crash, anyway.'

I searched her face, but her expression was clear. She raised her eyebrows in response to my stare, and I resisted the urge to frown.

My phone pinged in my hand:

> Laeli
>
> Come to mine at six? Other people will be there too. Chance to chill out after trials timetables come out this week

This message was followed by three weeping emojis, which I felt in my soul.

'Ugh, trials,' I said.

'*Ugh*, why would you remind me?' Mae groaned, flopping into my side half out of dramatics and half because the bus had taken a sharp turn around a roundabout, forcing her against me.

'Are you sure about Friday?' I asked, once she had righted herself. 'Sounds like there'll be other people there too, so you wouldn't be crashing a one-on-one thing.'

'Totally sure,' Mae confirmed. 'Double sure. If there are other people, that probably means Kasun too, yeah? I don't … really want to see him right now.'

I nodded, conceding.

To Laeli, I typed:

Amalia

I'll be there.

✱ ✱ ✱

It didn't take much to convince Kamilia to cover for me being out.

'That's perfect, actually,' she said, when I brought it up with her that afternoon. 'I've got a date with this cute guy from my anatomy class, so we can just tell Mum and Dad we're having a sisters' night. I can pick you up after so we get home together.'

She didn't mention helping me with the music festival, and neither did I, not wanting to push my luck. My patience paid off, however, because on Friday I got my answer.

While I was getting ready for Laeli's, which involved me trying to teach myself how to do a fishtail braid while growing increasingly irate, Kamilia came in.

'I think you should do buns,' she said, startling me. She was leaning against the doorframe, arms crossed. She gestured to the sides of her head, 'Like, two big messy ones. I think it'd be cute. Plus you have enough hair for it.'

When I stared back at her, clumps of hair tangled in my fingers, she sighed and walked over, making a *gimme* gesture.

Once she had taken over, her hands busy with my hair, she said, 'I'll do it, by the way.'

I winced as she tugged a comb across the back of my hair, pulling it tighter against my skull, then managed a smile. 'That's great!'

'On one condition,' Kamilia said, tugging at one of the buns to loosen it.

I looked at her in the mirror. She was focused on my hair, but had pulled both her top *and* her bottom lip into her mouth, which was a sign she was thinking hard.

'Okay?' I said, half-question.

'You have to talk to Mae. Properly,' Kamilia said, firm. 'Take it from someone who's been there, platonically and romantically. I would bet actual, literal money that there's going to be a moment where all the stuff you just went through is going to come up again. When it does, you have to face it. You have to face it honestly. Your relationship might depend on it.'

'I feel like you're projecting your break-up onto me,' I said, then felt a pang as her hands stilled.

Before I could say something to soften my words – or to work out how to suck them right back into my mouth – Kamilia spoke.

'Maybe,' she said quietly. 'But I'm not wrong.'

She finished my hair in silence.

After looking me over, she said, 'I'll be right back.'

What followed was a lowkey makeover that left my eyebrows – thick and unruly – now handsomely curved, my eyes hooded in a sultry rather than sleep-deprived way, and my cheekbones flashing. The buns reshaped my face too, making it look more defined.

'A little light, a little shadow and voila,' Kamilia said. 'No shadow needed under those cheekbones, though. They speak for themselves.'

Then, before I could react, she wrapped her arms around my shoulders from behind, pressing her cheek against my cheek and giving me a quick squeeze.

'Have fun,' she said, 'and remember our deal. When it's time to talk, *talk*.'

I nodded. This lie felt easy, because I wouldn't need to deliver on it. Mae and I were fine. There wasn't anything left to say. Right?

※ ※ ※

Kamilia dropped me off at Laeli's with a stern warning not to be 'as messed up as last time' when she came back to pick me up. Heart thudding in my stomach, feeling faintly nauseous, I braved the steps to Laeli's front door.

I raised my hand to knock, felt my heartbeat increase and my stomach roil, and took out my phone instead, typing out a message to Jake.

> Amalia
>
> **Are you at Laeli's?**

Long moments passed. My spine and armpits felt itchy with sweat. My hands left damp streaks on my phone. I pulled up Kamilia's number.

Before I could press call, the door opened.

'Heeey, Book Club,' Jake said.

He flopped against the doorframe, catching himself on one forearm. His eyes were bright, his face relaxed.

'You're drunk,' I said.

Jake raised his fingers to his lips, then was overcome with giggles. At my expression – somewhere between amusement and horror – he took a deep breath, pulled himself up, and made an attempt to project sobriety.

'I'm not driving today,' he said, 'so it's fine.'

I raised my hands. 'I'm not judging.'

He narrowed his eyes. 'You look like you're judging.'

'Maybe *you're* the one judging,' I shot back, 'because this is just my face.'

'Hi, face,' Jake said seriously. 'I'm drunk.'

Then, with some effort, he straightened from the doorframe, gesturing for me to come in. Our moment of back and forth had relaxed me, so I followed him into the hallway before my body could restart the anxiety machine. When we entered the living room, Jake managed to spoil my calm by announcing, 'I found her!'

The people arrayed around the room – one of whom was Kasun, none of whom were Laeli – proffered a series of greetings. I raised my hand and wished I could melt into the wallpaper.

Turning back towards me, Jake clapped his hands. 'Let's get you a drink.'

We found Laeli in the kitchen. She looked a little pink, but nowhere near as loosey-goosey as Jake.

'Amalia!' she exclaimed, pulling me into a hug.

When she drew back, she kept her hands on my arms and let her gaze roam over me.

'Nice hair,' she said. 'You look hot as. Jake, doesn't she look hot?'

Oh, no. Bad enough to have Laeli, beautiful Laeli, call me hot. Now I was going to have to keep my cool as Jake was forced to out me as stunningly average while doing his best not to hurt my feelings—

'She always looks hot,' Jake said absently, head in the fridge. Then, oblivious to the havoc that one sentence was wreaking on my psyche, he turned around, holding two ciders. 'Want one, Book Club? They're strawberry.'

I accepted the drink. Jake clinked the necks of our ciders and then headed out of the kitchen like nothing had happened. Like my world hadn't just tilted on its axis.

'So, we're planning to watch some movies,' Laeli was

saying. I focused on her and tried to make my face form an expression that suggested I had been listening the whole time. 'And we'll chill. I'll order pizza soon, so people aren't drinking on empty stomachs.'

'Very responsible,' I said, like the wet-blanket I was.

'I'm *super* responsible,' Laeli agreed, then grinned. 'Ready?'

I let her pop off my bottle cap, took a sip – one drink to loosey this goosey – then followed her into the living room. Space had been left on one of the sofas for both Laeli and me, so we took our seats beside each other. (I tried not to think about how many people had seen us kiss and drawn their own conclusions vis-a-vis appropriate seating arrangements.)

Jake had taken control of the remote before we had come in, and a frankly absurd amount of time was spent deciding what to watch. By the time a decision had been reached, I had sipped my way through half of my drink, and was relaxed enough to be smiling along with proceedings. Once the movie started, Jake paused to survey the room, and I realised all the seats had been taken. When his eyes lighted on me and he made his way over, my pulse began thudding in my throat. The memory of that first car ride came back to my mind unbidden, making me flush.

'Can I have a pillow?' he asked.

Trying to calm my heart – *obviously* Jake wasn't going to ask Laeli to budge over so he could sit next to me – I rooted around behind me and passed over a suitable specimen.

Jake dropped the pillow at my feet, and then sat down, pressing his back against the sofa *between my legs*.

Okay, so he wasn't *literally* between my legs, because my legs were crossed on the sofa – but if they hadn't been!

If they hadn't been!

I took a sip of my drink that was more like a gulp, and narrowly missed swallowing the wrong way. Gasping as quietly as I could, I tried to watch the movie and tune into the commentary that had sprung up around the room. I was succeeding until we were closing in on the end of the film and Jake leaned his head back and rested it against my shin. It wasn't this gesture specifically that broke my concentration, but more the series of actions – nay, events – that followed.

Over the last few weeks, I had become used to my sister doing something similar, crawling into my space and demanding affection like a moody cat. My muscle memory took over, and I reacted as I would have with her – which was to say, I reached out and ran my knuckles gently over the nape of Jake's neck, pressing my thumb into one of the thick muscles there that I normally worked loose for Kamilia.

I watched Jake's chest rise and fall. Then he shut his eyes.

My pulse thundered in my ears. Half of my brain was screaming at me to stop – what was I doing? This wasn't my sister! This was Jake! *Jake!* Instead of stopping, though, I took a small breath, keeping my hand steady.

Not letting myself overthink it, I kept rubbing, feeling tense muscles relax under my fingers. Jake tilted his head to the side, just a little. Once I felt the tension in his neck ease, I altered the path of my hand. Careful not to disturb his curls, I dragged my thumb from his temple to the nape of his neck, becoming distracted by the texture of the stubbly hair at the base of his skull and letting my knuckles rub against it for a moment before starting the path from his temple again.

Jake's chest rose and fell for a second time, and he sighed through his nose, tilting back against my shin more firmly, the stretch of his throat laid bare.

And I kept going.

When the credits started rolling, Jake's eyes fluttered open. Sitting up – I snatched my hand back – he got up and left the room without a word.

22

'Food break,' Laeli announced from beside me, which made me startle.

Someone turned on the light – the room had become progressively darker over the course of the movie as night set in. There was a general kerfuffle as people stood up to stretch, go to the bathroom, and get another drink.

I glanced at Laeli, who hadn't moved, and found her looking at me.

'What pizza toppings do you like?' she asked. While her tone was relaxed, her gaze was almost *too* focused.

'Oh, I'm easy,' I mumbled.

She touched my cheek, and I felt heat spread out from the point of contact.

'Love the highlighter,' she said. 'It makes your eyes super dark and pretty.'

'Thanks,' I said, managing not to say something like *your eyes are always super dark and pretty*.

Laeli's lips parted ever so slightly, like she was about to say something – but then someone was leaning over the back of the sofa, demanding her attention, and she turned away from me.

I got up, rubbed my hands on my thighs, and started walking.

When I blinked myself back into focus, I found I had made my way outside. The pool had its cover off. Not letting myself overthink it, I rolled up my pants and sat down, submerging my legs up to the shins. The cool lap of the water helped to temper the hot embarrassment that flushed through my system every time I thought of Jake, and the speed and silence with which he had stood up and left. It was like he had forgotten it was me running my fingers through his hair – or, worse, hadn't *realised* it was me and not Laeli – and when he did, he was so repulsed that he had to leave.

I buried my face in my hands. *God.* I should have stopped touching him the moment I realised what I had been doing. But I hadn't. All because I had got muddled by the fact that he had called me hot – that I had *deluded* myself into thinking he'd want to be touched by someone like *me*—

'Amalia?'

I lifted my face from my hands, glad that my eyes had stayed dry. Laeli smiled at me, then came closer, squatting down next to me.

'We've ordered pizza already,' she said. 'Sorry you didn't get a say.'

'Oh, I don't mind.' I tried for a smile that I hoped looked less wobbly than I felt.

Laeli watched me for a moment longer. Then she said, 'Can I join you?'

Well, I wasn't going to say *no, Laeli, you may not join me in your own pool*.

After she had made herself comfortable, the material of her skirt bunched in her lap, she said, 'I guess we didn't really talk about this explicitly, but I'm a lesbian. I like girls. Do you like girls?'

I nodded.

'*And* you like boys,' Laeli said.

This time it wasn't a question.

'Yep.' I focused on the warped shape of my legs in the water. 'I just think people are hot, generally. Not that I've acted on it much. Ever.'

'You do have a bit of a "don't come any closer" thing going on,' Laeli said, adding, in a confessional tone, 'When I first met you, I was kind of intimidated.'

I stared at Laeli. She looked back, smiling.

'I'm not intimidating,' I said finally. 'I'm like, the opposite of intimidating.'

'Well yeah, I know that now,' she said with a laugh.

As her laughter faded, I realised we were just staring at each other. And we were sitting very, very close. *Well. Why not? Why deny myself this?*

I put my hand between us, leaning into it, feeling the grooves between the tiles press into my palm. Laeli moved at the same time, body twisting towards me. When our lips met, she sighed a little against my mouth.

After a while, she sat back, laughing as she did so.

'So that's not actually why I came outside,' she said. 'That's kind of the opposite of why I came outside, actually—'

'Laeli!'

The yell came from inside, but it was close. Both of us turned towards it, then Laeli glanced back at me with a shrug.

'It can wait,' she said, reaching out and tapping me on the nose. Then she stood up in a graceful twirl and padded back to the kitchen.

I looked at the water for a few moments longer, then got up and followed.

Inside was the last person I wanted to see right now and simultaneously the only person I really wanted to see, which was a confusing way to say: it was Jake. His head was in the fridge, but he glanced up when he saw me, gaze skating over me before he refocused on the drink selection.

'Want something?' he asked, the words directed into the fridge.

'I'm okay,' I said, directing my words at the kitchen counter.

'You were hanging out with Laeli, right?' This was maybe the worst way he could have phrased it, especially as he followed it up with an awkward, 'One on one?'

'Yep,' I said.

'Good on you,' he said.

Then he closed the fridge door and left the kitchen. I stared at the countertop and let myself be consumed by the various agonies triggered by our brief conversation, beginning with *he couldn't even look me in the eye*, and ending somewhere in the vicinity of *he didn't even take out a drink*.

I went to the fridge and contemplated its contents, wondering if it would help restore a sense of normality for me to grab something for Jake like, *Hey, you forgot this, fool*, or if it was safer for me to just go back in empty-handed and pretend like we had had a normal, not at all stilted conversation.

I ended up taking out a drink, but I cracked it open before going back into the living room. If Jake was going to be weird, I was going to get tipsy.

✱ ✱ ✱

It worked a little too well.

I floated through the rest of the evening feeling numb and a little dizzy, checked out enough that I could brush off Jake's weirdness. When Kamilia appeared to pick me up – after I had given Laeli a hug goodbye and pretended not to notice that Jake was suddenly involved in a conversation with someone on the other side of the room – she took one look at me and said, 'Not as bad as last time, but we're going to have to do some laps to sober you up.'

'Laps?' I repeated, flopping into the passenger seat and beginning a short-lived war with the seatbelt, which was resolved by Kamilia prying it out of my hands and clipping it in for me.

'Yeah,' she said. 'Think of it like PE, except it's night-time and we need to do it for long enough that you don't get home visibly drunk.'

I opened the window, closing my eyes against the whip of the wind. 'And it'll make me not drunk?'

'Nah,' she said, 'but it'll waste some time so the alcohol can make its way through your system. And also I am punishing you because I *asked you not to be drunk*.'

'Not drunk,' I said, opening my mouth wider so I could enunciate.

Then I bared my teeth, intrigued by the sensation of the wind against them.

'Very convincing,' Kamilia said.

The park was dark and foreboding when we drove past, so Kamilia took us to get chips instead. We grabbed a table inside, just next to the door, and Kamilia bought me two bottles of water despite my protests, glaring at me until she was sure I was taking regular sips.

It was somewhere between sips of water and burning my tongue on the chips that I told Kamilia the updated situation. When Laeli's name slipped out in relation to the latest poolside kiss, I felt myself flush hot and then cold.

Kamilia picked up on my freeze immediately, and nudged the water bottle towards me.

'C'mon, keep drinking,' she said. Then, waiting until I had a mouthful of water: 'Anyway, who hasn't kissed girls?'

I choked a little. Kamilia gave me the kind of smile that said she had done that on purpose.

'Look, we all experiment,' she said. 'It's no big deal.'

I swished the water around in my mouth, nose scrunched.

'Okay, well, good for you, but I wasn't experimenting,' I said. 'I kissed her because I think Laeli's hot. I liked kissing her.'

There was something affirming about saying it out loud like that. Yes, I hadn't managed to convert my feelings into a full-blown crush (yet). That didn't mean that I wasn't attracted to Laeli. When I kissed her, I wasn't kissing her as an experiment. I was kissing her because I wanted to. Because, crush or not, she was … she was Laeli. I *wanted* to kiss her, in the same way I'd wanted to kiss Kasun, and wanted to kiss—

I wasn't going there, not right now. Not after tonight.

'Girls are super-hot,' Kamilia was saying. 'That's a normal thing to think. You're into this Jake guy, though, right? Tall, dark and handsome from the cinema?'

'Yeah,' I said, nose scrunch moving into a full forehead frown, 'but that doesn't mean I didn't like kissing Laeli.'

Kamilia shrugged like we were on the same page. I forced my frown to relax. I wasn't sober enough to pinpoint why exactly Kamilia's comment had got under my skin, so I ate a chip and let it go.

'Well, after the hair stuff Jake basically shut down on me,' I said, ploughing on with my account of the night, 'and it sucked. I think I might have ruined everything.'

'I don't think you ruined everything,' Kamilia said, giving my hand a pat.

'Counterpoint: *I* think I ruined everything.'

'Eat your chips,' she said, abandoning the hand-patting and nudging the water bottle back towards me. 'I bet by Monday everything will be fine.'

Everything was *not* fine.

Mae got weird and quiet when I brought up Laeli's movie night, but then insisted she was fine, and every time I tried to corner Jake he would find some polite, perfectly reasonable way to slither out of the interaction. The only positive was that Laeli was still talking to me, and cheered me up during visual arts class by regaling me with stories from previous gigs and music festivals she had attended.

As the cherry on top, Tetka Sabinka decided we needed to push back book club by a week because she hadn't had a chance to read *Wuthering Heights* yet, so I didn't get to hang out with my cousins on the weekend. What I *did* get was a surprise phone call from Tetka Mojca, who was finally ready to grill me about what I wanted to study. I found myself telling the truth, and was relieved when Tetka Mojca accepted my answer. When she offered to drill down into further degree options with me, I was surprised to hear myself agree.

Throughout the call I channelled Jake, taking a mental step back from ideas of *pressure* and *expectations* and treating the conversation as what it was: just a conversation, not an interrogation or a sermon or a test where I could only get my answers wrong. By the end of the call, Tetka Mojca and I had run through a number of sub-specialisations within biology (thank you internet), and I was feeling cautiously optimistic about listing marine biology as my first choice.

(I would be lying if I said *Moby-Dick* hadn't played a role in the choice: having whales in the back of my mind for most of the year had definitely left its mark on my psyche.)

This small win spurred me on to try for another. Kamilia had said she'd handle the music festival, but maybe, just maybe, if I played my cards right, I could get Mum to agree to the festival without Kamilia's help.

This meant that on Sunday when it was time for church, I said, as sweetly as I could, 'Can I come this week, Mum?'

My mother grabbed at her heart when I spoke. After taking a good few minutes to tell me off for startling her ('Oh Maria devica! Why are you sneaking around at an hour like this!'), she agreed. She shot me a number of suspicious glances on the drive over, and after Father Danijel had stopped by post-service to tell me how *wonderful* it was to see me again, and would I be coming more regularly? she pulled me aside and said: 'Okay, what is your scheme?'

'Scheme? In this, the house of the lord?' I gestured at the church around us.

'Malka,' she said, tone all warning. 'What are you planning?'

I threw caution to the wind. 'There's this music ... concert that Mae is going to, it's really ... carefully run, the cops are there and everything, so it's *really* well supervised—'

I had thrown too hard – my mother was looking alarmed. 'Why would the police be at a music concert?' she asked.

'Well, it's sort of an all-day thing,' I hazarded.

'So, a music festival,' my mother said. 'Like Woodstock.'

'Maybe?' I tried, which turned out to be the wrong answer.

My mother's expression shut down. She turned to the door, and I trailed after her, already tasting defeat.

'No, Malka,' she said, 'there will be no music festival.'

23

Kamilia didn't seem surprised or disappointed when I schlumped into her room later that day with the bad news.

'You didn't need to do that,' she said. 'I've got it under control.'

That was all I heard from her on the topic – until book club the next week. We were hosting, as usual, which meant Mum was in a frenzy of cleaning. She didn't notice that Elizabeta and Renata arrived early, or that they were ushered in by my sister and directed up the stairs before they could be seen. *I* noticed, however, and looked on suspiciously from the breakfast nook until my sister gestured for me to follow.

Once in Kamilia's room, I was directed to sit on the bed. It became apparent that I had been directed to do so in order for my sister and cousins to loom over me more effectively.

'Are you sure she's up to it?' Elizabeta asked.

'It was her idea,' Kamilia said.

'It'll be fun,' Renata said, smiling at me.

I smiled back, then stopped when Elizabeta said, in portentous tones, 'I don't know. If it was *just* Amalia ... but you said her friend wants to come, too? When a lie gets too big ...'

Which was how I found out that for years (years!) my cousins had been running a ruse involving *other* cousins (theirs, not mine – this was a scheme that ran cousins and cousins deep), that allowed generations of cousins (cousins!) (generations of!) to attend music festivals.

The ruse was simple: go on regularly scheduled camping trips, many of which were real, some of which other, non-cousin family members attended. They were such a staple within the family that even I knew about them – I had wriggled out of attending them more than once. The beauty was in the believability: if you swapped out one camping trip in every three or four for a different type of expedition, who would ever know? There wasn't any phone coverage where they camped, so nobody could expect regular calls and texts. As long as you set off and then returned with the right equipment and took a handful of photos to feed the illusion, nobody's parents would be any the wiser.

'We're trusting you to be cool about this, Malka,' Elizabeta said, once they had finished explaining.

'Absolutely,' I said. 'This is great. This is some deus ex machina stuff. Deus ex familia? Is that anything?'

'She's not being cool about this,' Renata said, shooting a look at Elizabeta and Kamilia.

I raised my hands. 'No, no. I'll be super cool about it. Promise.'

✱ ✱ ✱

By the time we filed in for book club, Mum, Tetka Sabinka and Tetka Mojca were already arranged around the coffee table, Tetka Mojca positioned strategically between her sisters. I was the first of the cousins to come through the door, and the relief on Tetka Mojca's face at my entrance was palpable.

'—for the second time this year,' Mum was saying, gripping her mug.

'This is the *first* time I have suggested delaying a session, *thank you*, Barica,' Tetka Sabinka shot back, offering me a tight smile when she noticed me hovering near the door.

'Yes, that's my mistake,' Mum said, tone sharpening, 'with that infernal whale you cancelled altogether.' To me, she said, 'Where is your sister?'

Kamilia appeared behind me on cue, taking my shoulders and guiding me into the room. Renata and Elizabeta came in moments later, cutting the tension by beelining for our parents' generation, depositing kisses on cheeks and, in Elizabeta's case, a plate of brownies on the table. Soon after, Dad appeared to pass around coffees.

Once we were seated and caffeinated, Tetka Mojca cleared her throat and said, 'Do you know Kate Bush?'

By the end of the session, both Mum and Tetka Sabinka were so befuddled by and irritated with Tetka Mojca's extended and repeated digressions on the musical career of noted eighties sensation Kate Bush that they seemed to have forgotten they had begun the session at loggerheads. Ganging up on Tetka Mojca seemed to have cheered them up too, and, judging by the small smile Tetka Mojca was hiding behind her coffee mug, she wasn't complaining about the ease in tensions.

Once Elizabeta's suggestion for the next book club had been approved – over the next month we'd be reading *The Odyssey* – Kamilia said, 'Malka and I were thinking we'd join Renata and Elizabeta on their next camping trip.'

I hid behind my mug, hoping I wasn't visibly tense as I braced myself to be on the receiving end of a suspicious look from my mother.

Instead, Mum clapped once, smiling at us. 'Good for you girls to spend some time together. Only: Malka, bring your homework. All right? And take pictures for me, okay? And call me on the drive there and back.'

I exhaled, maybe too loudly, because Tetka Sabinka looked at me oddly. Kamilia kicked my foot, and I made myself smile.

'Thanks, Mum,' I said.

Just like that, the music festival was on.

✱ ✱ ✱

Once I was able to slink away from book club, I texted Mae:

Amalia
> Mill Hill walk asap!!

I got a thumbs up, and, after telling my parents where I was going, I hurried to the front of the house, setting myself up on the front fence to wait. When Mae arrived, I hopped off and grabbed her arm, walking at speed away from the house.

'Steady on,' Mae laughed, taking a few running steps so we were level with each other and reorganising our arms so we were looped elbow-in-elbow. 'Where's the fire?'

'It's happening,' I said under my breath, shooting a look back at the house to make sure there were no family members nearby who could overhear us.

'What?' Mae said, which was fair.

'The music festival,' I said, once we reached the end of the street and I was satisfied no one could listen in. 'Kamilia sorted it.'

Mae's eyes widened, then narrowed. 'How?'

I explained the 'cousins' scheme. Mae's eyebrows climbed.

'Damn,' she said, finally. 'I wish I had cousins. That's smart.'

'Your parents should be fine with that, right?' I asked.

'Is there going to be adult supervision?'

She was trying to keep her expression neutral, but I knew Mae – she was starting to let herself get excited.

'Elizabeta is twenty-two – twenty-three now, actually,' I said. 'She's coming. She could give your parents a call, maybe? Reassure them?'

Mae was nodding, biting down at the edge of a smile. 'Okay. Okay. This might actually work.'

Suddenly, Mae stopped, dragging me to a halt with her.

Taking both my hands, expression serious, she said, 'Are we actually doing this?'

I nodded, grinning. 'We're doing this.'

Mae let out a sound between a laugh and a scream, starting to bounce up and down. I bounced with her, carrying us in a giddy circle.

When we calmed down and began walking again, Mae asked, 'So what made you want to do this, anyway? You never said.'

'Oh!' In my rush to sell the idea to Mae, I had clearly forgotten to mention its source. 'Laeli asked if I was going, and I was like … I hadn't been planning to, but actually that sounds fun.'

'Oh,' Mae said.

I glanced at her, then back at the road – we were crossing over towards the park now. 'Oh?'

'Cool,' Mae clarified, which was about as useful as no response at all.

We walked further.

'I would have thought a music festival wasn't really your thing,' Mae said finally, tone light. 'Noisy, crowded, kinda grotty – not your favourite things.'

'Sure,' I said slowly, feeling my hackles rise. 'I think I'll survive, though.'

First Kamilia and now Mae. Was it so hard to believe I wanted to go to a festival? That I wanted to push out of my comfort zone? I'd been doing it for months – more than once at Mae's request – but suddenly it was hard to believe?

We stepped to the side and let a string of bikes pass.

'How did Laeli convince you?' Mae asked.

'I don't know.' I stepped back onto the path. 'She didn't, really. It just sounded … fun.'

Mae and I had disentangled at some point, and had both crossed our arms. Taking a deep breath, I dropped mine.

'Why do you ask?' I said.

Mae sighed, dropping her arms too. 'Forget about it, it doesn't matter. I'll talk to my parents about camping, but I think it should be fine. We need to buy tickets in advance, right?'

I nodded, watching her carefully. All the excitement seemed to have drained out of her. Now she just looked tired. I made a conscious effort to relax my own expression, realising that it had gone tight.

'Yep – I checked earlier and there still seem to be some tickets left,' I said.

Mae only nodded. We continued into the park in silence.

A restless frustration simmered under my skin when I got home. Though Mae had seemed to be back in good spirits by the end of the walk, I couldn't shake the sense that we'd had a fight without actually fighting. The content of the not-fight was also confusing to me. Was Mae annoyed at me for suggesting we go to this music festival? Had I offended her simply by choosing to do something she didn't think I'd want to do?

Once I was in my room, I threw myself onto my bed, taking out my phone. After shooting a quick message to Laeli, letting her know I'd be coming along to the festival – she sent back a string of enthusiastic emojis within moments – I opened Jake's contact, scrolling through our messages.

My fingers hovered over what I'd typed on the screen.

Hey, so I know you've been avoiding me, but guess what? I'm going to be even harder to avoid because I'm coming to Lotophage!

I had circled away from sensations of agony whenever I thought about Jake, and was starting to slide into the territory of pissed off. Okay, so he didn't want to be touched by me. Fine. What was irking me was that he hadn't even let me apologise – I hadn't been allowed to get through more than a 'Hi, how are you' before he was finding a reason to slip off somewhere else. And why was he so disgusted, anyway? He had been fine with some level of touchy-feely before. He had *initiated* touchy-feely. I wanted to know why this one time had been so bad. I wanted to learn about his boundaries so I could respect them. Instead, I had been cut off.

I closed my chat with Jake, reopened it, closed it again and put my phone away. I spent a few moments lying on my stomach, wallowing, then rolled off my bed and padded to Kamilia's room. She was at her desk, and looked up with her eyebrows raised when I appeared in her doorway.

'Does this mean you *have* gone to a music festival before?' I asked.

Kamilia rolled her eyes. 'Obviously.'

The weeks leading up to the festival were a blur of midterm exams and, directly on the heels of that, trials preparation, which meant that I didn't have much spare time to stress about Mae and the not-fight, Jake and his avoidance, or the potential for my parents to become suspicious of my sudden interest in camping. Before I knew it, Mae was knocking at the door the morning of the festival, a densely packed backpack slung over her shoulder. Kamilia and I were putting the finishing touches on our own 'camping bags', our mother peering over our shoulders and suggesting that maybe we should consider some warmer clothes to combat the early winter chill, *and what about thermal leggings? You can never go wrong with thermal leggings.*

I couldn't say that wearing thermal leggings to a music festival seemed like a quick route to heat stroke, so I shoved them into the top of my pack and shrugged on a thick flannel for good measure, donning my hiking boots – dusty from disuse – as a final touch. The plan was to drive to the festival in Elizabeta's car, which meant I'd be meeting Laeli and Jake (if he didn't try to avoid me at the festival) somewhere there.

It was during the drive that the nerves hit me. What if my parents somehow worked out what we were up to? If they did, would this be worth it? Kamilia and Mae had been right: I didn't like noise, or dirt, or crowded places. I didn't know most of the bands. I was going to be two hours' drive from home – four hours by train.

I was going to be in the middle of nowhere.

Oh, no. I was freaking out.

By the time we got to the festival, I had quietly worked myself into a state of dread.

The festival's car park was full of people in a variety of outfits ranging from the practical – plenty of flannels and jeans were on show – to the outlandish, with glitter featuring heavily. While the car park wasn't directly beside the showgrounds, it was close enough that the thump of muted bass and the howl of vocals carried to us, dimmed only slightly by the sounds of the crowds.

My driving companions were busy wriggling around in the car, changing out of their camping gear and into their party gear. As I had made no such distinction between outfits, I got out and leaned against the side of the car, turning my face towards the sky and closing my eyes. It was a good day for being outside. The sun warmed my cheeks, my nervous sweat cooled by a breeze which carried the chill of early winter. The pause calmed me enough to accept a makeover from Kamilia, who insisted on layering on and around my eyelids with varying amounts of gold eyeshadow and glitter. She finished the look with a pattern of rhinestones around my eyes that matched her own, giving my cheek a pinch when she was done.

'You look *so* cute,' she said, then pointed a finger at me. 'Remember: if Mum and Dad call or text, do *not* answer. *Maintain* the illusion.' When Mae got out of the car in her party gear, Kamilia pointed a finger at her too, before turning it back to me. 'You will both meet us back at the entrance by nine-thirty, or we *will* leave without you because our motel is *not* close to here and their front desk closes at ten-thirty.'

Mae nodded. I gave Kamilia a thumbs up. Kamilia nodded back at Mae, then pinched my cheek again.

'Okay,' she said, clapping her hands together in a frighteningly accurate imitation of Mum. 'Let's go.'

When we got inside, Mae beelined for the covered bar in the eighteen and over section. I was tempted to ask if she wanted to eat something first, as the only thing she'd had all morning was a hash brown on the road, but bit my tongue.

'Where do we start?' I asked, once Mae reappeared, drink in hand.

Mae took a swig of her drink and gestured towards the main stage.

I let her lead.

Mae was on a mission to be as close to the front of the crowd as she could get. I, on the other hand, was becoming overwhelmed by the crush of people around us. As she threaded us through the crowd, trying to get us closer to the stage, the bump and jostle of the people we passed made me feel like I was being fast-tracked through a large digestive tract. The set had started. The sun was hot. Everything was too close.

Just when I was hoping for some more space, Mae was pressing into my side, mouth tickling my ear, her voice too loud. 'I think I see Laeli.'

'What? Where?' I asked, disoriented by how loud Mae's voice was, and by how loud everything *else* was. It took me a moment to understand what she was saying.

Mae's hand was tight around my arm. 'Would it be weird if we joined them?'

'What?' I asked again, shrinking back from the hot waft of alcohol that came off her breath.

'She'd be happy to see you, at least,' Mae said.

Her voice was too loud, too close. One of the speakers screeched, and I winced.

'I think I'm going to duck out for a moment,' I said.

Mae looked at me, then back towards the stage. 'But I love this song.'

'You don't have to come with me.' My voice came out sharper than I intended.

The noise of the crowd was making it hard for me to think. All I wanted was to get out.

Mae stared at me, then let go of my arm.

'Okay,' she said, 'fine. Just text me where you are, all right?'

I nodded.

Without her grip on me, I was cut adrift. The crowd pushed forwards, and I let them push through me. The crush of people thinned out closer to the back, until I was twisting my shoulders to brush past people rather than moving like a square peg trying to slip through a round hole. When I was free of the crowd, I took a moment to breathe, filling my diaphragm to capacity and holding the air until my chest began to burn.

'Oi, Book Club!'

There was only one person who called me that. I turned back to face the crowd, still catching and holding each breath, hands on my hips. Jake was making his way towards me, the stragglers at the back of the crowd moving out of his way – probably because he was built like a rugby player, a fact that was all the more apparent as he had opted for a tank top, leaving his arms on full display. There was something unfairly endearing about the fact that he had a shirt sleeve tan.

He was also wearing a bucket hat.

I heard myself blurt, 'Going fishing?'

Jake shrugged. Even once he had stopped walking, he kept moving, bouncing on the balls of his feet, fingers curling and uncurling into loose fists. At my words, a smile flickered across his lips, and he moved closer, flipping off the hat so I could see what was written on the top: *women want fish*.

'Very silly,' I commented.

Jake flipped the hat back onto his head with a grin. 'How are ya, Book Club?'

'Better, now you're not avoiding me,' I said, because my mouth was nothing but trouble.

Jake took the bucket hat off again, rubbing his fingers across the stitches on the brim.

'That wasn't great of me,' he said.

The reply shocked me into silence. I had been *sure* any mention of ... anything would send him running back into the depths of the crowd. I rubbed the back of my neck, finding the strands of hair there matted with sweat.

'No,' I said. 'Or yeah, but also nah. I've been wanting to apologise.'

Jake's fingers stilled on his hat.

'I'm sorry if the way I touched you ...' I paused, feeling heat sweep through my cheeks. 'I'm sorry if I made you uncomfortable by ... touching you.'

'You didn't,' Jake said, almost interrupting me with the force of his reply.

'Okay.' I crossed one arm over my body, gripping my arm where Mae had been holding me minutes before. 'But I obviously did, because you've been avoiding me ever since.'

'Amalia,' Jake said, flipping the bucket hat on and then pressing his hands to the back of his head, squinting into the middle distance. 'Please believe me when I say you didn't make me uncomfortable.'

'Okay,' I said, letting my arms drop. 'Still, I think it's important to like ... to know your boundaries, and know when you want me to – to stop touching you.'

'Amalia, I promise, I have never not wanted you to touch me,' Jake said, then looked immediately, wildly, embarrassed. 'Forget – just – I'm not uncomfortable – I followed you out here because you looked stressed. That's why I'm here.'

I wondered what I looked like now. Jake, despite assertions to the contrary, was starting to appear both uncomfortable and stressed.

I have never not wanted you to touch me.

Surely he meant, *I promise I have been fine with all the times we have touched like platonic friends do.*

What if he meant more than that, though? What if he meant what it sounded like he meant?

'I don't like crowds, but I'm feeling okay now,' I said. 'I just needed some air.'

And something to distract me.

'Hey,' I said. Jake had gone back to bouncing on the balls of his feet, and was avoiding eye contact, though he paused when I spoke. 'If you're not desperate to get back to a set, want to grab some food?'

24

The fairground the festival was nestled within was sprawling and surprisingly hilly, the grass alive and green in patches despite the beating it was taking today. After texting Mae where we were going, Jake and I wandered away from the set, starting a loop of the grounds – I didn't feel the need to rush to the food, and it seemed like Jake didn't either. Neither of us said anything, but the silence wasn't heavy. I let myself focus on the world around me, and the longer we walked, the more relaxed Jake's posture became.

When he shoved his hands into his pockets and squinted at the sky, the line of his shoulders loose, I asked, 'Have you been to one of these before?'

Jake dodged around a bottle on the ground, tilting his head towards me. 'Oh, yeah. Better if you can get into the eighteen plus gigs, though.'

'Alcohol?' I guessed.

Jake shrugged. 'Older folks know concert etiquette better, too. Not as messy as these kids.'

I chortled, swaying in towards him, our arms brushing. 'Oh, these kids.'

'Yeah,' Jake said, looking at me now.

I swayed back into my own space, putting my hands in my pockets. *Steady.*

'So, no crowds?' he asked.

'Is that a surprise?' I countered.

'You never know,' Jake said, then took a deep breath, letting his head drop back so the sunlight hit his cheeks. 'Music's different.'

After exploring the geographical boundaries of the festival, we stumbled on a line of food trucks backed up against the fencing that separated us from the outside world. I made a beeline for the one displaying a plastic leg of meat attached to a vertical spit on its roof. Beside the truck was a tent where the actual spit was set up, the scented smoke wafting in a *come hither, we have doner kebabs* way.

Jake headed for the food truck advertising potatoes on a stick, meeting me back at the kebab truck and wordlessly handing me a large lemonade.

When I had my kebab, we found a patch of grass to park ourselves on. I took off my flannel and used it as a makeshift picnic blanket.

'Any book club news?' Jake asked, once we were settled.

'We're reading *The Odyssey*,' I offered.

He nodded. I nibbled my kebab, finding my mind turning back to our previous conversation.

'What did you mean before by "music's different"?' I asked.

Jake didn't seem fazed by my conversational about turn. 'I mean, like, crowds. Music crowds are different from regular crowds.'

'Explain.'

Jake adjusted his hat so it was covering his face, then settled back down. He said, through the fabric, 'It's just different.'

I kicked his leg, and he swatted at me, then propped himself up on his elbows, letting the hat slide off his face so he could look over at me. 'I can try to show you what I mean?'

I squinted towards the nearest stage, taking in the size of the crowd.

'If you hate it, we'll get out,' Jake said. 'Swear.'

I took a bite of my kebab and sighed through my nose. Jake grinned.

'All right, Book Club. Eat up. We've got places to be.'

✳ ✳ ✳

Jake and I worked out which of the next sets we were interested in, and, when it was almost time, we set off. The act we'd agreed on was performing on the only covered stage, and I felt some relief when we passed into its shade. We arrived in that in-between moment when the previous crowd was dispersing, the new crowd moving to fill the empty spaces. Jake put his hands on my shoulders and directed me through the gaps, until we were close to, though not exactly at, the very front.

'Don't want you to get pushed against the barricade,' he explained.

This set was a band I actually knew, and I felt a spark of excitement when the frontwoman got behind the mic, tuning her guitar as she addressed the crowd. The space was fuller now, though I didn't feel the true size of the crowd until the first song started. Then the jostling really began. It was like before, the crowd undulating and squeezing, foreign hands brushing against my arms, my thighs, my butt, all with the plausible deniability provided by a moving mass of people.

'Ames.'

Jake wasn't as close as Mae had been, so the volume of his voice wasn't startling. He leaned into my side. 'How are you feeling?'

'Stressed,' I said. 'People are touching my arse.'

He nodded, rather than laughing or waving me off. Then he stepped back. Just when I thought he was about to disappear into the crowd, leaving me alone in the crush, I felt him behind me, close but not so close that he was pushed right up against my back. He rested his hands on my shoulders again, palms a gentle press against the sides of my neck.

'Is this okay?' he asked, ducking his head beside mine so he didn't have to raise his voice.

I nodded, and felt his fingers flex around the motion before they slid to cup my shoulders.

Cocooned like this, with Jake taking the brunt of the crowd's movement, I felt my heart rate slow, my stress fading. Jake was swaying, and I swayed with him. The music was loud, but it had lost some of its overwhelming power. It was like the sound was water, and I had been spitting it back. Once I relaxed into it, it moved through me. I could feel it thrumming in my fingertips, pooling in my toes.

Jake's hands moved off my shoulders, skimming my arms almost absentmindedly. He said something, but his voice was hoarse, and I leaned back, turning my face closer to his.

'You can take up space, if you want to,' he said. 'If you want to dance.'

Jake's hands moved to my wrists, and I laughed as he raised one of my arms, making it undulate like I was a one-man wave. I cooperated as he moved my other arm to complete the motion. His face was pressed into my neck, and I could feel his grin. His breath against my skin sent a cascade of tingles down my spine.

After that, I temporarily lost my mind.

The weight of him, the pressure of his body against mine, made me sway back. I pushed into him, seeking closer contact. His grip on my wrists spasmed for a moment, and the sudden tightness of his hands, the heat of his palms, made my stomach heavy. I twisted towards him, just slightly, and my cheek brushed his. When he exhaled, the sound was tight and uneven. His breath grazed my lips—

The lights changed, a cascade of red lasers cutting through the crowd and lighting the backs of my eyelids. I opened my eyes. Jake had pulled back. His hands were on my shoulders again, his body a safe distance from mine.

I closed my eyes again, feeling the pleasant heat inside me curdle into shame.

Dammit.

We kept a polite distance for the remainder of the set, Jake's hands dropping away from my shoulders.

When it was over, and we were moving with the crowd back into the body of the fairground, he said, 'We should see where everyone else is.'

I nodded, silent. Taking out my phone, I checked to see if Mae had replied.

Nothing.

I texted:

Amalia
Where u?

When I glanced at Jake, he was also focused on his phone. I looked back at mine and opened my messages with Laeli. I sent:

I kept my eyes on the screen, and was rewarded a few seconds later by typing bubbles from Laeli's end.

'Laeli says they're at the main stage,' I said.

Jake nodded, and we set off.

The silence that accompanied us as we walked was not a comfortable one. Jake was right beside me, but it felt like he wanted to walk ahead and disappear. I, personally, wanted to bang my head against a wall. I couldn't believe I'd misread the situation like that. Jake blurting out something that sounded like sexual innuendo had been an accident, and I had been too swept up in my crush to accept that. I wouldn't make that mistake again.

To distract myself, I opened the group chat with my cousins and sister to see if I'd missed anything. Renata had sent a blurry selfie taken at a set about forty minutes ago, and it seemed like Kamilia and Elizabeta were currently debating what to eat and when.

Out of distractions and closing in on the main stage, I stopped. It took Jake a moment to notice, but when he did, he drew up short a few paces away. Neither of us crossed the space.

'Jake,' I said, 'about the … when we were dancing—'

'We were just dancing,' he said. 'I promise, Amalia. I wanted you to enjoy the set. That's all. I didn't mean to do anything—'

I raised my hands, resisting the urge to press them to my stomach instead. My insides felt all shaky. I had been wrong. I had been *so wrong*, and I had messed this up a second time.

Jake was still too far away, his fingers curling and uncurling.

'Nothing happened.' I smiled so hard my cheeks hurt. 'It was a good set. I had fun.'

Jake's hands loosened. 'Okay.'

I nodded, mouthing the word back to him. Trying to convince myself it was true.

'Hey!'

Laeli had come up behind us, and waved when we made eye contact. I was too distraught to appreciate how cute she was in a red bandana, scarf crop top and a pair of thick gold earrings, but managed a smile anyway.

'Hey,' I said. 'You look great.'

'You look *cute*,' Laeli said, drawing out the word. 'Where have you been?'

I pointed in the direction of the covered stage, then checked my phone as a way to resist the urge to take a peek at Jake. My screen was bare of notifications. Still nothing from Mae.

Jake had moved past us, heading for a group standing at the fringes of a nearby set. Laeli came up beside me, hooking her arm through mine and directing us to follow.

'Have you seen Mae?' I asked as we walked.

Laeli shook her head.

We drew level with the group Jake had disappeared into. I could see him and Kasun standing together with a few other guys, some from our school, some not. A girl with long, dark purple hair and a nose ring was standing near them. When my gaze landed on her I found she was already looking at me. She turned away when we made eye contact.

'So?' Laeli asked the group at large. 'Where next?'

There were some breakaways, but by and large everyone moved towards the biggest stage – the only one I hadn't been to yet. I grimaced at the sky. I was starting to regret the fact that I hadn't brought a hat. As though reading my thoughts, Jake appeared beside me, flipping his bucket hat onto my head.

'Women love fish,' he said solemnly, when I raised my eyebrows.

'Women love fish,' I confirmed, adjusting the hat on my head.

I was glad he turned back to Kasun then, because my eyes filled. Now wasn't the time to cry, though. Jake and I were good. We weren't what I'd hoped, but we were good.

Now I just had to find Mae.

25

The crowd was easier this time. I closed my eyes and focused on the music, trying not to think about the hands and the bodies touching me, or the fact that Jake was at least two people away from me. Laeli kept close to me, and I focused on her. When she danced into my space, I moved with her. When she took my hand and raised it above her head, I led her through a spin. When she leaned in to kiss me—

Her lips were sweet and soft. It was nice. It also wasn't the mouth I wanted to be kissing.

At some point, I felt Laeli tense against me, and I wondered if my thoughts were coming through in my kissing. I pulled back. Her gaze was focused over my shoulder even as she leaned in towards me. I turned, following her gaze, and saw the girl with the long purple hair kissing another girl I also didn't know almost directly behind us. A few things clicked into place at once.

I looked back at Laeli, and found she had refocused on me, her mouth tight, her eyebrows caught in a furrow. Without letting myself overthink it, I reached over and pressed my thumb gently to the skin between her eyebrows, smoothing over the frown lines. Laeli's expression relaxed, though her mouth stayed tight.

'You want to step out?' I asked.

She shook her head, doing her best to smile. 'I'm fine,' she mouthed.

We didn't kiss again during the set.

Afterwards, I stepped away from the crowd, trying Mae's number. After a few rings, she picked up.

'Where are you?' I asked, trying not to let my anxiety seep into my voice.

'Where are *you*?' Mae shot back. 'I went to the food trucks but couldn't find you.'

I felt a stirring of guilt – I had forgotten to text her when we got to the main stage, too distracted by Laeli's presence and Jake's sudden distance.

'You didn't text me,' I said instead. 'I asked you where you were.'

There was silence on Mae's end. I rested one hand against the back of my neck, digging the tips of my fingers into the base of my skull.

'Well, I found your family,' Mae said.

'Good,' I said, after a beat.

An apology was on the tip of my tongue – yes, Mae hadn't texted me where she was, but I hadn't either – when she said, 'So are you with your friends?'

I dug my fingers more firmly into the back of my skull, feeling pressure build there. There was nothing wrong with what Mae had said, but there was something in her tone …

'I'm with Laeli and Jake,' I said.

'Okay,' Mae said. 'Well, we're heading for the bar and then the covered stage.'

'Got it,' I said. 'I'll come to you.'

'Cool,' Mae said. Then: 'You don't have to.'

I let my hand drop back to my side, blinking against the shock of Mae's words.

'Why wouldn't I?' I asked.

'I don't know.' That edge to her voice was back. 'Maybe you have plans.'

'My plans are to hang out with you,' I said.

'Okay,' Mae said. 'I'll see you soon then.'

'Okay,' I echoed.

Mae hung up. I stared down at my phone, a sick feeling rising in my throat.

'Are you all right?'

I was surprised to find Laeli right next to me, her frown back.

'Where are you going now?' I asked, because the answer to her actual question was, *I don't know.*

What was going *on* with Mae? Was I reading something into nothing? It didn't feel that way. Then again, maybe I was being oversensitive after the Jake event. Maybe I was reacting to nothing.

'Not sure,' Laeli said, looking over her shoulder then back at me.

It was starting to get dark now, the floodlights around the stages flickering on. Where had the time gone?

'I think I'm going to the covered stage,' I said. 'That's where Mae is.'

'Sounds good,' Laeli said. She glanced down at her phone, typed something out, then said, 'Jake and Kasun are staying at the main stage.'

That was probably for the best. No point hanging around Jake after I had made him uncomfortable. I looked at Laeli again, who was typing on her phone again, lower lip squeezed between her teeth.

The words *Was that your ex, kissing another girl?* were on the tip of my tongue.

'I'm going to go meet Mae,' I said instead.

I knew the answer already. No point rubbing salt in the wound.

I found Mae quickly, mostly because she was with Elizabeta and Renata, and Renata was easy to spot thanks to her neon yellow get-up and the fact that she was flailing to the music like a tube man in front of a car dealership.

'Malka!' Elizabeta exclaimed, pulling me into her side when she caught sight of me.

'Sorry I'm late,' I said, glancing between the three of them. Mae had smiled at me when I had appeared, which made me feel marginally less weird, but now she seemed more focused on the stage and the drink in her hand than me. 'Were you waiting for me? Is that why you're so far back?'

That had been the other reason they'd been so easy to spot: they weren't quite at the very back of the crowd, but they were far back enough that the crowd was thin around them. I had been able to make my way to them without needing to deploy a single 'excuse me'.

'Mae said you didn't like the crowds,' Elizabeta said. 'So we thought we'd hang out here instead where it wasn't so intense.'

I felt a swell of warmth as I looked over at Mae again. She caught my eye and offered me a tentative smile. I threw my arms around her, and after a second she wrapped one arm around me in return.

'Thank you for thinking of me,' I said.

'Of course,' Mae grumbled. 'You're my best friend, aren't you?'

'Obviously.'

Before I knew it, we were closing in on the end of the night.

'Last set,' Kamilia told us – she had joined us one set ago – clapping her hands in another startling imitation of Mum. 'What's it going to be?'

I checked my phone: Laeli had texted me that she was back at the main stage a few minutes ago.

'Main stage?' I suggested.

'Is that where Laeli is?' Mae asked, clearly having noticed my phone check.

'Who's Laeli?' Kamilia said.

'Amalia's new friend,' Mae said, then added, 'I'm going to get one more drink. Anyone want to go to the bar before the main stage?'

'I'll come,' Renata said.

Mae nodded. Before I could say anything she was winding her arm through Renata's, pulling her away. I watched them go, then looked at Kamilia, who was already looking at me.

'That was weird,' she commented.

'She's been ... kind of weird all day,' I admitted.

Kamilia tsk-ed. 'You promised to deal with whatever was going on with you two as a condition of coming to the festival.'

'We dealt with it,' I snapped. 'The Kasun thing is – it's fine.'

Kamilia seemed unconvinced.

'What's the Kasun thing?' Elizabeta asked.

'Nothing,' I said, trying not to snap at her too.

Apparently I didn't succeed, because Elizabeta raised her hands in surrender. I took a deep breath. 'Let's just go.'

When we got to the main stage, the crowd was dense enough that I had no hope of spotting Laeli.

I texted:

> **Amalia**
> I'm here, where u?

A few moments later, she texted back:

> **Laeli**
> near front right speaker!!!

'I've got to find my friend,' I told Kamilia and Elizabeta.

If Mae was going to go off without me, then I'd do the same.

After what felt like a lifetime of pushing around and through people, I spotted Laeli. It was like the first sight of land after a year at sea, and I found myself becoming mercenary in my efforts to get to her, elbowing my way through the last clumps of people until I was by her side.

'Amalia!' Laeli exclaimed when she saw me, wrapping her arms around me and gifting me a grin that made my heart flutter.

'Hey.' I smiled at her and then glanced around us. Jake and Kasun were nearby, Kasun shooting me a sunshine smile when we made eye contact. 'What did I miss?'

'Not much,' she said. 'Want to dance? I promise I'll protect you from the crowd.'

'My hero,' I sighed, and Laeli's smile got even bigger.

She slipped behind me, putting both hands on my waist and swaying me back and forth. I let her move me, laughing. It wasn't like it had been with Jake, because Laeli was smaller than both of us, and also because Laeli ... well, she wasn't Jake. But it was nice.

When Laeli wriggled back around so she was beside me, leaning up into my space, I leaned down and let our lips meet.

'What are you doing?'

The words were loud enough to cut through the music. Laeli and I pulled apart, and I looked behind me – Mae was stalled in the process of pushing through the crowd to me.

'But you like *Jake*,' she said.

My eyes popped. I twisted my head towards where Jake stood – too far away to have heard, thank goodness, and totally disconnected from this conversation. But still, *way* too close for comfort.

'Shut up,' I snapped. '*Shut up*, Mae.'

Mae stared at me.

'Who *are* you?' she said finally – then turned and dived back through the crowd.

'Damn,' I hissed, turning to follow her.

Only then did I realise Laeli still had a grip on me. It was loose, but her hand snagged mine when I started to move.

Double damn.

'Laeli, I'm sorry,' I said. 'I didn't mean to – about Jake – I'm sorry.'

She shook her head. I stared at her a moment longer, then went after Mae.

✱ ✱ ✱

By the time I caught up, Mae was panting like she had run a marathon. Still, she didn't slow down – if anything, she sped up when she realised I was closing in on her.

'Leave me alone!' she called over her shoulder.

'No!' I called back, accelerating.

Mae broke into a jog. 'I don't want to talk to you! I don't even know you!'

I started jogging too, my lungs immediately burning. 'Can you – stop?'

'No!' Mae yelled back, though she had started to slow despite her words.

'I'm – sorry – for telling you – to shut up,' I panted, managing another stumbling burst of speed. 'I do – like – Jake. I just – didn't – want him – hearing.'

Mae stopped, leaning on her knees, hair falling in a tangle around her face.

'Why were you kissing Laeli?' she asked the ground.

I put my hands on my hips, leaning backwards and puffing in a few breaths.

I thought of my sister. It would be so easy to deflect, like she had. To say, *well girls are hot, and they're fun to kiss*. To say, *I was just having a bit of fun*. But this had been a secret for long enough. Mae deserved to know.

'I'm bisexual,' I said.

I meant for the words to come out clear and confident,

but I was still trying to catch my breath, so they came out on a wheeze instead. Mae squatted down, resting her elbows on her knees. I squatted to face her, pushing her hair out of her face.

'How do you feel about that?' I asked.

'Is she your girlfriend?' Mae said. 'Are you emotionally cheating on your girlfriend with Jake? *Why wouldn't you tell me you had a girlfriend?*'

Before I could respond, she pulled away from me. I jerked up, ready to start the chase again, but she fell onto all fours and threw up instead.

'Oh,' I said. 'Oh, no.'

Crouching back down, I pulled Mae's hair out of her face, giving her a clear run at the ground.

When she was done, I said, tentatively, 'Laeli isn't my girlfriend. I've just kissed her a few times because … because she's cute, and I wanted to. And I think I led her on, so I'm feeling a bit awful about that. Can we come back to the me being bi thing? Are you – are you okay with that?'

Mae sat back on her heels, and when I looked at her face, I saw that she was crying.

'Oh,' I said slowly. 'Okay. Is that … Are those homophobic tears?'

Mae started laughing. 'I thought you were replacing me.'

'*What?*' I exclaimed.

'You start making all these new friends, and you're hanging out with Laeli all the time, and then it turns out you didn't even tell me you had a crush on the *guy you were setting me up with* and it was like, are we even friends anymore?'

The words came out in a torrent. I stared at Mae as though she'd thrown up again.

'I only started talking to new people because *you* wanted to go out,' I said.

'I *know*,' Mae said, bitter.

'I was *never* trying to replace you.'

'It felt like it,' Mae mumbled.

We eyed each other.

'Why didn't you tell me you were feeling like this?' I said finally.

'Because jealousy isn't cute,' Mae said.

That startled a laugh out of me, even though I felt a bit like screaming. Laeli? All this weirdness had been about *Laeli*?

Mae pushed herself up.

'I need water,' she said. 'My mouth is really messed up right now.'

I glanced down at the pile of vomit and winced. 'That's a good plan.'

As we walked to the taps by the line of porta-potties, I checked my phone. When my screen lit up, I stopped so suddenly that Mae made it a few more steps before she noticed I wasn't with her anymore.

'Oh, no,' I said. 'No, no, no …'

'What?' Mae said. When I didn't say anything, she repeated, more harshly, '*What*, Ames?'

I showed her my screen, and watched her expression drop.

I had six missed calls from Kamilia, three from Renata, one from Elizabeta, and a string of texts the latest of which was just a line of exclamation marks.

It was past nine-thirty.

They had left us.

26

I called Kamilia as Mae washed her mouth out at the taps.

It rang for half a second. 'I told you!' Kamilia said, before I could speak. 'I told you!'

'Did you actually *leave*?' I asked.

'Yes! We *actually left*, because if we *hadn't* we would have *nowhere* to sleep tonight!' she said, voice rising.

'I can't believe you'd actually leave!' Panic drove my voice up into a yell by the end of my sentence.

'I can't believe I thought you'd be able to handle this!' Kamilia shouted back. 'I can't *believe* I thought you'd actually be able to follow *clear instructions!* You—'

There was the sound of a scuffle.

'Hey, Malka,' Renata said.

'Put Kamilia back on,' I said.

'So … I'm not going to do that. We actually need to brainstorm a solution.'

I realised one of my hands was in the air, stalled mid-gesticulation. Taking a deep breath, I lowered it, clenching it into a fist when I noticed it was shaking.

'Okay,' I said. 'Okay. Mae and I are together. If we head for the car park right now, could you double back for us?'

'Sorry,' Renata said, sounding genuinely apologetic. 'We're already cutting it fine. We need to stay en route – but once we've checked in, Elizabeta can circle back around and pick you two up?'

Kamilia said something that sounded angry. Elizabeta made a faint affirmative sound.

'When would that be?' I asked.

There was a pause.

'I'm guessing, like, two hours?' Renata said.

A wave of dizziness rushed over me. I looked over at Mae, who had finished rinsing out her mouth and was now watching me with concern.

'You can't make it to us sooner?' I asked. 'Mae's not feeling good – she's just thrown up, and I think it might be better for us to be—'

'If it was possible, we'd be there in a heartbeat,' Renata said gently. 'You're going to have to hang tight, okay? I promise, we'll come as soon as we can.'

'Okay,' I said in a small voice.

'As soon as we can,' Renata repeated.

I heard Elizabeta yell something in the background.

'Elizabeta wants to know if you're safe,' Renata said.

'Are we safe?' I echoed.

Mae shrugged. I took a deep breath, trying to steady my heart, which was pumping double time.

'We're fine, I guess,' I said.

'Good,' Renata said. 'Love you. See you soon.'

'Love you,' I repeated.

Renata hung up.

I crouched down, hugging my knees. After a moment, Mae crouched down next to me. We crouched there together in silence, festivalgoers stepping around us to make their way to the porta-potties. The rush of the taps flicking on and off provided intermittent blasts of white noise. Despite my best efforts, each flash of sound jolted me back into the present.

'What's the plan?' Mae asked finally.

'They won't be able to come back for two hours.'

Mae took a deep breath, digesting that information.

'How did your friends get here?' she asked.

'The friends I'm replacing you with?' I shot back. Then I sighed. 'Sorry. I don't know.'

'Okay,' Mae said, doing a good job of not reacting to the jab. 'Maybe check with them? See if they can give us a lift, or get us close? Or if they're planning to stay another two hours we can hang out with them.'

I nodded slowly, then took out my phone. After a moment of deliberation, I called Laeli.

Nothing.

We were almost back at the main stage when I spotted Jake. Steeling myself, I directed us towards him, waving when he caught sight of us. After a moment's pause, he waved back, though the smile he offered us was small.

When we drew level with him, I felt compelled to ask, 'What's up?'

'Laeli wants to head out,' he said, putting his hands on his hips and blowing out a sad little sigh I wondered if he was conscious of making. 'Something happened during the set and she's ... she wants to leave. I've called our ride; we might all head back with her.'

Guilt weighed heavily in my stomach. *This is my fault.*

When Jake shot me a confused look, I realised I must have said it out loud.

'Laeli wanting to head home isn't your fault,' he countered.

Mae stepped up beside me. Despite looking as dishevelled as ... well, as someone who'd just thrown up on all fours in the dirt, her eyes were bright, her expression focused.

'Sorry to hear about Laeli,' she said, sympathetic. She paused for a moment, then smiled with a self-deprecating little squint. 'We've actually just missed our ride. Any chance we could hitch one with you? Only if there's space, obviously.'

Jake was already nodding. 'Yeah, for sure. We have Kasun's family car so there'll be space. Where are you guys heading?'

I zoned out as Jake and Mae started to talk logistics, trailing after them as they headed for the festival exit.

We found Kasun near the gates, wearing a dirt patch in the grass as he paced back and forth, his attention on his phone. To his credit, he didn't seem startled or put out when he noticed us, giving Mae and me a nod before his attention settled on Jake.

'Where's Laeli?' Jake asked.

'She's gone to, um ... she's gone to the loo before we leave,' Kasun said, shiftily enough that it was clear Laeli had not in fact 'gone to the loo' but was likely crying, freshening up after crying, or both. I felt that guilty twist in my stomach again.

Silence unspooled between us.

I was just starting to get fidgety with the quiet when Mae jumped in. 'Okay, well, if we're just waiting for her, let's find somewhere to stand that's not right in front of the gates.' She began herding us towards a clear patch of fence nearby. 'By the way, we already asked Jake,' she said, addressing the words to Kasun with an air of determination, 'but we were hoping to get a ride back with you – with all of you.'

I chanced a look at Kasun. He was watching Mae with an expression that seemed studiously comfortable. Mae, in turn, was doing her best to radiate calm confidence, but her back was a little too straight, her shoulders tight.

'That's all right with me,' Kasun said quietly.

We reached the fence. There was still no sign of Laeli.

'Jake said we're taking your family car?' Mae was seemingly intent on keeping some thread of conversation going.

'Yeah,' Kasun said. 'When my family go down the coast they let me borrow it.'

I frowned, remembering a long ago conversation with Jake, which had treaded similar ground. My frown deepened as I tried to remember the details of it, and I heard myself say, 'Do your family go on holidays without you a lot?'

I regretted the words as soon as they were out. I did *not* know Kasun well enough to be asking things like that.

Kasun just smiled, though. 'I do get invited, don't worry. My family is just ... complicated.'

Mae was nodding – she had heard this before, then.

Still, Kasun seemed content to rehash his life circumstances. 'I'm the second-oldest kid – me and my older sister are like a year and a half apart. My parents ... they had us pretty young, then they – they didn't actually separate, but ... anyway, they worked things out, and now I have three more siblings.'

So he was one of five. Wow.

It was hard to imagine. My house already felt crowded enough with four of us. I imagined having three more siblings on top of Kamilia, all younger than me, and couldn't suppress a shudder. How did Kasun get anything done in that house? He probably didn't get much peace. Him staying home while his family holidayed suddenly made a lot of sense.

'What about you?' Kasun asked. It took a moment to realise he was talking to me specifically. 'I know Jake's situation, and I know Mae's an only child. I think Jake mentioned you had a sister?'

'Oh,' I said, floundering for a moment. Jake had talked about me in enough detail to mention I had a sister? When would that have even come up? 'Well, there's not much to tell, but …'

And, for the first time since pre-drinks at his house, I found myself having an actual conversation with Kasun. I talked about my sister, and my cousins, my mum and her sisters.

When book club came up, Jake chimed in. 'Did you ever finish *Moby-Dick*?'

I startled, staring over at him. Jake glanced at me, a smile tugging at his lips.

'I … have not,' I said, slowly. Then I raised one hand, adding, a touch defensively, 'Yet.'

Jake half-laughed. 'Hey, I'm not judging. It's not like I finished it either.'

My ears pricked up. 'You started it? When?'

'I did,' Jake admitted, 'after we talked that first time.' Then he cleared his throat, turning his attention to Kasun. 'Hey, have you heard from Laeli since she went to the toilets?'

Kasun shook his head. We all digested this information.

'Someone should check on her,' Mae said. She shifted her gaze to me. 'Amalia?'

I stared at Mae. She levelled a look at me. Ah. So she suspected like I did that Laeli's snap decision to leave, and now extended absence, might have something to do with me. I took a deep breath, then nodded.

'Yep,' I decided. 'I can go look for her. I'll catch her up on the plan.'

It was time to face the consequences of my own actions.

I checked the toilets closest to the entrance, calling Laeli's name and hovering awkwardly near the porta-potties until I decided she probably wasn't there – I figured of all the places to sneak off for a moment alone, festival toilets did not rate high in either comfort or privacy. Branching away from the loos, I began scanning the area nearby, keeping my eye out for quiet corners.

It was as I was passing by the medical tent that I noticed someone sitting cross-legged in the shadows next to it, eyes trained on her ankles as she fiddled with a bottle of water.

'Laeli?' I tried.

The girl looked up, smiling a wobbly sort of smile when she saw me – it was definitely Laeli, though at some point she'd shrugged on the big bright green jumper I remembered seeing around Kasun's waist earlier, and her eyes were puffy and red, which suggested crying had occurred in the not-too-distant past.

'Hey Amalia,' she said, voice clogged. She sniffed, straightening. 'Sorry, did Jake or Kasun send you? I'm okay, I just needed a quick breather before we left.'

My heart twisted. Not letting myself overthink it, I folded onto the ground beside Laeli.

'You shouldn't apologise,' I said. 'I'm – I'm the one who's sorry.'

Laeli stopped fiddling with the water bottle. 'Why are you sorry?'

'Why?' I stared at Laeli. Then the words were exploding out of me: 'Of *course* I'm sorry! I didn't – I should have told you sooner. It wasn't fair that I was kissing you without being honest with you. About – about my feelings. That was *awful* of me. That was *cowardly* of me. I …'

I trailed off. Laeli was squinting at me, which wasn't the reaction I had expected.

'What?' I asked, patting my face. 'Is there … is there something on me?'

Laeli, doing her best to bite down on a smile, shook her head. Then, to my horror, her eyes filled with tears.

'Oh, no,' I said, half on a moan, as Laeli buried her face in her hands and started to cry.

I reached out, putting both my hands on her shoulders, and gave them a few pats.

'I'm sorry, Laeli, really,' I said.

'I'm so selfish,' Laeli hiccupped.

I stopped patting, letting my hands rest on Laeli's shoulders in a way I hoped was both gentle and reassuring. 'You're not selfish.'

Laeli's face emerged from her hands then, her eyes large and wet. 'I knew.'

'You knew what?' I asked.

'I knew – I was pretty sure – you liked Jake,' she said, lowering her voice to a whisper on Jake's name. 'You didn't have to say anything. I know what it looks like.'

My whole chest lurched. I glanced towards the medical tent as though Jake might materialise from within it at any moment. 'But – if you knew … why …?'

'Why kiss you? Well, why did you kiss me?'

'Because … I wanted to,' I said.

Laeli shrugged one shoulder, giving me a watery smile. 'Yeah. And I sort of figured it was … better. I wasn't going to break your heart. It wasn't mine to break.'

I felt that lurch in my chest again. Laeli reached out, and I took her hand.

Then I frowned. 'But if you knew, why are you … here?'

Laeli took a deep breath, looking at our hands. 'It's been over – properly over – with my ex for a few months. But I think … a part of me didn't believe it would stick. Seeing her kissing someone else … I get I'm a total hypocrite, but I … it was like I realised it was actually over. And then you left and there was nothing to distract me and she was still there but I was alone and—'

Laeli pulled her hand out of mine, pressing it back over her eyes. Her mouth twisted, her lips trembling. I watched her, my hands pressing into fists, trying to squeeze out the emotions rising in me so I didn't cry with her.

'I'm so sorry,' I said, knowing I sounded like a broken record.

Laeli's mouth tensed, then relaxed. She dropped her hand from her eyes.

'I needed it,' she said. 'I needed to see it.'

I nodded. Laeli focused on me, taking a deep breath.

'But I am selfish,' Laeli said, softer. 'It wasn't just that I knew you had a crush on Jake. I realised – after the movie night at my house – I realised that Jake had feelings for you, too, but that as long as we were … anything, he would never act on it.'

My hands spasmed, my nails biting into my palms hard enough to hurt. I blinked at Laeli, mouth half-open, trying to think past the noise in my head. That wasn't – he didn't – he *couldn't*—

'I kept saying "this will be the last time",' Laeli said, not seeming to notice that my brain had turned to static. 'But I was so hurt and you were … and it was selfish. I'm sorry.'

'That's not right,' I managed, finally.

Laeli cocked her head.

'He – he doesn't,' I said. 'I – he—'

Laeli took my hands in hers.

'I'm sorry,' she said again, more firmly. 'And I think we should break up.'

At my goggle-eyed stare, Laeli laughed.

'You know what I mean,' she said. 'No more kissing. I've got to work out how to – to be alone, and you … you've got to think about some things, I guess. Just—' Laeli narrowed her eyes, shaking a finger at me. 'Don't go breaking his heart, okay?'

I managed a strangled laugh at that, if only at the absurdity of it all. While I was relieved almost beyond comprehension that I hadn't been the reason Laeli had snuck off for a cry, she was wrong about Jake. She was just … she was wrong.

At least that meant I wasn't at risk of disappointing Laeli. I couldn't break a heart that was never mine to break either.

We sat there in silence for a while longer, Laeli opening her bottle and taking a few gulps.

'The people in the medical tent gave it to me,' she explained, when I glanced at it. 'I think they think I'm very drunk. I wanted to go back earlier but they suggested I sit down and have some water first.'

'Well, I'm here now. I'll look out for you.' I pushed myself up, offering a hand. Laeli took it without hesitation. 'Shall we?'

Laeli's smile was stronger this time. 'We shall.'

When we got back to the group, looks of relief washed over Jake and Kasun's faces before they crowded forwards like mother hens, Kasun throwing an arm around Laeli's shoulder and Jake checking her unsubtly for signs of damage. Mae and I locked eyes while the three best friends were distracted, and she raised her eyebrows in a way I figured meant, *Is it sorted between you two?*

I nodded, then I flicked my eyes towards Kasun, hoping I was conveying a similar question.

Mae shrugged, then nodded, crinkling her nose at me.

'Good timing, too,' Kasun was saying, pulling Mae and I back into the conversation. 'Sounds like Jake's sister is outside with the car.'

Mae dropped into step beside me as we turned towards the exit, threading her arm through mine and bumping my hip gently. I bumped her back.

Kasun's people mover was stalled next to the kerb a few metres away from the exit gate, the driver leaning out of the window and locked in an animated argument with two festival workers in high-vis vests. When she saw the group of us, her ferocious expression broke into a smile, and she ducked back into the car, beginning to reverse towards us in spite of protestations from the festival staff. We hurried to meet her.

'All right, kiddos?' she said, when she had come to a stop in front of us.

When I could see her properly, it wasn't hard to guess that she was Jake's sister. They had the same eyes: dark, with a hint of mischief. They paused on me and then Mae.

Her eyebrows spiked. 'Mae?'

I looked at Mae, who was staring at the woman, startled. 'Gizem?'

'You know each other?' Jake asked, glancing between them.

'I do some admin at her law firm,' Mae admitted.

Gizem shot Mae a small smile, eyes crinkling at the corners. The expression made her look even more like Jake.

Memories of conversations I'd had with Mae about her work resurfaced. Was this …?

'The cool lawyer,' I heard myself say.

Mae turned immediately red. Gizem's gaze slipped back to me, and her eyes twinkled.

'Must be,' she said. 'Small world, huh? Well, get in before our friends from the festival grab their pitchforks.'

27

I hadn't realised the excitement of the day had drained me so much until my eyelids drooped and, between one blink and the next, Mae was gently shaking me awake.

After conveying a groggy thank you to Gizem for the lift and exchanging goodbyes with Laeli, Jake and Kasun, we picked our way down the path that ran alongside the front office of the motel my family had booked, scanning the doors for number seven. It wasn't hard to spot, in the end: the door was open, Kamilia standing in the doorway with her arms crossed. She didn't move as we walked towards her, though her expression tightened. Then, suddenly, she was lunging forwards, wrapping me in a tight hug.

'You're such a pain in my arse,' she muttered.

I gave her a squeeze. 'I'm sorry we weren't there on time.'

Finally, she let go of me, stepping back and re-crossing her arms.

'Since you two are the last here, you're stuck with the kids' bunk beds,' she said. 'Elizabeta and I are taking the queen bed.'

Inside the main room, we found Renata sprawled out on a foldout sofa bed in the centre of the space. Elizabeta, who was in the middle of pouring hot water into an array of mugs, looked over at us with a tired smile.

'Glad you two are safe,' she said. Renata sprung up to pull us both into hugs. 'I'm making kamilica. Want some?'

Getting ready for bed was an extended process, as there was one bathroom and five of us. Finally, though, I tumbled into the bottom bunk, hair wet, the skin on my face tingling from some type of apricot facewash Renata had decided I needed to try out. Kamilia was still in the bathroom, making the most of the shower, and I could hear Renata and Elizabeta murmuring and laughing from the main room as they flicked through TV channels.

I was just starting to feel the slow, swirling tug of sleep begin behind my eyes, when Mae spoke.

'You still awake?'

'Mm,' I said.

There was silence for a moment, and then Mae was clambering down the ladder, nudging me until there was enough room for her to stretch out next to me.

We lay there, shoulder to shoulder, Mae's body a warm weight against mine. When my eyes were beginning to droop again, she said, 'When did you know you were bi?'

I was tempted to reply, *can't this wait till the morning?*

Instead, I blinked my way back to consciousness and said, my voice dragging a little with sleep, 'Sort of ... end of last year, beginning of this?'

'Okay.'

Silence stretched between us.

'Why didn't you tell me?' she said.

I hummed as I mulled that over. 'I guess I thought it didn't really ... like, I wasn't dating anyone. Why did it need to be said? I think, though ...'

'You think?' Mae prodded.

I realised I had trailed off, sleep rising up against my consciousness and pulling me, briefly, under.

'It was new,' I said. 'It was mine.'

'Was that why you didn't tell me about Kasun?' she asked.

'Sort of. You liked him first. I didn't want to make you ... uncomfortable. Especially not once you'd actually started dating.'

'I wish you had,' Mae said quietly. 'I know we'll ... I knew there'd be a day when we wouldn't tell each other everything anymore. I thought ... maybe in uni. Or maybe when we have jobs and houses or maybe if one of us moves away. I didn't realise it was already happening.'

I moved my head in a slow nod. 'I'm sorry. I really am, Mae.'

I felt her take a deep breath. 'I don't want there to be any secrets between us anymore. Okay?'

'Okay,' I agreed.

'Good. So I have something to tell you.'

'Is it that you and Kasun are actually dating now?' I asked.

Mae let out sharp gasp of laughter. 'Definitely not. It was good talking to him today, though.'

I made a noise I hoped was supportive. Sleep lapped at the edges of my thoughts; the tide was going out, now, and it was carrying me with it—

'I'm gay.'

I opened my eyes.

'You're what?' I said to the slats above my face.

'I'm gay, Amalia.'

I propped myself on my elbows, looking down at Mae, sleep forgotten. I opened my mouth, then closed it.

Then: 'For how long?'

'My whole life, I guess,' she said. She was watching me carefully, playing with the edge of a blanket. 'But I worked it out pretty recently.'

I lay back down, turning onto my side. Mae shifted too, so we were face-to-face.

'When I think back, it seems obvious,' she said. 'Like, I always managed to crush on the most unattainable boys. Boys I barely even talked to, and who probably would never talk to me. Then suddenly I was working on this project with Kasun and he actually – he seemed to like me? And I didn't stop to ask myself if I really, actually liked him back. I was ... excited. It was something new.'

Mae swallowed, gaze drifting away from me. 'Eventually I started to realise that it wasn't actually Kasun I liked. I liked his attention, and I liked the thrill of sneaking out and trying new things. I liked the world he opened up. I enjoyed his company, but I started to realise I didn't actually like him in ... other ways. When we kissed – I thought maybe then everything would work out. That I'd realise I was wrong and it would all fall into place. It didn't. Kissing him, I felt ... nothing.'

She swallowed again, looking back at me. 'I thought, okay. Well, maybe I can still be friends with Kasun. *Just* friends. Then suddenly I'm on a date with him, and his hand's open on the armrest between us, and I know – not just that I don't like Kasun, but that the whole thing is ... wrong. That it's *all* wrong. So I called you, but I couldn't ... I couldn't explain it. He hadn't done anything bad. It just *felt* ... it wasn't right and I didn't know – or maybe I didn't *want* to know – why.'

Mae smiled at me then, a small, tired smile. 'And there was Laeli. She starts at our school, she's beautiful, and she's also openly gay.'

I hadn't meant to speak, but found myself half-squawking, 'You knew Laeli was gay?'

Mae laughed. 'She was *not* secretive about it. Like, she didn't come up to me one day and say, "Hey, by the way I'm gay". It was a ... known thing, though.'

'How didn't *I* know that?' I wondered.

'You were up Agatha Christie's butt at that point, I'm not surprised you totally missed it,' Mae said, not without affection. 'Anyway, Laeli ... I couldn't stop thinking about her. I thought maybe I didn't like her, for whatever reason. Turns out I was plain old jealous. To make it worse, of all the new friends you could have made ...'

She trailed off, and I absorbed that. It must have been a double blow: not only had Mae been worried about losing me, she thought she was losing me to someone who had done the work Mae was only just starting to realise was ahead of her. Like I was trading Mae in for an upgraded model.

'I'm sorry,' I said.

Mae waved her hand at me. 'You making a new friend isn't something to be sorry for. I was ... caught in my own head. And it's not like I was a great friend during all that. When I found out you had a crush on Kasun, I – I took out my ... confusion and frustration about my feelings on you. I *wanted* to be mad because of something silly like – "oh, no, you want *my man*. How *bad*."' She grated out a laugh. 'You were being a good friend, trying to set me up with the person I had been talking about for, like, a year. Except that made me face myself sooner than I maybe would have otherwise. I kind of hated you for that, a bit. I wasn't ready. But that wasn't your fault.'

I reached out, finding Mae's hand and lacing our fingers together, pulling our joined hands to my heart.

'I wish I'd told you I was bi sooner,' I whispered. 'If I had told you earlier, it would have been different. We could have done this together.'

'Who knows,' Mae said, giving my hand a squeeze before pulling back and tucking her hands under her cheek. 'I was … there was a lot going on, in my head. Maybe I would have been mad at you anyway. I was mad at Laeli for less.'

'I wish you *had* told me,' I said. I clasped my hands together, like I was trying to wring my emotions out with them. 'I wish that *I* had told *you*. I wish that we had trusted each other with that.'

'Me too.'

My lip wobbled, and I bit down on it, determined not to cry. Mae scooted closer so we were almost nose to nose. She closed her eyes, letting out a little sigh.

'I don't blame us,' she said. 'I don't. It's scary. You never know for sure how people will react. Even people close to you.'

'I guess.' I closed my eyes too, taking a deep breath before saying: 'I've got your back, though. Always. I've got you.'

I couldn't see Mae's face, but I knew she was smiling when she said, 'I've got you, too.'

✳ ✳ ✳

After going for a bushwalk the next day and taking a handful of photos that could be shown to our parents – and making sure that any lingering glitter and rhinestones had been fully disposed of – we embarked on the drive home. Instead of going home from mine, Mae followed me up to my room, dropping her bag at the base of my bed and launching herself at my pillow. I stared at her as she made herself comfortable. She raised her eyebrows.

'Did you think we were all done last night?' she asked. 'You need to catch me up on everything with Laeli and Jake. No secrets, remember?'

I flopped down at the far end of my bed, bouncing once with the force of it. 'Yeah, but there's nothing really to say.'

'Obviously untrue.' She sat up and brought my pillow with her, hugging it to her stomach. 'Fill me in. C'mon. You can start with the first time you kissed Laeli.'

I sighed. Then, still lying flat on my back, I started talking.

✳ ✳ ✳

'So Laeli and I "broke up",' I concluded, raising my arms in the air so my air quotes were visible, 'because she thinks that if Jake thinks we're together, he's not going to make a move on me. But Jake definitely doesn't like me. He's made that pretty clear.'

'Has he?' Mae asked, sounding doubtful. 'Sounds like he thinks you're hot and he freaked out because you touching his hair during that movie night made him horny—'

'It did not!' I shrieked, sitting bolt upright and glaring at Mae.

She snorted, then continued, '*And* he told you he always wants you to touch him? Yeah. He's into you.'

'He didn't say that, exactly,' I mumbled, lying back down.

Even though I couldn't see Mae anymore, I knew she was pulling a face at me.

'He's not,' I insisted.

'Okay, well, even if we put *all that* aside – his best friend is telling you it's true. Why would she lie? Telling you this is, like, actively against her own best interests.'

I glared at the ceiling. 'I don't think she's lying. I think she's wrong.'

Mae smacked me in the stomach with my pillow. I *oof*-ed.

'You're being very frustrating right now,' she said. 'It's so obvious.'

I wrestled my pillow from Mae so I could throw it at her. Mae, rudely, only laughed.

'I'm not hearing any better reasons. Just – stop hitting me with the pillow! – just talk to him. Lay it all out.'

'I basically did that,' I sniffed, sitting back on my heels.

'He thought – probably still thinks, unless Laeli's talked to him – that you're dating his best friend,' Mae pointed out. 'Even if she has, he probably won't try anything, because it sounds like he's disgustingly loyal and romantic, and probably wants you and Laeli to get back together if he thinks it'll make you happy. Tell him you're not dating her. Go from there. Okay?'

I wrinkled my nose at Mae, then sighed, giving her one more half-hearted whack with the pillow. 'Fine.'

Mae grinned.

After Mae left, I started to strategise.

What would I open with?

Hey, Jake, I'm not actually dating Laeli. Anyway, remember how you said you wanted me to touch you all the time? Just wanted to circle back to that and check if you meant platonically or if you wanted us to explore each other's bodies.

Should I abandon words entirely and try to seduce him? No, I had (sort of) tried that already, and it hadn't worked. Words needed to be involved. Powers of seduction were … not my strong suit.

What *was* my strong suit? So far my strengths seemed to lie in waiting for someone else to kiss me, which had been more successful than expected – though, clearly, not quite successful enough.

Should I send him an *email*? Was that a thing people did in situations like this?

I had never so dearly wished that I was a bird. If only I could flash my plumage and be done with this.

Ten more minutes passed.

I glanced at *Moby-Dick* on my bedside table, and thought of my latest conversation with Jake in Kasun's car. Finally, when the mental agony got to be too much, I took out my phone and searched 'crochet patterns'.

Maybe the best way to think about this was not to think about it at all.

28

The 'ignoring it' strategy worked great – until my next maths class with Jake on the Monday. When I walked into the room and saw him balancing on the back two legs of his chair, gesturing about something to Kasun, my heart went *badump-a-thump*. When he saw me, he didn't smile exactly, but his eyes crinkled, and *ugh. Eugh. Yeuch!*

He raised his eyebrows at me. I schooled my expression into something that was neither eugh nor yeuch, and sat down next to Mae with great dignity.

She ruined this by leaning over and saying, 'What's the plan?'

'What plan?' I shook my books out of my bag.

'Oh, so it's like that,' Mae said. 'Got it.'

I groaned, leaning forwards and pressing my face against my open workbook.

'Just tell him you're not actually dating Laeli,' Mae said. 'You don't even have to bring up your feelings straightaway.'

'What if I don't talk about it ever?' I countered, then turned my face towards Mae. 'Do you think Laeli's told him?'

'We talked about this. Maybe she has, but chances are he's gotta hear it from you, Ames. Also, Laeli is not a messenger pigeon,' Mae said. 'It's not her job to be your Cupid.'

'Maybe you could tell him?' I suggested.

'You're being a baby.'

I turned my face back into my workbook.

✷ ✷ ✷

Days passed. I continued to fill my brain with thoughts of crochet. It was starting to look like I was closer to making a doily than sitting down and having a proper talk with Jake.

On Friday afternoon, I embraced cowardice and visited the yarn shop near the local shopping centre. After the visit, buoyed by my recent purchases (a crochet hook, a ball of blue yarn and a couple of darning needles, which I would apparently need), I ducked inside for a bubble tea. Because I was a coward, I did a furtive scan of the food court before going in.

'What are we looking for?' someone said behind me, stalling me in the middle of craning my head around a corner.

I turned around to face Jake.

'You,' I said, truthfully.

'Cool.' Jake seemed unfazed by this revelation. 'What's up?'

Oh, well. Time to be brave.

'Want a bubble tea?' I asked.

Jake stuffed his hands in his pockets. He was in his work clothes, with a non-work hoodie thrown over them.

'Sure,' he said. 'I'm getting dumplings, if you want anything. Shift starts in twenty.'

Twenty minutes.

I could do this.

✷ ✷ ✷

When we sat down, Jake's knees bumping mine under the table, he said, 'Kasun and Laeli are coming over to mine tomorrow. Nothing special, just hanging out. Want to come?'

My brain, churning as it was with thoughts of crochet and crushes and Jake's knee, which had come to rest pressed against mine, was not being helpful in the words department.

'Tomorrow,' I managed to say.

'Yep,' Jake agreed, stuffing a dumpling into his mouth.

I watched him as I took a sip of my drink. He seemed … totally normal. Like the weekend had never happened. Surely, if he did have a crush on me, he'd be acting as weird as I was?

'You can bring Mae along, too,' Jake added.

'Do you think Laeli and I are dating?' I blurted.

Jake's eyebrows stilled. He put another dumpling in his mouth.

I reminded myself I was being brave.

'Laeli and I were never dating,' I said. 'We kissed a couple of times, but that's it. We're just friends.'

Jake kept eating his dumplings. I forced myself not to fidget. How on earth had Laeli decided Jake had feelings for me? I could *not* get a read on his thoughts beyond, probably, *I am eating dumplings*.

'Okay,' he said finally. 'Other fish in the sea. Don't worry. We'll find you a hot girl.'

'Or guy,' I said.

This caused the first visible change to Jake's expression, his eyebrows puckering. I felt a flare of annoyance. When I next spoke, I could hear it colouring my words.

'You know I like guys too.'

Another expression change.

'You had a crush on Kasun,' Jake said, 'that I haven't heard anything about since you started making out with Laeli.'

Jake presented this as though it constituted a clear explanation. As though point A was negated by point B. I took another sip of my drink, this one angrier. Jake, sensing a change in the waters, slowed his dumpling intake. I leaned forwards and put my drink down.

'You're right,' I said. 'I don't have a crush on Kasun

anymore. I have a crush on another guy. One that I'm starting to second-guess, honestly, because right now he's being a bit of a – a *goose*.'

Jake seemed to have forgotten about his dumplings.

This was not how I had imagined the conversation going at all.

'I'm bisexual, Jake,' I said, when Jake didn't say or do anything.

His phone alarm beeped. He looked down at it like it was a foreign object.

'My shift's about to start,' he said.

'Great,' I snapped. 'Do you have literally anything else to say?'

He studied his dumplings. When they didn't present him with a comeback, he refocused on me.

'My sister …' He trailed off.

'*Enlighten* me.'

His phone was still beeping. He stood up, rubbing one hand across his cheek, then dragged his fingers through his hair, fuzzing his curls like he'd been electrocuted on one side.

And then he left.

'I'll kill him!' Mae said, rubbing circles on my back.

I stayed facedown on my bed, arms bunched under my pillow.

'Can't believe I couldn't imagine anything worse than Jake telling me he didn't like me back,' I mumbled. 'I didn't think him just … *not believing* I could have a crush on him was an option.'

'People can be awful.'

'But Jake's *not* awful.' I lifted my head. 'He's funny and kind and—' I buried my face in my pillow again.

Mae gave me another reassuring pat on the back, then I felt the bed shift as she got up. A moment later, my desk chair squeaked and sighed, so I figured she was making herself comfortable.

'How many jackets do you have on this chair?' she asked. Then: 'Is this my leather jacket?'

'Maybe,' I muttered.

I heard the whump of fabric being lifted and sifted through. 'Is this *Kasun's* jacket? From that beach party? And this is Jake's, right?'

'*Maybe*,' I muttered again.

'You are *such* a little thief,' Mae said, sounding impressed. 'Also, I think it's time to bring in the official Jake translator.'

I called Laeli.

'Okay, I have a theory,' she said, once I had explained the situation.

Mae raised her eyebrows at me. Despite the fact that she had been the one to suggest I call Laeli for help, she came over camera-shy when Laeli video-called, and was now sitting on my desk chair, knees pulled to her chest.

'You said he mentioned Gizem?' Laeli asked.

'The last thing he said to me was something-something his sister,' I said. 'The last thing! Then he left!'

'No, that makes sense actually,' Laeli said.

I threw up my hands. Mae draped her leather jacket around her shoulders.

'You know Jake's sister Gizem is gay, yeah?' Laeli said.

Both Mae and I nodded.

'She identified as bi at first,' Laeli said. 'Then later came out as gay. And then there's me – oldest friend, also a lesbian. My ex was also someone else who started out identifying as bi and ended up re-identifying as a lesbian. She used to joke about it being a "stepping-stone" sexuality. She definitely did that in front of Jake more than once.' Laeli paused, looking at me and then away. 'I should have ... pushed back against that more. I know it's not true. But I sort of thought ... that's *her* truth. Anyway. I know better now.'

I nodded slowly, breathing through the twisting feeling in my stomach. I knew where Laeli was going with this.

'It's possible,' Laeli said, 'that Jake's internalised the idea of bisexuality as a ... a stop on the way to being gay.'

I thought of talking to Kamilia, and the casual way she had dismissed the possibility I could like women because of my attraction to men.

'So because he's seen me kissing you, he's decided I don't actually like men?' I guessed.

'Something like that,' Laeli said, offering me a smile that was more like a grimace.

'Right,' I said, because I wasn't sure what else to say. 'Thanks, Laeli.'

'I'm sorry, Amalia,' she said. 'Do you want me to talk to him?'

I thought about it for a moment, then shook my head. 'No, that's okay. But thanks.'

Laeli looked like she wanted to say something else.

After opening and closing her mouth, her frown deepening as the silence lengthened, she said, finally, 'Are you going to go to Jake's? Tomorrow?'

'I don't know,' I said.

It was the truth.

When I hung up, I just sat there, trying to breathe. I felt like someone had closed their fist around my heart. Mae got up from the chair, coming to sit beside me on the bed, and wrapped me in a hug. I slumped into her, letting her squash me against her side, and took a few deep breaths.

'Want to watch a movie?' she suggested. 'We could make some cookies too, maybe?'

I nodded, succumbing to distraction.

After Mae had gone home later that evening, I went to my sister's door. I stood outside it for approximately two minutes, shifting my weight from foot to foot, before the door opened.

'You know you can knock, right?' Kamilia said. 'Or were you skulking out there for fun?'

'I don't skulk,' I said, not making a move either towards or away from the doorway.

Kamilia waved me across the threshold. 'Whatever. You're being weird. What do you want?'

I meandered past her, making my way to the edge of her bed and picking up the whale toy that sat, pride of place, among her pillows.

'I sort of told Jake I liked him,' I said, 'and he sort of didn't believe me.'

Kamilia blinked and sat down at her desk. 'I'd say I'm sorry, but *what*?'

'Yeah.' I could feel my insides turning in on themselves. 'Sounds bad, right?'

Kamilia crossed her legs, propping one elbow on her knee and hunching forwards so she could rest her chin on her fist, eyes narrowing. 'Okay, let's analyse this. Did you say it like … *ha-ha, wouldn't it be funny if I liked you*?'

'No,' I snapped, putting the toy down and pacing back to the door. Then, softer: 'No. Maybe I'm not being … So I didn't lead with *I have a crush on you*.'

Kamilia nodded, eyes still narrowed in concentration. 'Okay, so I'm thinking that was your problem.'

I let out a half-laugh, sagging against the doorframe. 'Yeah, the problem was definitely what I led with, because I told him I was bisexual and he didn't believe me.'

Kamilia straightened. Her expression did … something. I didn't know. I was deliberately not watching her. I had noticed a flaky bit of paint on the doorframe and was focusing on that instead.

'It was kind of a deja vu moment,' I continued, reaching out to press my pointer finger into the paint, 'because it reminded me of when I was talking to you, and I said I liked girls, not just boys. And you said something like "everyone thinks girls are hot, Amalia", like I wasn't telling you something important. Like maybe I wanted you to say, *that's cool, Amalia, thanks for sharing.*'

The paint flake came off on my fingertip. I looked at it for a moment, and then rubbed it off against my thigh.

'Anyway, good talk,' I finished.

'Malka,' Kamilia said.

I took her in then, seeing her furrowed brow and the way her lip was twisted into her mouth. I rubbed my palm against my T-shirt, like my whole hand was covered in paint flakes that needed to be wiped clean.

'Malka,' she said again, more firmly this time. 'Come here.'

I deliberated for a moment, hovering in the doorway. Then I walked to her. When I was within grabbing distance, Kamilia took both of my hands in hers, keeping her gaze on me until I locked eyes with her.

'That was thoughtless of me,' she said. 'I didn't realise what you were saying. Or … I did, but I … I responded badly. I didn't realise it was important to you.'

I didn't say anything. I felt frozen in place.

'Hey,' Kamilia said. 'So you like girls too. That's cool.' She squeezed my hands, trying for a smile. 'Thanks for sharing, Malka.'

A weight lifted from my chest.

I burst into tears.

I slept in late the next morning, unwilling to breach consciousness and face the day. Finally, though, I sat up in bed, pulling my phone out of its charger and dragging it into my nest of blankets with me. I opened up my chat with Laeli.

Amalia

Hey, I'm not going to make it today. Could you do me a favour tho?

The reply came back near instantly:

Laeli

Anything!!!

I paused for a moment, fingers hovering over my phone screen, then wrote:

> **Amalia**
> Could u come by mine? I have jackets I need to return to Jake and Kasun. thought today would be a good opportunity

> **Laeli**
> Of course

> **Laeli**
> Send me ur address. I'll be there in arvo – will swing by urs first before Jake's

> **Amalia**
> Thanks Laeli

Laeli sent me back a heart emoji.

It was for the best, I told myself, sliding my phone back onto my bedside table and then groping around until I got a grip on the copy of *The Odyssey* I had found waiting for me in my room when I got back from 'camping', courtesy of Mum.

I had been meaning to return Kasun's jacket for a long time and now, with Jake … it would be a clean break. No more reminders. My crush on Kasun was already a faded memory. I'd get there with Jake too.

I opened my book, and did my best to distract myself.

A couple of hours later, Dad sidled into my room, doling out a mug of coffee, a cut apple and a kiss on the forehead, before retreating without a word. Mum came in shortly after, frowning when she found me still in bed and coming over to feel my temperature before announcing that my floor was a mess and she would give it a vacuum. Even Kamilia made an appearance, coming in once Mum had finished vacuuming. She pulled my desk chair over to my bed so she could hold her phone in my face and demand I rate a selection of celebrities by relative attractiveness, pulling a face no matter what I said.

I knew my family could tell something was wrong, and I appreciated that none of them were prying just as much as I appreciated the company. When Laeli arrived that afternoon and I descended the stairs, I felt watchful eyes chart my journey to the door, the exchange of jackets carefully monitored. Once I was back in my room, Mum appeared within fifteen minutes and deposited a plate of strudel next to me along with a warning not to expect any more special treatment. Five minutes later, she was back with a mug of warm milk and honey, which she put down beside the strudel without comment.

I pulled the strudel into my lap, and kept reading.

I was up to Odysseus's homecoming when there was a scratching of nails against my door.

'What is it?' I called.

Kamilia bumped open the door, surveying me with her hands on her hips. 'There's a boy at the front door.'

I blinked at her.

'What do you mean?' I said, finally.

'Boy,' Kamilia said, pointing towards the front of the house. 'Door. For you.'

I blinked again, feeling a flutter of something in my chest.

'Okay,' I said. 'Um. Give me a moment.'

Kamilia shrugged, but she was looking at me shrewdly as she stepped back into the hall and closed the door behind her. I stared blankly after her for a moment, and then burst into action, shifting my book and empty plate onto my bedside table with a clatter and launching out of bed.

Shucking my pyjamas, I sprayed myself with deodorant and then threw on a T-shirt and jeans, not bothering with a comb and twisting my hair up into a messy bun instead. Then I took a deep breath and headed for the front of the house.

Jake was waiting for me on the front porch. His curls had slowly been growing out over the months I'd got to know him, and they were rumpled now, like he'd been tugging at them on the drive over. His dark eyes were bright, his jaw tight. He was also holding … books. A stack of books.

'Laeli told me you weren't coming,' he said.

I paused in the doorway, resting my hand against the wooden frame.

'It's my fault,' he said.

It wasn't a question. I stayed silent. Jake's jaw ticked.

'I'm sorry,' Jake said, taking a step towards me. The words sent a jolt through me, and my fingers tightened on the doorframe. Jake kept talking. 'You ... caught me off guard, but that's not an excuse. I'm sorry I assumed one thing when you were telling me another. I'm sorry that I tried to argue with you when you were telling me something important. I'm just – sorry.'

I swallowed, digesting his words, feeling something in me lighten by increments as I did.

'Okay,' I said, finally.

'Okay?'

I nodded, once, decisive. Then: 'Why do you have a bunch of books?'

Jake frowned, then looked at the pile in his hands as though only just remembering they existed. When he looked back at me, his expression shifted into something determined.

'So I didn't finish *Moby-Dick*,' he said, 'although I tried. I'm still trying. I read *Emma* in a week, though. I liked it. I thought she was a bit of a dickhead, but I – I liked the end. The Agatha Christie was good – don't think I'm really into old-school murder mysteries, though. I didn't guess the final reveal, so that was cool. Then – *Wuthering Heights*. That one messed with my head. I liked it, but that doesn't mean I'd read it again. And I started *The Odyssey* last week. I—'

I let go of the doorframe, stepping towards Jake. He stopped talking, watching me approach. When I was in front of him, I reached out, running my finger along the spine of the book on top of the pile. There they were, one on top of the other. A stack of book club picks, all with creased spines, some bristling with crowns of sticky notes. I wondered absently if Jake was the type of person to annotate as he read.

Jake seemed to be holding his breath.

'When did you read these?' I asked.

'When you told me about them,' he said.

I looked away from the books then, finding Jake already focused on me, gaze intent on my face. 'Why didn't you tell me?'

'I couldn't.'

'You couldn't?' I echoed.

Jake shook his head. His gaze flickered to my lips.

'It would have been obvious, then,' he said. 'How much I think about you. How much I want to know about the things you like, and the things you don't. If I couldn't have you ... how could I have talked about it?'

I stared at Jake as he spoke, his words filling me with a warm, heavy feeling. When he finished, I took one final step towards him, hooking my hands under the books and sliding them out of his grasp.

'I'm going to put these down now,' I said.

Jake only nodded. When I straightened, he gazed at me for a long moment. I gazed back, feeling myself beginning to smile. I watched Jake's eyes spark in return, crinkling at the corners. He cupped my face between his palms and I let him draw me in towards him, my own hands drifting to his hips.

'You know,' I said, when his lips were a breath away, 'I'm going to need an official ranking after this. Worst to best. We'll have to put *Moby-Dick* in its own category for now, but—'

Jake laughed, and kissed me.

Epilogue
Six Months Later

'I don't know if I can do this,' Jake said, glancing over at me with an expression bleeding such raw vulnerability that I had to swallow a giggle, given the context.

He was sitting on my desk chair, spinning himself around in circles – literally and figuratively. I was sitting on my bed, putting the finishing touches on a crochet doily that I was going to force my family to use as a table centrepiece for the rest of time, because it had taken me too long to make to not be cherished forever.

'Want a distraction kiss?' I asked, still focused on my crochet.

A moment later I let out a yelp of surprise – Jake had flopped down on the bed next to me, hard enough to make me bounce. After shooting a look at the doorway, he pulled me down for a kiss, following it with another glance at the door before sneaking a second, and then a third.

'Was that a good distraction?' I said, when he pulled away.

'It'll do,' Jake said, eyes crinkling, though his smile stayed small – clearly the kissing hadn't quite done away with his nerves.

'Okay.' I hummed. 'Other distractions, other distractions ... Oh! I told you that Mae got into her communications degree?'

Jake nodded, slipping his arm under my waist so he could pull me against his side. I let myself be moved, rolling so I was snug against him and tucking my cheek against his chest, crochet temporarily forgotten. University offers had started coming in for those of us who hadn't received any early acceptances (Laeli had got an offer in November for a science degree that would let her study astronomy and astrophysics). Though I wasn't planning on changing my preferences for a boy, I was secretly glad that Jake and I had been accepted into the same uni – Jake for an arts degree with a history major, me for a science degree with a marine biology major.

Were either of us completely committed to our choices? No. But making a choice felt brave regardless, and I found myself excited to step into the unknown – especially if I could do it alongside the silly, kind boy lying beside me.

'Aren't Mae and Kasun going to some open day event today?' Jake asked.

'Oh, right!' Kasun had, unsurprisingly, been accepted into a Bachelor of Arts with the intention of majoring in philosophy, though according to Mae he was considering deferring the offer and getting a year of life experience before going back to school. 'I wonder if Mae can convince him to start at the same time she does. She's kind of nervous about not knowing anyone at uni.'

'Nah, she'll have a great time,' Jake said. 'And you'll still be right around the corner.'

I nodded, tracing a finger over his heart. Jake was right. A lot was changing, but a lot was still staying the same. Despite being done with high school, I wasn't moving anywhere new yet, and neither was Mae – when we needed each other, we'd still only be ten minutes away.

I felt Jake's eyes on me, and tilted my head up so I could look at him properly.

When we made eye contact, he said, 'You know those little crochet tops? You should make one of those.'

'Not a fan of the doily?' I glanced across him at my pile of crochet materials.

'I love your doily, Eyebrows.' Jake paused to reposition me so I was fully resting against his chest, before continuing: 'And I love that you spent ten billion hours making it. I really do.'

'But?'

Jake raised both his palms in an *imagine it* gesture. 'Little crochet top.'

'Noted,' I said.

Jake grinned at me, waggling his eyebrows before threading his fingers through my hair, guiding my mouth back to his. His other hand began to play with the hem of my shirt.

'Kids, it's time!'

Mum. It was like she had some sort of sixth sense for teenagers making out.

Jake let me go with a groan, woeful expression returning. I didn't manage to stifle my laugh this time.

'You're going to do great,' I said. 'You're smart and thoughtful and they're probably going to eat you alive down there, but – it'll be in a loving way.'

'You say the sweetest things,' Jake said, with just enough gravel in his voice that he couldn't quite play it off as a joke. Pushing us up and giving me one last peck on the lips, he continued, 'I don't know if I believe the bit about it being in a loving way, though.'

'Probably for the best. Let's not keep them waiting.'

Downstairs was set up as it always was: the nice crockery was out, slices of strudel still steaming where they sat on the coffee table. My book club family were arrayed around the room holding mugs of coffee, and looked up when we entered.

Holding Jake's hand, I sat us down on the last available sofa. Despite keeping what I hoped was a reassuring pressure against his palm, Jake stayed rigid for at least the first twenty minutes. Only once my aunts got into a spat about the novel's romantic plotline did he start to relax. Thirty minutes in and he was enjoying a slice of strudel.

His time to shine came almost halfway through the session. My mother, weary of familial opinion-sharing, swivelled in her armchair, pinning Jake with a look. 'Do you have any thoughts to share?'

Jake straightened, putting his strudel in my lap and clearing his throat.

'Thanks for having me at your book club,' he said, earnestly enough that I saw both of my aunts visibly melt. 'I'm … super honoured. Uh. Okay. So, to start with – I thought I'd talk about the set-up.'

Acknowledgements

Writing has always been a very solitary hobby for me – before I started on my journey to publication, the number of people who had read my work could probably be counted on both hands. Now that I'm writing these acknowledgements, I can say with certainty that this is no longer the case, and I'm so deeply grateful to all the people who have helped turn this manuscript from a solitary project into a real-life book.

Starting from the pre-query days, thank you to my very first readers: Mum, Dad, Claire, Jocelin and Peter (and to Andrew – while technically not a first reader, thank you for taking the time to sit down with the story). Whether it was sending me messages of encouragement post-read, offering thoughts on how the manuscript could be improved, or answering my specific questions about their thoughts on plot and characters, you all made me feel confident in my decision to push forwards with querying.

Querying is one of those processes that authors and aspiring authors discuss with dread. When I started querying, I braced myself for rejection after rejection, telling myself that it would be *totally fine, really* if no one expressed any interest in the manuscript, and that I would happily shelve it and try again later. I was so convinced this novel would go nowhere that I didn't quite know what to do with myself when my lovely agent, Vicki Marsdon, not only offered to represent me but then landed me a deal with the fantastic folks at Allen & Unwin in a matter of months.

Thank you, Vicki, for seeing the potential in my manuscript, and thank you to Anna McFarlane, publisher extraordinaire, for seeing the same and acquiring the book for Allen & Unwin. Anna and Nicola Santilli, you have been an amazing editorial team of two, our editorial rounds have allowed me to develop and refine the manuscript into a book I'm really proud of. Nicola, I'm really going to miss our editorial meetings/catch ups – the sight of your spacey background never fails to make me smile. Thank you for being the best editor a debut author could ask for.

A second thank you to my mum is necessary, too: thank you for being another set of eyes for all things Slovenian and Catholic; our conversations prompted some moments of introspection on the nature of our cultural identity, which made me think more deeply about what writing from lived experience looks like. Thank you also to Josephine Jožica Gorey for letting me benefit from your knowledge of the

Slovenian language, your feedback and corrections were invaluable.

Thank you to Daniel Gray-Barnett for the most amazing cover. It matches the tone of the novel perfectly, and your rendering of Amalia and Jake in particular gives me butterflies every time I look at it. Thank you also to Amy Daoud for your work on the book's design, all the cover and internal flourishes are wonderful.

Thank you to both Erin Gough and Dr Jodi McAlister for your early endorsements: as a debut author, it means so much that you were willing to give your stamp of approval to an unknown voice.

Thank you to my magic physio, who unsticks my ribs, makes sure my shoulders are sitting evenly, and knows exactly what to do when I come in 'twisted up like fusilli'. This entire process would have been significantly longer and more gruelling without your treatment.

The list of thank yous go on: thank you to Vanessa Lanaway for a fantastic final proofread – sorry for the confusion about school terms! Thank you to Reem Galal now and into the future, I'm so excited to continue working with you on getting this book (and me!) in front of readers. Thank you to Isabelle Webb for being my patient point of contact as I collected together my author info and photos, and Deborah Lum for reaching out on behalf of Marketing. Thank you to the Publishing Director, Eva Mills; the Head of Marketing, Simon Panagaris; the Education Marketing Manager, Carolyn Walsh; and to the Sales, Marketing and

Rights teams respectively. And to all the other teams and individuals I haven't listed but who gave their time and effort to *The Set-Up Girl*: thank you, thank you, thank you!

So many people contributed to getting this book on shelves, and I'm so grateful to all of you.

My final thank you goes out to the readers. I hope you had as much fun reading this as I had writing it.

About the Author

Sasha Vey is an Australian author who enjoys writing about the everyday dramas of teenagers experiencing the (often messy) transition into young adulthood. Sasha's debut novel, *The Set-Up Girl*, is a YA romantic comedy. When not writing or working, Sasha can be found on the piano or resisting the urge to start another crafting project.